The Happiness In Between

Center Point
Large Print

Also by Grace Greene and available from
Center Point Large Print:

The Memory of Butterflies
Wildflower Heart
Wildflower Hope

**This Large Print Book carries the
Seal of Approval of N.A.V.H.**

The Happiness In Between

Grace Greene

CENTER POINT LARGE PRINT
THORNDIKE, MAINE

This Center Point Large Print edition
is published in the year 2021 by arrangement with
Amazon Publishing, www.apub.com.

The text of this Large Print edition is unabridged.
In other aspects, this book may vary
from the original edition.
Printed in the United States of America
on permanent paper.
Set in 16-point Times New Roman type.

ISBN: 978-1-64358-874-2

The Library of Congress has cataloged this record
under Library of Congress Control Number: 2020952820

Everyone wants, needs, to be loved and appreciated. I encourage my readers to look for opportunities to share love and appreciation with others and offer a helping hand. Whether the need is in an animal shelter, an adult memory care unit, or protecting the weak from abusers, be aware and provide support and encouragement whenever and wherever you can.

I dedicate this book to those who offer love and kindness, and to those who need it. Through the efforts of all who care and act upon it, may we all be blessed by the seeds of kindness we sow.

Chapter One

Sandra Hurst didn't call ahead. She drove through the night across Virginia, from Martinsville to Richmond, with her music turned up loud to shut out unhappy thoughts. She focused on home—on running away to home—because sometimes running away was the sensible choice, sometimes the only choice. She envisioned her parents' driveway bordered by trim, mature hedges of Japanese holly and sheltered by long-lived dogwoods. It was too early in spring for the dogwoods to be showing off their pink flowers and foliage, but she wasn't coming home to admire the view. All she wanted was to park in the driveway and doze quietly in the car. She wouldn't bother anyone. She'd wait until the sun was up and her mom and dad had started their day.

The neat, tree-lined streets were familiar and peaceful in the dark. It felt like home, though she hadn't officially lived here for a long time. A large brick house in an established neighborhood just off the Boulevard in the urban suburbs, before the city became downtown living—she'd never thought much about it, but as an only child, she'd assumed the family home would shelter her parents for years to come and still be there for her, or for her to deal with, in the distant future. It was the house she'd grown up in. Home.

She hadn't thought that way twelve years ago when she left for college. Life was ahead of her, and all good things were possible because she'd always done what was expected of her. She'd been the good, obedient daughter who brought home near-perfect report cards and the responsible young person teachers and neighbors praised. A nice person. Tonight, she was hoping for comfort, at least for the physical comforts. She didn't expect sympathy, but her parents wouldn't turn her away. In fact, she could help them. As Dad's memory had grown faulty, the weight of managing their personal and business affairs had fallen on Mom. Mom had been talking about simplifying their lives, downscaling, and perhaps moving to Florida. Some of her friends had already made the move south.

As Sandra pulled into the driveway, she saw lights on in the living room. Was there a problem with Dad? Or was someone awake and waiting for her?

She parked and cut the engine. The porch light came on. The front door opened, and bright light spilled out from the foyer, along with her mother's shadow. Mom stood in the doorway silhouetted in her fluffy bathrobe.

She didn't open the storm door, didn't come

halfway out, and didn't offer a hand with Sandra's suitcase. She stayed inside, watching, as Sandra hitched her purse up on one shoulder and tried to ease the car door closed so as not to disturb the neighbors. She carried her small suitcase up the steps, and, in the end, her mother did open the door wide and allow her inside, so that was something.

"Is Dad OK?" Sandra asked. "You're up early."

"Trent called."

Of course he did. She set her suitcase beside the chair.

"I didn't expect him to realize I was gone until morning. I left a note, but it's like him to call anyway, to stir things up. I'm sorry. I'm sure it was alarming to be awakened in the night by the phone."

"Stir things up? He was worried." Mom closed the door and locked it. "He wanted to know if you'd called us. Perhaps you should have."

"I wanted to tell you face-to-face."

Mom was wearing her pink bathrobe and pink leather slip-ons. Her brown hair was short, curly, and naturally highlighted. Sandra had inherited her dad's straight black hair. She'd also inherited her mom's large, dark-brown eyes, and this wasn't the first time they'd engaged in a staring contest. Sandra knew this game was impossible to win, and she broke off from her mother's gaze.

9

Sandra walked to the kitchen and pointed at the fridge. "I'm thirsty. Mind?"

Mom's behavior was odd. She'd stayed in the hallway and was now standing in the kitchen doorway.

Her mother. Her childhood home. Shouldn't Mom have asked if she was all right? If Sandra was hungry or if something was wrong? That's what Mom had done when she'd left Trent before. Apparently it only worked that way the first time one's daughter left her husband and divorced him. Mom continued to stand in the doorway, her hands in the pockets of her robe, her lips pressed together.

"Mom, won't you talk to me?"

Her mother frowned. She pulled her hands from her pockets and waved them as she spoke, but she kept her voice almost whisper-low, for Dad's sake, of course.

"I don't understand you, Sandra. I didn't understand the first time, neither of us did, but we tried to, and we helped you. Now I have your father to consider and my own health, too. I urge you to work this out with Trent, but I can't get in the middle of it, not again."

Unfair! Sandra wanted to shout. Instead, she forced down the shame that made her face burn. Her mother's words were true. She took a deep breath, then said softly, "There's nothing to work out. I'm sorry my mistakes inconvenience you."

She paused before asking, "Where else would I go?" Sandra pretended not to hear the whine in her voice and ignored the prickling of tears in her eyes. She wouldn't cry. Not here, not in front of her mother.

Mom closed her eyes and sighed, then looked at Sandra again. "You can stay here, but only for a little while. We signed with a real-estate agent today. The house is going on the market at the end of the week."

Sandra turned her back to her mother and reached into the fridge to grab the orange juice. It gave her a moment to collect her thoughts and control the slight shakiness that had suddenly overwhelmed her and was showing in her hand. A familiar shortness of breath threatened. Anxiety. She coughed to force it away. "You're selling the house?"

"I told you before. Your father and I are moving to Florida. We're going now before he's . . . while he can still enjoy it."

"Good. Sounds good." Sandra nodded. "I understand. Makes sense." What else could she say that wouldn't sound foolish or self-serving? "I'm surprised, that's all. I didn't know you were that far along in the planning."

Her mother crossed her arms and sighed. "I told you. Perhaps you were focused on your husband and your marriage?"

"Or should've been? Is that what you mean?"

Sandra pressed her hand to her forehead. "Sorry. I'm tired. I've been driving most of the night . . . well, almost four hours, but I haven't slept in a while. Do you mind? I'll bring in my other stuff tomorrow. I have what I need for tonight in my suitcase."

Mom shook her head. "I don't mean to seem unwelcoming, but understand that within a few days, people will be coming through the house, viewing it. We are busy packing and cleaning. We're hoping for a quick sale."

Sandra pretended not to understand what her mom was saying: Don't get too comfy—was that what she meant? Panic tried to creep in, and Sandra stopped it. She could turn this around. She could show her mother this could be a good thing for the family. She forced a smile. "Well, then, I'm glad I'm here to help."

"What about Trent?" Mom asked.

Sandra stared, this time at a total loss for an acceptable response. "We'll talk tomorrow, Mom. Or I guess that's actually later today, right? I'm going to grab a few hours of sleep. Unless you've already packed up my bed?" She'd tried for a joking tone, but it fell flat.

Still standing in the doorway, her mother asked, "Are you going to call him? He's worried."

"No."

"If he calls back?"

"Tell him it's over and not to contact me again."

Sandra moved close to her mother, wanting to hug her despite the lack of warmth and welcome, but Mom's hands went back into her robe's pockets, and she moved aside.

"Thanks, Mom," Sandra said. "Sorry to be a bother."

In the daylight, after having slept for a few hours, Sandra saw the truth of what her mother had said. Many of the furnishings in the house were already gone. In storage? Boxed? Sold? That included most of the framed photos in her bedroom, from the dresser as well as the pictures on the wall. Her childhood room. She was an adult now. She had no real claim except that of sentimentality, but she'd expected to find *home* as she'd driven through the night.

Her mother had left two framed photos on the dresser. One showed Mom with her siblings and her parents. Sandra recognized her Aunt Barbara and Uncle Cliff with their sister as young adults. With them stood their parents, Sandra's grandfather, whom she'd never known, and her grandmother. Sandra barely remembered her grandmother despite being her namesake. She was also the only grandchild. Yet, never had she called the woman "grandmother" or any form of it. That's how the Shoemakers were, at least in her experience.

The other photo was of Sandra with her

parents. Was she destined to be the end of the line for the Shoemaker family? Her dad's family was different. Dad's family had spread far and wide. She didn't know her distant cousins, but she knew they existed. It was funny to have had so much family but to feel so alone.

Sandra returned the frames to the dresser and went to see what else had changed.

In two of the upstairs rooms, boxes were taped and stacked. Markers were used to identify the contents. She recognized her mother's penmanship, the perfect slants and loops not in the least compromised by uneven, yielding cardboard surfaces. Other boxes were open, their flaps wide and beckoning. Dad was standing among them in the guest room.

The sale would happen quickly. Sandra knew it. That's how her luck ran. And, given her mother's welcome, she wasn't expecting an invitation to move to Florida with them.

"Dad?"

He was randomly picking up items and shuffling them between boxes. Only the taped boxes were safe from his busy hands. Sandra went to stand beside him. He smiled broadly. He was dressed well, his hair was combed, and his eyes were bright. He looked like himself. The vague motions, the lack of focus and direction in his expression, betrayed his reality.

"Cassandra. Hello, dear. When did you get home?"

She hugged him. "Middle of the night. You were sleeping."

"How is your husband?" Dad frowned. "Is he here?"

"No. I came alone."

"I see."

"What do you see? Other than boxes?" she joked as she kissed his cheek.

"The last time you came home without him you divorced."

His eyes were on her, but he couldn't hold his concentration, and he looked away. She hooked her arm in his and put her head against his shoulder. Standing there, not seeing his lost eyes, she could pretend for a few seconds that she had her father back. But then his hands began to fidget again, and she felt a slight tremor run through him as if something in him was resetting. His memory, she supposed.

Sandra sighed. "You're right, Dad. That's true. We're going to divorce again."

She released his arm and took his hand, wanting to explain to him, to tell her dad everything. But dementia had been creeping up on him, becoming more noticeable and undeniable over the past year. If this was a good day for him, she wouldn't ruin it by reminding him that her worthless husband was cruel.

"No one can say I didn't try." She gave him a smile and another hug. "Are you OK up here?"

"Yes, lots of work to do. Cleaning, you know." He was staring at the boxes again. He reached in and selected a book. "Is this yours?"

"No. Not mine." She accepted the book from him. As a child she'd often held this book in her hands, running her fingers over the pebbled texture of the old leather binding and the embossed lettering on the cover. Mom had cautioned her many times not to mess with her father's books. Dad had never minded.

She smiled at him. "It's a book of stories and poetry. Poe. One of your favorites. 'Is all that we see or seem . . .' " She paused, waiting for him to say his part. He was watching her, but he didn't respond to her cue. She touched his arm and finished the verse for him. "But a dream within a dream."

"What is that?"

"Edgar Allan Poe. One of your favorites." She laughed quietly. "With you living and teaching in Richmond, he'd have to be."

"Oh. Well, then I should read it."

"Reread it, you mean, though it's been a while, I'm sure."

"Really?" He picked up the book again, looked at the flyleaf, and thumbed through the yellowed pages. "Looks good."

She touched his silver hair. He'd grayed young. He was still young, barely retirement age. For two decades he'd lectured on American

16

literature at a nearby college. This morning those memories were absent. It was so tempting to tell him, to remind him, to push him to remember, but she stopped. It wouldn't be a help to him, and it would cause him dismay and confusion and cause her frustration and grief.

"You can read it when you take a break." She took the book, put it back in the box, and patted his arm. "I'll talk to you later. I'm going downstairs to say good morning to Mom."

He nodded but pulled the book back out of the box. He stood there looking at it.

Sandra found her mother working in the kitchen. Small appliances and cookware were arranged and stacked on the granite counter. Empty boxes waited on the floor to be filled. One appliance was actually on duty—the coffeemaker. A few cups of the dark brew were ready in the carafe.

Sandra grabbed a mug and poured a cup. "Mom, about those boxes upstairs? Dad moved things around, so you might want to check before taping them up."

"The open boxes in the guest room? No worries. Those are for your father to . . . pack. He wants to contribute. So long as he doesn't open the taped boxes, it's good."

"Can I help?"

After a pause, she said, "Maybe later."

"He called me Cassandra."

"It's your name." She twisted the paper around

the mixer and wedged it into a box next to another wrapped item.

"True. It's . . . it's been a while, I guess. I'm not used to hearing it. Doesn't matter."

"He's been going back in time more and more."

Sandra nodded and spread a piece of white packing paper on the counter. She set the electric can opener on top. As she folded the paper over it, Mom stopped her, saying, "I'll do it. Otherwise, I'll lose track of what's where."

Sandra pulled her hands away from the paper and stepped back.

Mom finished wrapping the can opener and put it into the box. She gestured at her daughter. "You are so thin. If you're dieting, please stop." She added, "What are you going to do about your marriage?"

Caught between the dieting remark and the one about her marriage, Sandra hesitated. She decided the "thin" comment was just one more criticism and skipped to the marriage question. "I can't go back. It's over."

"I remember when you said that before."

Frustrated, Sandra raised her voice. "You're right. What do you want me to say?" Sandra bit her lip, shocked by how rude she'd sounded. She didn't want to add to her mom's worries. "I tried. I truly did." She grabbed the loaf of bread from the counter and hovered where the toaster used to be. It wasn't in its usual place. It was over by the stove, and it wasn't plugged in.

"I've cleaned it, and I'm about to pack it."

"No problem." Sandra settled for butter from the fridge. "Buttered bread will be fine."

"Tell me," Mom said. "Tell me about Trent. Tell me what he did. Tell me why."

"He . . . he's always watching me, judging me. He has a mean streak, Mom."

"He's controlling. You knew that. If you didn't know it at first, you certainly did by the time you divorced. So what's new? What is it this time?"

Sandra felt cornered. "It's hard to explain. I feel like a prisoner in my own home. Trent . . ." How could she tell it so her mother would understand? "When he's there, I have to watch what I do and say. He sets traps, little traps, and then watches. He waits for me to make a mistake so he can lecture me."

"Has he hit you?"

"No, but . . . he takes things. My things. They disappear if I don't put them away quickly enough or if I leave something out that I'm working on. He doesn't admit it, but it's what happens. Sometimes they show back up later. Sometimes not. He locks me out of the house if I'm away too long. And when he isn't there, Leo is. Leo is like an extension of him."

"His dog?"

Sandra looked away. "I know how it sounds." She slapped the counter lightly. "Leo. He snapped at me. I didn't mean to surprise him, but he's always hiding around corners. He's like a stand-in for Trent when Trent's not there, watching me all the time. I can't take it anymore."

"Leo snapped? Were you bitten?"

"No, Mom. That's not the point anyway. The point is there's no peace whether Trent is there or not." The words almost choked her. They tore her up inside, but when she said them aloud, they sounded so petty and inane. "I can't do anything right. When I told Trent that Leo snapped at me, he kicked him."

"Trent kicked him? Was Leo hurt?"

Now she'd gotten her mother's attention. Over a dog. Sandra regretted mentioning the incident.

"He's fine. You never liked dogs anyway. Why do you care?"

"No one, not even an animal, deserves to be mistreated."

"That should also include me, shouldn't it?"

Mom sighed and rubbed her temples. "I don't understand, Sandra. Tell me what's different this time. What's different from the first time you married and then left him?"

Her mother's expression said so much, Sandra felt defeated. She let it drop.

She could've made stuff up, exaggerated, but she wouldn't. She might be a failure and a spine-less coward, but she wasn't a liar. How does one prove what hasn't been witnessed?

You shouldn't have to prove it, not to the people who love you.

When Sandra didn't respond, her mother threw up her hands and turned away. "We helped you with the first divorce. This time you're on your own. I already have enough on my plate. Too much." Mom spoke with her back turned as she wrapped the cooking pans in paper. "You make your choices, you live with the results or remedy them, but it's on you. You're an adult, Sandra. You have to take care of this yourself."

Sandra took her coffee but left the bread half-eaten on the counter. There was so much she wanted to tell her mother, almost too many words and emotions to sort them into coherent thought. She would've tried harder, though, if she'd thought her mother would understand.

Bottom line: what she needed right now was a divorce.

Trent had managed the money. He'd given her an allowance out of which she paid for food and small things. She'd tried to squirrel away a dollar here and there, but it wasn't much and certainly wouldn't pay the legal fees for a divorce. Over the last few weeks, she'd smuggled clothing and personal items out of the house and stashed them in brown plastic lawn and leaf bags. Disappearing suitcases might be noticed; Trent was very sharp that way. He wasn't likely to miss a few plastic bags from the large boxed roll in the garage. She hid the bags in the trunk of her car. Trent never used her car, so he wouldn't see what she was up to. But cash was the problem, and to get some real cash, enough to fund a divorce and to support herself, she needed a job. That was her primary goal, and coming home to Richmond was the first step toward it.

Thus far, the plan wasn't going well. This morning, she'd emptied the car, carrying the plastic bags up to her room while her mom wasn't looking. Sandra didn't need any sharp remarks; she needed space to lay out the clothing and miscellaneous items and make plans. She'd have it all sorted and packed away again shortly. Here in her old bedroom, despite many of the knickknacks and personal items already being gone, some of her old clothing was still in the drawers and closet. She put together an outfit that would serve for job hunting, then set aside pajamas, a couple of pairs of jeans, and a few shirts. The rest would go back in the car. But first she went to the room with the open boxes and found Dad's Poe anthology. She took the book from the box and returned to her room.

Dad didn't remember the book. Mom didn't want or care about it. If she had, she would've put it into a taped box. The typeset letters inside formed poems and stories, but the book represented memories to Sandra—specific memories of her father that belonged to the two of them and now, apparently, only to her.

She sat on the edge of the bed and opened the cover, not specifically intending to go to their poem, but after years of use, the pages parted naturally at "A Dream Within a Dream." They were Poe's words, but for her, they were inextricably linked to the sound of her father's voice reading them aloud:

Take this kiss upon the brow!
And, in parting from you now,
Thus much let me avow—
You are not wrong, who deem
That my days have been a dream.

The poem continued, but her memories suddenly hurt, especially in view of her father's condition. She closed the book.

Sandra found waterproof bags in the pantry. She wrapped the book carefully, along with the two framed photos her mom had left on the dresser. The package was too large to add to her keepsake box, so for extra protection, she worked it carefully into the middle of one of the clothing bags.

She stowed the bags safely in her trunk, leaving nothing of value in the bedroom except for a few clothing items in the dresser drawer, nothing to disturb or distract realtors or buyers. Her mother would have no reason to complain.

She started the job search the next day, targeting temp agencies, and the interviews seemed promising, but she hadn't completed a college degree and had little practical job experience. The few jobs she'd had since leaving college hadn't lasted. Now here she was, thirty and almost back to where she'd started. As her mother had said the last time Sandra was in this position—one couldn't reap what one had never sown.

Drained but not discouraged, Sandra walked into the house and closed the front door softly. She slipped off her shoes and walked barefoot to the stairs.

Her mother spoke from the dining room. "Did you find a job?"

Sandra stopped in the wide doorway. Mom was boxing up documents and papers. Over her head, all eighteen bulbs in the crystal chandelier glowed. Those lights reflected in the beveled glass front panels of the china cabinet. The cabinet shelves were now empty of bone china and crystal. Small boxes marked in big red letters as fragile were stacked on the floor beside it.

"Where are you going, Mom? I mean, where in Florida?"

"We bought a condo outside of Tampa. Not a mansion, but big enough."

"Do you have pictures of it? I'd love to see where you'll be living."

"Of course. I'll show you this afternoon. I go over them every day with your father. But be careful what you say. I don't want him getting worried about not coming back here. The new place will be home soon enough. He'll adjust."

Land mines. A lot of land mines were laying there, in wait, for Sandra to stumble over. To upset Dad. To disappoint Mom.

"After we're settled, and you're all settled with your life, you can come down and visit." Her mother added, "Speaking of getting settled, how'd it go with the job hunt today?"

"Nothing for sure yet, but it looks promising."

"I see."

Sandra felt dismissed. "I have an interview tomorrow." It was a lie. She was sorry she'd said it even as the words slipped from her lips.

"Good. I hope it will come to something." Mom crossed her arms. "I left some things on your bed. Amazing what one finds when going through things for packing."

Quietly, Sandra went to her room to change. Mom had left a manila envelope on the bed. Sandra tipped the contents onto the coverlet. Photos spilled out. Wedding photos. The sort that friends and family take at the reception and give to you later. These were from the first wedding almost ten years ago. The second wedding had been very different, with the two of them at the courthouse, each with a friend as a witness, and

25

not one minute of it had felt right. But at this first one, there were so many smiling faces, including the bride and groom. Her parents looked happy, too, as they leaned in to a group photo with Aunt Barbara and Uncle Cliff.

Trent was handsome, no question about that. A wholesome, good-humored face. Strong blue eyes. Broad shoulders. Short, sandy hair. He wore the tux well. And she looked good, too, in white lace and satin. So much younger then and so naive it had exuded from her. What had Trent called her? A blank canvas, primed and ready, and he wanted to be with her for every brushstroke. She'd heard what she wanted to hear, and to her, at nineteen, his words had sounded romantic and loaded with promise. The wedding was like a fairy tale, and the reception had lots of food, laughter, music, and dancing. Life was perfect . . . until the party stopped and their married life began.

Trent didn't call her cell phone because she'd left it behind. He called the house phone instead, and her father answered.

"Sandra? Who is . . . ? Oh, I see. Uh-huh." He called out, "Cassandra?"

Dad was standing in the kitchen looking confused. He held the phone away from him but didn't cover the speaker.

"Cassandra, there's a man asking for you. He

said his name is Trent. He's saying things like you're lost, that you hurt him. He talks like he knows me, but I didn't do anything wrong. I didn't, did I? Sometimes I get confused, but . . ."

She took the phone from his hand. "I've got it, Dad. No worries. It's someone playing a trick. A bad joke." She pressed the mouthpiece against her shoulder and gently pushed his arm. "You go help Mom clean the house, OK? I saw her in the bedroom." She waited until he was halfway down the hall before she put the receiver to her ear and said, "Trent?"

Nothing. The call had ended.

She hadn't heard the phone ring. It didn't matter. Dad's dementia hadn't yet involved imagining phone calls, much less from Trent. Trent had accomplished what he intended, she guessed. He might not have set out to upset her father, but having done so, he probably considered it a job well done. People were as weak as their weakest links, he liked to say. Their vulnerabilities. Trent was right. Anything that hurt her father hurt her. Trent knew that. Sandra put the receiver back on the hook.

When her mother had fussed at Dad over the years, it had hurt Sandra. She felt protective. She'd try to sympathize with her father, but he would always say, "Be patient with your mother. She is a wonderful woman. She has many fine qualities, but she's not a dreamer, Cassandra.

27

My head is always stuck in books. Without your mom, who'd make sure the electric bill was paid or food was stocked? She's efficient and no-nonsense." He ruffled his daughter's hair. "Without Mom to handle the business, we wouldn't have the latitude to dream, would we?"

She'd been Cassandra then. By the time she'd finished middle school, no one called her that anymore. By that time, she'd decided she wasn't a dreamer. She didn't know what she was. She was lost somewhere between her parents and fit in nowhere. Luckily, she didn't have to worry about it much because Mom knew everything and made all the decisions. Sandra went along. Mom was usually right, and life was simpler that way. Truly, it wasn't a bad life. Not at all. Compromise was the early approach she'd taken in her own marriage. She'd thought she and Trent would work out their differences and make a solid marriage like that of her parents. After many wasted years, she'd learned that compromise worked only if both people were playing by the same rules. Sandra's rules were the ones she'd learned from her parents. Trent's rules . . . well, he'd gotten them mostly from his father but put his own spin on them. He called them points of failure. And never the twain would meet.

She was a slow learner. When she'd agreed to marry him a second time, she still believed she could help him. She believed his promises. But his promises meant nothing. They'd only ever been a means to an end. His end. His goal.

So he'd called her parents' house and found her here. No surprise there. In times of trouble, where else would she go but home?

Sandra came down the next morning to resume her job hunt. Again today, she was dressed like a woman in search of a professional gig, aside from her bare feet. She carried her heels and stopped at the door to put on her sandals.

Her mother nodded. "You look very nice. Except for the shoes."

"Yes, I'll change them before meeting with the agencies." She pointed to the heel tips. "I'm protecting the floor."

"Good luck," Mom said.

Sandra grabbed her purse and keys and went outside. It was a perfect spring day. The sky was blue, and the sun was bright but gentle. When she reached the driveway, she froze in disbelief.

The trunk was open. Empty.

Dumbfounded, she tried to process what she was seeing. Someone had raided her car. The box in the backseat with her personal items and keepsakes was gone. The glove box had been rifled through, as well as the center console. A blouse, a slip, and some lingerie were strewn about, abandoned on the driveway and in the bushes, but for the most part, her stuff was gone.

The bags in the trunk, including the one with the photos and her dad's book, were gone.

Everything, except what was on her person and upstairs in the bedroom, was gone.

All gone.

Chapter Two

She dashed up the front steps and into the house, running straight to the kitchen to the house phone. Mom was on the line, the receiver to her ear, chatting.

Sandra waved to interrupt her. "I need the phone."

Her mother frowned and mouthed, *What's wrong?*

"My car was broken into. Someone stole my stuff. I have to call the police."

Mom held up her hand. "One second." She spoke into the phone. "Barbara, I'll have to call you back. See you soon." She hung up and turned to her daughter. "Did you leave the car unlocked?"

"No, of course not."

"Did they break a window or what?"

"No, the car isn't damaged." Sandra sat at the table, her hand on her face, deflated. "Trent has a key."

Her mother stared. "You think your husband drove all the way here to harass you? Well, I suppose he might have . . . but to steal your clothing? Really? I can believe he'd want to see you, but surely he'd come to the door." She paused as if waiting for a rebuttal. None came.

"You probably left the car unlocked. Someone took advantage, hoping to find something worth keeping or selling. They do that, you know, in every neighborhood. Opportunists check the cars to see if they're locked."

Sandra called the local police, but doubt and frustration had crept into her anger and taken its heat. They said they'd send an officer to take a report, and Sandra was surprised when they actually did. The police were busy these days. Old clothing stolen from a car, but with no actual damage done to the car, didn't rate high as a crime. Still, this was a respectable neighborhood, so the police cruiser drove up and parked at the curb. She went out to speak with the officer. He examined the exterior of the car and then inside.

"No sign of tampering or force. Are you sure you locked it?"

"I am."

"Any valuables missing?"

"Clothing. Toiletries and personal things." Her eyes burned, the tears welling at the thought of her father's Poe anthology. "They weren't worth a lot, maybe, but they were important to me."

"If you didn't leave it unlocked, then is there someone with a key who might've interfered with the car and the contents?"

There was. She didn't want to say his name aloud, nor acknowledge the fact of him. She pushed out the words. "My husband. Ex-husband. He has a key, but he lives in Martinsville. Hours away."

"Which is he? Husband or ex?"

"Technically still my husband."

"He has a key, you said?"

"Yes."

His expression remained impassive, but she sensed the change in his overall demeanor. She tried to read his face but couldn't.

"Domestic." He seemed to consider the situation for a moment before speaking. "I'll write this up so you'll have a report, but there's really nothing here for me to investigate. If you believe this was done by your husband, consider keeping a record of events and encounters, harassments, in case you need the information for litigation or otherwise." He then asked, his eyes wearing a kinder look, "Ma'am, has he been violent? Any cause for concern for your safety or physical well-being?"

"No." Trent played games with her mind, but he'd never been physically threatening. It might have been easier if he had been. She was sure she was wrong to think that, but at least she'd have something to point to. And physical violence would surely have forced her to leave him sooner the first time and stay away instead of giving him that ill-advised second chance. Perhaps that was one of those choices her mother was talking about. Maybe this was the price she had to pay for choosing Trent twice.

After the officer drove away, she turned toward the house. Her mother was at the door waiting.

"No help," Sandra said. "Probably Trent. Domestic."

Mom nodded as they stepped inside. "He wrote a report, I see. I have a hard time believing your husband would come all this way and not ring the doorbell. There hasn't been so much as a telephone call, not since the one your father answered. But instead Trent steals your clothing from the car?" She raised her hand. "But stranger things have happened."

They walked to the kitchen, where Sandra grabbed a glass and filled it with water. Her throat was so dry. She drank several sips before speaking.

"No, Mom. This is exactly like Trent. There is nothing at all strange about this. Pettiness. Vindictiveness. Manipulation. All dedicated to dominating me." She sat at the kitchen table and sagged, not trying to fight the hopeless feeling wrapping itself around her. "Trent wins again."

Her mother walked over to the kitchen sink and stared out the window. The curtains were still hanging from the rod, but the knickknacks were gone from the sill. She turned back to her daughter. Her arms were crossed, but she wore a calculating expression. "Too bad you don't have the car title." But she said it with a slight lilt at the end, as if it were a question.

"I do." This car was the only asset in her name. It was a used car, not fancy, but it had been a goodwill gesture, a conciliatory move on Trent's part when he'd schmoozed her back into marriage. "I do have the title. It's upstairs in my suitcase."

"Sell it, then. Take the car to a dealer and get what you can for it. Your father's old car is in the garage. He hasn't driven in almost a year. It's old, and I was going to donate it, but it runs, and Trent won't have a key for it."

Sandra shivered. If Trent caught wind of this . . . If he had any kind of idea that she might sell his . . . No, this was *her* car. This wasn't his business. But it would be better for all concerned if she could get it done quietly and under Trent's radar.

"Good idea. Thank you. I don't want Trent to know."

"He won't unless you tell him. And where's your phone? That fancy one you had?"

"I left it. Trent would shut it off anyway, and he might have used it to find me."

Mom shook her head, looking amazed. "I don't think he'd need the phone to find you. You don't hide very well." She walked off but then stopped and turned back. "Get one of those phones like Barbara has. They're cheap, and you buy minutes as you need them."

She was referring to a burner phone. Very low-tech.

"The house phone will be disconnected soon, and you need your own. Also, call the car dealership today, the one on Broad Street. Your dad and I have done business with them for years. Ask for Bert Davis. Tell him you're our daughter and what you need. If he can help, he will. Then drive over there tomorrow, and I'll come pick you up when the sale is done."

"Trent will know."

"How?"

Sandra shrugged. "He always does. He's dedicated. That's what he calls his behavior. He's dedicated to me, to helping me. He's out there somewhere watching."

"That sounds like an exaggeration."

Sandra smiled, not pleasantly and not in agreement. "You don't know him, Mom. Not the real Trent. Early in our marriage, I was planning to attend the first session in a lecture series of writers and poets at the community college. I thought it would be fun and different. A reason to get out. Trent wasn't happy about it, but he said I should do what I thought best." She forced herself to breathe. "So I went. I parked and went into the building and discovered the speaker had canceled. I didn't stay long. I was inside for maybe thirty minutes. Anyway, when I returned to my car, it wouldn't start."

Sandra stood, her hands clasped. "It was getting dark. No one was parked near me, and the few people who were out there were all strangers, so I called Trent. He didn't answer. I had to leave a message. I didn't have money for a tow truck. I sat in the car and waited." She remembered how it had felt. Marooned. Forgotten. Helpless. "It was a long wait, but then he drove up. Some little thing in the engine had come loose. He fixed it in the space of a heartbeat. Some cap or plug or something." She wiped at her cheek and found a tear.

"Mom, he'd been there the whole time. That road he drove up on came from the maintenance area behind the school. No outlet back there. He'd sabotaged my car and then left me to wait."

"Did you ask him about it?"

She nodded. "Yes. I confronted him. He said he'd called the school earlier in the day and discovered the session had been canceled. He wanted to see what else I might be up to. As if . . . as if I might be sneaking around on him. He said he drove to the school to see if I'd actually gone there. He denied sabotaging my car but admitted he'd deliberately made me wait."

Sandra looked at her mother. She couldn't read her face. "I thought about it. I felt like I'd actually done something wrong, had brought it on myself. In the end, no real harm was done, right? Except to my feelings and to my trust."

She looked down at the table, staring at her hands. "He apologized, Mom. He said he was sorry. He said that it was important to always have options, a backup plan. He said he was glad I had learned that. He was sorry my feelings were hurt, but that this small lesson might save me from greater hurt next time."

Sandra put her hands over her face. Stupid. She was the very definition of futile.

Her mother cleared her throat. "Call Bert Davis and sell the car. If Trent is somehow tracking you, he'll assume the car is going to the dealership for repairs. Misdirection can be a useful tool. Let's make it work for us."

Sandra's car wasn't fancy, and this was essentially a distress sale, so the money wasn't great. Still, it was something, and Sandra was holding a check for $5,400 when Mom pulled up to the curb.

"Will your bank cash it for me?" she asked.

"Of course." Mom gave her a long look. "Are you really going to carry that kind of money around with you?"

"What choice do I have?"

"Get a checking account?"

"Maybe. When I find a job, I'll need a bank account. Until then . . ." Sandra tucked the check in her purse. There was no way she'd risk Trent getting his hands on her funds. He could find a bank account. She didn't doubt that for a second. But she didn't say it out loud because her mom would never really understand what it was like to be watched and controlled. No, the money was safer with her. "After the bank, can we stop at the store to get that phone?"

Mom sighed. "Yes, but be quick. I have to pick up your dad from day care."

Sandra stood at the windows watching the street through the screening of the same dogwoods, holly, and lilacs she'd seen her entire life. She'd given up the job hunt until after the house was sold and the move was done because Trent was out there, she knew it. She hadn't spotted him yet, but he was nearby, and she didn't want him to see that her transportation had changed.

Trent didn't, couldn't call. He didn't have her new number, and the house phone was now disconnected. He had her mom's cell number, but he hadn't called her. She would've said so if he had.

Dad's car was at the local mechanic's shop. They were doing an oil change and replacing the tires, among other things. The garage owner was an old friend of her parents. A friend of the family. That was a perk of longtime roots in the same city. Dad's family had been in Richmond forever. Mom had moved here when they married. To help their misdirection plan, Joe, the mechanic, had towed away Dad's old car with most of the few belongings she had left already in the trunk. After the tune-up, he would keep it in an unused bay. The storage was free but not the repairs. Sandra felt her stash of cash slipping away.

What would Trent think when her car didn't come back from the dealership? And when the movers came and the garage door opened, and he saw that only her mother's car was parked inside, would he assume Sandra was leaving for sunny Florida with her parents? Maybe.

Would he finally go home and find someone else to beguile and control? Was anyone else naive enough to not only fall for him but to stay long after the truth of his obsession had become obvious?

Sandra stayed inside. She helped pack and clean and sort items of all descriptions for donation or trash. Neighbors hauled away the discards and dropped off donations to the Salvation Army and Goodwill. She was useful in the house and, within these walls, she didn't risk meeting Trent face-to-face.

Everything moved too quickly. When potential buyers came to view the house, Mom and Sandra left together and parked down the street, waiting until the prospective buyers left. On one such trip, her mother said, "I wonder if these people will make an offer. What do you think? Any guesses?"

Sandra nearly choked. She cleared her throat but refused to answer.

"Sooner or later, someone will make that offer, Sandra. The sale will happen. You could go to Cub Creek. Your aunt has plenty of room there."

She was offended. She let the sentence hang in the air unanswered for a moment before saying, "Cub Creek? Aunt Barbara's house? I hardly know her."

Her mother gripped the steering wheel. "Maybe it's a good time to get to know her better. She was fond of you when you were little."

"Please." If Sandra made a list of what she didn't need, it would include a nosy aunt she hardly knew and a place she hadn't visited in years and had never missed, located in the middle of nowhere with no opportunity to find employment. "No thanks, Mom. I need to find a job."

Mom nodded. "It was a thought."

The couple who was viewing the house came down the sidewalk with the realtor. As soon as they were gone, Mom and Sandra returned to the house, and Mom immediately went back to packing and sorting. Sandra wished she could slow her down. Or slow down time. She was watching her life, her history, devolve—deconstructing into bits and pieces wrapped in paper and crammed into boxes, then summed up with scribbled words in black marker.

The first lookers returned a week later and, after a second walk-through, made an offer. They wanted a quick possession. *Of course they do,* Sandra thought to herself. Mom was delighted. Dad was oblivious. The closing would be in two weeks. Two weeks, and then what would she do?

Time was cruel and contrary. It passed, regardless of her wishes or plans, and the final day arrived. Sandra watched her mother fold and layer the last clothing items into her suitcase, keeping out what she and Dad would need for that night and the next morning. Sandra was waiting to carry the case downstairs for her.

"How will you manage the car trip on your own? I mean, Dad can't drive, so . . ."

"We'll do fine. We can go as slowly or as quickly as we need to." Mom lowered the suitcase lid and zipped the top closed.

Sandra waited. Desperation drove her. "I could help, you know. Both with the drive to Florida and to get you settled down there."

"We'll be all right." Mom stepped back to allow Sandra to pick up the suitcase. "Don't roll it. You might scratch the floor." She touched her daughter's arm. "Wait a minute, Sandra. There's something I want to suggest to you."

Her heart lifted. Florida?

"It's about your Aunt Barbara."

"Aunt Barbara?" she echoed. "What about her? We already discussed this, didn't we?"

"I've asked her to come to Florida for an extended visit. I've been asking her all along, but she was reluctant. This morning she called to say she'd like to come. I'm thinking she'll be there for about two months. It would be good for her, and I could use her help."

"What?" Sandra felt her jaw tighten. Aunt Barbara? Really?

Hadn't she just offered her assistance to her mother and father? Where had her aunt been during all the packing and sorting? Mom acted like she didn't, or couldn't, hear her daughter. Sandra was choosing her words, ready to repeat her offer to help, when her mother spoke again.

"She's worried about her house and leaving it empty."

"Mom—"

"We think a house sitter is the answer."

Sandra gasped. She was still standing in the bedroom holding her mother's suitcase by its side handle as an icy anger settled around her, and she shivered. Her jaw felt so tight she could hardly speak. "House sitter? Me? And Aunt Barbara goes to Florida? Now I see."

She set the suitcase on the floor.

"That's right." Mom's tone was suddenly bright and upbeat as she moved briskly around the room, busy again as she checked the already empty dresser drawers for the hundredth time. "I thought of you. I didn't tell her you'd do it because I didn't want to speak for you. Frankly, I didn't know how you'd react." She turned to face Sandra. "It's out in the country. You know where she lives. You said you were hoping to stay in town and find a job, but the movers will be here tomorrow morning to get the furniture and boxes and then . . . well, where will you go?" Mom placed her hands on the dresser. "I told Barbara you might be willing to stay at the house while she's away in exchange for room and board."

That cold anger felt brittle inside Sandra. It wanted to shatter, and she fought it. "Room and board, Mom? I need a job. I need to earn money. I can do that in Florida and help you and Dad at the same time."

"I think that what you need is a place to rest and be alone. It's quiet out there at Cub Creek. I don't mean to sound cold, but I think you've been confused for a long time." She touched her daughter's arm and lifted it by the wrist. "You get thinner and thinner." She sighed and released her. "You need to figure out what your future looks like instead of just going from one thing to the next."

"I've been under stress for a long time. At least give me credit for effort. I've suffered, but I've tried." Sandra pressed her hands together and held them to her face, but for only a moment. Her anger turned hot. She held up her palms toward her mother as if warding off unpleasantness.

44

"Mom, I appreciate all that you have done for me, throughout my life and in recent times. But frankly, one thing I wish you'd done, both you and Dad, was to have loved me enough to teach me survival skills. Doing the right thing doesn't guarantee anything in this life. You sent me out into the world like a lamb among hungry carnivores." She stopped abruptly, gasping again. One hand went to her side to press against a shooting pain.

Nearly breathless, she continued. "I did everything that was asked of me. You, Dad, my teachers. Everyone. It was like a contract, right? I listen, I learn, I follow the rules, and everyone is happy. In college I chose the right major and signed up for the required classes and . . . I tried to tell you it wasn't working for me. You and Dad said to apply myself. Work harder. Make friends, but the right friends, you said. Trent looked right. He was strong. He was certain about everything. But it was a lie. I did everything everyone wanted, yet you broke the contract. Every one of you." The last words burst from her. "Here I am, the only one still trying. The rest of you are concerned with yourselves, with your own lives, while I'm left alone."

Sandra closed her eyes and tried to visualize relaxation and peace. The ache eased almost immediately, and oxygen filled her lungs. She opened her eyes, both glad and guilty that she'd exposed her anger and frustration, had taken them out on her mother. Now what? It was Mom's turn, and Sandra waited.

Mom bit her lip. She kept all expression from her face. When she spoke, she didn't mention either her daughter's outburst or her obvious physical discomfort. She kept her tone soft and level. "If you change your mind about house-sitting for Barbara, let me know." She walked out of the room and into the hallway, then stopped and turned back to face Sandra.

"Tomorrow the movers will be here. Dad will go to the day care for the day, and when the movers are done, I'll pick him up from there and head south. Will you be here tomorrow?"

Her mother spoke coolly, calmly, as if refusing to acknowledge that Sandra's entire life, from the cradle to present, had become nothing more than a caravan moving on to the next life stop. This time without her. Without their child, grown or not.

Sandra felt deflated. She was done with forcing the issue, and she responded equally coolly. "I'll help with the movers. You haven't asked for my help, but I can give it, so I will."

"Cleaners are scheduled to come in the day after tomorrow to sweep and such. If you like, I'll cancel them, and you can do that for what I would've paid them."

Paid help. Despite the sale of the car, a little more cash could make a difference.

46

"I would've done it for nothing, but since you're offering, I'll take the job."

Mom nodded, then continued into the next room to recheck the nooks and crannies for forgotten items she valued and didn't want to leave behind.

The next morning, Sandra kissed her dad goodbye. She gave him an extra hug, which seemed to please yet confuse him. Mom left the house with him that morning as if today were no different from the ones before. For him, it may not have seemed different because he paid no attention to the stacks of boxes or to the bare surfaces devoid of knickknacks.

Mom returned with a box of doughnuts. The coffeemaker wasn't packed. It sat on the counter, hard at work, brewing, with a stack of cardboard cups beside it.

"Sugar and caffeine," Mom said as she offered a doughnut to her daughter. "Today is a day for breaking rules."

The lines in her mother's face seemed deeper, and the dark areas under her eyes were almost violet. When it came to the movers, she seemed content to let Sandra do most of the directing and fussing. Sandra noticed she was drinking coffee almost constantly. As far as the move itself, it went OK, but it continued into the afternoon. When the men finally slammed the back of the truck closed and left, Mom was eager to do the same. She seemed hurried, distracted, and stressed. She kept repeating that she had to pick up Dad, so despite the countless instructions about how and when Sandra was to leave the house, as if she'd never managed her own home or her own moves, she simply listened.

"Return the broom and cleaning products to the next-door neighbor tomorrow when you're done."

"I'll leave with you. Then you can drop me off one street over, and I'll come back via the alley and the back door."

Mom frowned and sighed, though the sigh sounded more like a groan.

"I know you don't get it, Mom. Please trust me on this."

They made a show of locking the front door and walking to the car. Sandra carried the suitcase and put it into the trunk, then climbed into the passenger side, and they drove off.

Mom stopped at the end of the street, and as Sandra moved to leave the car, her mother said, "I know things haven't worked out as you'd hoped, but don't go silent, Sandra. That's what you do when you have troubles. You think I'm being cold and harsh right now, but please keep me informed, and don't forget about Barbara's offer."

Sandra exited the car, and her mother drove away to begin the next phase of her life.

The alley was neat and clean, and Sandra let herself in through the back gate and the kitchen door. One more night at the house. She had stashed a couple of blankets and a pillow in the closet with her suitcase and tote bag before the movers arrived and affixed a note to the door threatening anyone who opened it. "Do Not Pack," it said. She arranged the blankets on the floor in the living room and listened to the silence, the echo of quiet, with the creak of the wooden floors and the occasional squeak of plumbing for accompaniment. The appliances had stayed, so there were also the little clicks and knocks and whirs from the refrigerator. She heated the last frozen meal in the microwave and ate it with a plastic fork. The final bag of trash would go out the door with her in the morning.

The burner phone rang. Her mom had planned to drive to North Carolina, as far as Rocky Mount, before stopping for the night. She told Sandra they'd stopped in Roanoke Rapids instead. Her voice was tight with stress. Dad was having issues with the distance.

Mom said, "Hold for a minute, please?"

Sandra heard Dad saying he didn't remember the drive home taking this long before. Her mom responded with the cadence of someone having repeated the same statement several times, that they weren't going to the old house tonight but were going on vacation to Florida. He'd always liked Florida, hadn't he? He agreed, sounding pleased, that yes, indeed, he'd always liked Florida, and it was fun to go there on vacation.

Mom returned to their conversation. "You're all set to clean, right? Broom clean is what they say, but I want it to look nice for the new owners."

"Easy. No problem."

"It always takes longer that it looks. Don't put it off."

Sandra groaned. "I won't. I'll take care of it. Worry about yourself and Dad."

"He's frowning again."

In the background Sandra heard him say, "Meg, honey, I don't recall the trip home taking this long before." There was a pause and he added, "This isn't my bed."

"I have to go," Mom said.

Sandra felt badly for her, but only a little. Her mother could've had her daughter's help on that trip, and her gratitude, too, if she'd wanted it.

The house was already so clean that sweeping and dusting seemed needless. Sandra did it anyway and shined up the bathroom mirrors and fixtures, too. When she was done, she returned the broom and other items to the neighbor, getting there by way of the back door and alley. Mrs. Combs pushed aside the curtain over the backdoor window for a peek before opening the door.

"Well, hello, dear."

Sandra handed her the bucket of cleaning items, the broom, and the mop. "Thanks so much."

"You are welcome, of course. Enjoy Florida, dear."

Easier to say thank you than to explain. "Yes, ma'am."

"I'll miss your mama and daddy. Hard to imagine better neighbors. Tell them I say so."

Sandra nodded. "Good-bye."

Mom didn't call until almost suppertime. "Sandra. Did it go OK today?"

"Are you asking if I cleaned the house, returned the supplies to your neighbor, and locked the doors behind me?"

"I guess that means you did. Well, we're staying near the Georgia line tonight. Hopefully we'll drive the rest of the way to Tampa tomorrow."

"How's Dad?"

"Better. He seems to have settled in to the trip." She added, "Have you considered house-sitting for Barbara?"

Sandra was in her car. When she left the house, she'd snuck out via the back door, and a cab had picked her up one street over. After picking up her car from Joe, she was now parked in front of a hotel. Everything she owned, including a box of food items she'd gleaned from her mom's pantry, fit easily in the trunk. It was sobering to consider that.

"When does she need me?"

"You could go whenever you're ready. She has plenty of room out at the old house."

Sandra hadn't seen her aunt since prior to her last wedding, and that had been by chance at her parents' home. Despite being family, they had no real bond or relationship. Sandra had been a little closer to her uncle, but that was back when she was a child, and he'd died a couple of years ago.

She ran her finger lightly across the dashboard, leaving a track in the trace of dust the sun highlighted. Was her refusal due to pride or stupidity? Her mother didn't want her in Florida. She wanted, instead, to send her daughter off to Cub Creek, the Shoemaker homeplace. Sandra was invited now because it suited the family's convenience. Because the family circle was closing again, this time in Florida, with Sandra left out. Left behind. Put aside. Always on the outside. Clearly her mother preferred to be with her sister than her daughter.

Mom knew her best, right? Sandra rested her forehead against the cool glass of the window. Mom shouldn't get her way, right away, every time. Thanks to the sale of the car, Sandra had enough cash to manage for a while. Though, being honest, even that was thanks to her mother.

"Let me know when she'll be leaving. I'll drive out there so she can join you and Dad down in Florida at your new place. I'll be fine on my own." Snarkiness was front and center in her tone, and she didn't care.

"Be smart, Sandra. Go now. There's no reason not to." Her mother's voice was suddenly muffled as she spoke to Dad, then she resumed her normal tone. "He's going to have trouble sleeping tonight. He thinks all beds should be the one he's accustomed to regardless of where he is at night. Anyway, will you call Barbara or should I let her know?"

"You'll be calling her anyway, so you can let her know."

Her sigh was audible. "I will. You have her phone number. I'll give her yours. She has always had a good opinion of you, so please try to be courteous. Don't take your annoyance with me out on her. Oh, and I almost forgot. She has a dog. You'll need to take care of the dog, too. Should be simple."

"A dog? What kind?" she asked, thinking of Leo. "You know I don't like dogs any more than you do, and they don't like me."

"Honestly, Sandra, it's just a dog." She sounded exasperated, but she paused, and when she spoke again, her tone was smooth and reasonable. "It's an older animal your aunt got at the pound. It won't be any trouble. I'm sure you can manage."

For the first two nights, she stayed at a nice hotel in Short Pump. Checking in without a credit card felt awkward, but with her driver's license and cash payment in advance, there was no problem. It was a lovely room, but she'd stood there that first day, looking at the furnishings, and felt odd. Almost alien.

She knew what was wrong. This wasn't a "we're on a trip or vacation" hotel-room stay.

How long would she need to be here? She had appointments at two temp agencies in the morning. One was a follow-up appointment. If, by some happy chance, she got a job tomorrow, would it start immediately? Right now she had enough cash for a first month/security deposit and a second month, too, at a decent apartment. Would they rent to her if she didn't have an official employer? She couldn't show any past income.

Don't borrow trouble, she told herself. *Keep moving forward.*

Sandra treated herself to a nice meal and then strolled around the shopping mall, but she held tight to her cash. When she had a job, she'd lighten up on the spending freeze. Trent hadn't trusted her to manage the budget, but that was on Trent, not her. She could do this.

The temp agency appointments in the morning didn't result in immediate interviews elsewhere. She knew she shouldn't be discouraged, but that second evening she sat in the hotel room and watched TV too late. The next morning, she slept through the free hotel breakfast. She lay in bed undecided about next steps. At ten a.m. she called the agencies again, but they had nothing to offer.

Two nights plus meals and a tank of gas. A fair chunk of her cash. She couldn't do this for long.

She downscaled for the next two nights to an inexpensive but still decent motel. Safety was the important thing. She checked through her belongings in the trunk and opted to bring in her purse and tote bag with her. The tote bag was roomy enough for her toiletries, a change of clothing, and the newspaper she'd picked up.

This place wasn't great, but the door locked. There was a bed and a table, both bolted down, and a chair that wasn't. The mattress sagged, but the linens and furnishings looked clean. All in all, not bad. She spread the newspaper open on the table to read through the job listings. She'd be back on track in no time. She could have a job as soon as tomorrow.

In the morning, Sandra made the calls. Some said the jobs had already been filled, and others instructed her to submit her application via computer. When she said she didn't have one, they sounded surprised and doubtful.

"I'm in the middle of moving back to the area. Would it be possible to come to your office and apply?"

"Sure. Or go to a library and use a computer there."

Sandra applied in person. One job was at a wholesale store, and the other was as a receptionist. Now she could only wait.

After the second night in the bolted-furniture hotel, a roach surprised her in the bathroom. He scurried away, but after that fright, as her heart rate was returning to normal, she was glad she hadn't seen him scuttling around during the night.

She couldn't possibly stay here another night. As she left, hurrying, she fumbled her keys, and they fell into a chair. She moved the cushion to retrieve them and saw tiny insects digging into the upholstered crevices. They were fast and soon gone from sight. Bedbugs?

Quickly, she snatched up her tote bag and purse and hugged them to her, then abruptly held them away from her. She needed to inspect them. She wanted to complain at the desk but went straight to the car first. She emptied her bag's contents, one item at a time, examining each before putting it into the car. In the end she tossed the tote bag into a trash can because the seams were impossible to adequately check. She examined her clothing for wildlife and found none, but she couldn't shake the feeling of creepy-crawlies on her skin.

Giving up and not bothering to complain—not even wanting to go back into the building—Sandra drove to a park and spent the day there, reading the newspaper and a magazine she'd purchased. She had peanut butter, crackers, and a bottle of water from her food box. She watched people jog around the lake or fish or throw Frisbees. Occasionally, she gave in and checked the odd itch or scratched, because she couldn't help it.

That hotel had made her feel safe enough but ultimately had cost her peace of mind.

If she spent her money on motels, especially nicer ones, it would be gone too soon. She weighed the risk versus the expense. Did she believe in herself or not? Those jobs could call soon, or the temp agencies might come up with an opportunity. She wanted to be in a position to take advantage of them, not stressed and exhausted.

As the afternoon passed, she had to decide. Sandra persuaded herself that belief in her plan would make it work. She treated herself to a nice dinner at a nice restaurant and an ever nicer hotel and dropped an easy two hundred plus. She slept badly.

The next day, she returned to the park and her picnic table. She ate peanut butter and counted her funds and felt a little sick. The money was going fast, and she could do better. She had to plan. Plan and stick to it.

When would her aunt call? Maybe staying in the country for a while wouldn't be so bad. She could worry about getting a job later. In fact, she could get that rest her mother kept talking about and also manage the job search and have interviews lined up by the time her aunt returned from Florida. That idea gave her new hope.

Meanwhile, what would she do tonight?

She had her car. The weather was mild. Really, it would be like camping, right? The car would be like her camper.

She checked out mall parking lots, commuter lots, and rest areas close to the city, choosing a commuter parking area within a mall parking lot. She spent the evening in the mall and grabbed supper. She returned to her car before the mall closed and watched. The cars pulled in and out. People walked across the lot in groups and in singles. No one paid any attention to her or her car. If challenged by mall security, she was ready with an excuse and a smile and prepared to drive off. She still had money. She didn't have to stay here. This was more like an experiment. An adventure. And no one ended up bothering her at all. Unfortunately, it wasn't good for getting a good night's rest.

The next day, exhausted, she drove to the park. Sitting at her picnic table, she screwed the top back on the peanut butter jar and closed the roll of crackers, fastening it with a twist tie. What seemed on the surface like a simple life was surprisingly demanding. Her thinking seemed foggy, no doubt from stress and lack of sleep. Her sense of rationality was slipping. Lack of sleep or not, that was ridiculous. She tried to nail it down. Other people survived hardship. They drew on their resources, whatever they were, and on their inner strength. This was a temporary situation. She still had cash, and she'd have a normal life soon.

Sandra held the phone in her hand and checked the slip of paper to make sure it was still in her pocket. She could call her aunt. Or give it another day or two?

She could drive out to Aunt Barbara's house. But what would Barbara report to her sister? That poor Sandra was a wreck and couldn't manage on her own for a few days? Trent would be proved right. Sandra didn't make good choices. She didn't have survivor instincts.

Maybe her aunt had made other arrangements or decided not to go to Florida after all. But if so, Mom would've called. In fact, Mom had called several times. The first was to ask how Sandra was doing. Sandra hadn't answered her calls since. Her mother would've known immediately by the sound of her voice that things were going very wrong.

Didn't Sandra have friends? A couch to crash on? She'd been so isolated the last few years. Trapped with Trent, so to speak. The friends she'd stayed in touch with after high school and college had fallen away during the divorce and the remarriage. Her best friend, also her maid of honor in the first wedding, Tammy, would've understood, but she had died several years ago in a car accident.

Never mind. There were logical, rational reasons for how she'd ended up in this spot—reasons that had nothing to do with personal failure. And there was a logical, rational path for getting back to where she belonged. A real life.

So if it came down to sleeping in the car and washing up in restrooms for two or three nights, given the time of year, it wouldn't be bad weather-wise. She'd done OK last night. Tonight she'd sleep better. But that confidence lasted only until dark.

At night everything changed, and despite her resolve, the fear rolled in and overwhelmed her. Someone might break into the car, either targeting her or breaking into the car to steal, and find her there, alone and defenseless. Each noise, no matter how small and innocent, screamed of threats.

Barbara still hadn't called. Sandra smoothed the crumpled scrap of paper with her aunt's phone number, then dialed. It went to her aunt's voice mail.

Sandra cleared her throat. "Hi, Aunt Barbara. Long time since we've spoken. Mom said you needed someone to watch the house." She paused, took a breath, and then finished the message. "So I wanted to make sure you had my number." She recited it twice. "Call me. Thanks."

Her veneer of calm began to crack. She was past fooling herself, and it frightened her that over such a short time, no more than a few days, she could feel disassociated with the rest of the world and regular people.

Breathing almost hurt her lungs, especially in the tightness around the edges. She reached up and scratched her itchy scalp. Not infested. It was only anxiety. Still, she checked under her fingernails for anything squirmy.

She needed to know whether she was still invited to stay at Cub Creek. If not, then she needed to conserve her cash to get an inexpensive apartment. Either way, she couldn't keep living this way.

That night, she returned to a commuter lot. As she'd done the prior nights, she climbed onto the back floorboard and pulled a blanket over herself. But every gust of wind, every crunch of gravel nearby, frightened her. Before dawn, drained and stressed, she drove to a quiet early-morning diner and washed up in their restroom. She purchased breakfast and lingered over a coffee refill. Feeling more rational, she returned to the car. Somewhere in all that activity, she'd lost the money envelope.

Frantically, Sandra retraced her steps. She went

to every place she'd been during the past twenty-four hours. She relived those hours a thousand times, some in actual physical retracing. She searched the car repeatedly, but to no avail.

She had money in her purse, but the majority of her cash was gone. Sitting at the picnic table at the park, she cried, grateful there was no one to see her misery. She was almost ready to see Trent. She held the phone in a tight grip. Was he nearby? Watching her? Was he still in the Richmond area hunting her? He could get here quickly, if he wanted to.

Tempted and horrified, she threw the phone. It flew over the picnic table, hit the ground beyond, and skidded toward the lake. Panicked, she flung herself after it, scrabbling at the ground to retrieve it before it could fall through the thick grasses at the water's edge.

Sandra huddled there clutching her phone. Clearly she hadn't hit rock bottom yet. Pathetic, yes, but not ready for Trent. Never ready for Trent. She almost panicked again when she imagined what rock bottom could be. If it could be worse than this . . .

She returned to the car and searched it one last time, and then finally gave up hope.

Her mother was right. Trent was right. She wasn't a survivor. She was a natural victim. Trent had explained the points of failure to her many times. He'd learned them from his father. Per Trent's points, there were two types of people. If you weren't a survivor, then you were a victim. For natural victims like her, failure was inevitable.

The last time they'd discussed that particular point had been during their second marriage. They were living in Arizona, and she now viewed it as the beginning of the end, the final end, the last gasp, of their unhappy second attempt. He had fired up the grill and was cooking thick steaks out by the pool. She'd seen the new, shiny motorcycle in the garage and was angry.

"You bought a motorcycle?"

"You bet. Decided I deserved a treat."

Sandra waved away the smoke drifting over from the grill. "Didn't I tell you I needed a new outfit for that job interview? You told me we couldn't afford it." She pointed back toward the garage. "What you spent on that bike could fill my closet. The insurance alone will cost a fortune."

"You don't need a job anyway, Sandy. I earn enough for both of us."

"Trent, you're the one who's always talking about being a survivor. Survivors support themselves, right? In times of trouble, they aren't dependent upon others."

"You, a survivor? You have me. You don't need to worry." Trent turned the steaks on the grill. "See? I can cook."

She tried to explain it from another angle. "It's

more than that, Trent. It's about partnership and fairness, too. You've spent a lot of money without talking to me. We're supposed to be working on our communication. You know I want things to be good between us."

Trent turned fully toward her, his smile gone. "Is that it? Are you saying that if you don't get what you want that you'll make sure things aren't good for us?" He slapped his hand with the spatula, heedless of the grease and bits of beef transferring to his hand.

She moved to the other side of the pool. "That's not what I said."

He nodded, his expression easing. "You're right, Sandra. I apologize. I remember my dad telling me that being a survivor is all about knowing what you want and doing what is necessary to get it. If that's you, then go for it. Do what you think is best, Sandra. You won't hear another word about it from me."

And she had. She'd gone to the mall the next day while Trent was at work, and she'd purchased the perfect silk blouse and a red skirt for the job interview. She'd stood taller, feeling as if she'd made a stand, had drawn on her inner strength, had faced Trent down. He'd seen he was wrong, and it had all worked out. That evening, he made a joke of shuddering at the cost on the price tags but had complimented her appearance. Before he got his revenge.

Inner strength? What a sick joke. The kind of joke that strong people played on those who weren't. She looked inside, and instead of her own voice, all she could hear was Trent's.

The itchy-scratchy scalp was wearing her down. It was the soap, she told herself. She washed her hair every day. She hated the look of oily, dirty hair. But it was hard to wash soap out of long hair in a restroom sink.

Aunt Barbara didn't call, and Sandra realized she wasn't going to. She thought of calling her mother. Poor Mom. Down in Florida with a husband who could no longer manage on his own and who needed the full attention of his wife.

Sandra no longer phoned the temp agencies. She'd been a pest. Desperation did that to people. The managers asked her not to call every day, that if they had something for her, they'd contact her. They hadn't, and she understood now that they wouldn't. That hope was gone.

Dreams colored her sleep with images of bed-bugs infesting her car and lice burrowing in her scalp. When she woke in the night, she understood that her world was only going to get darker.

In the morning, she was lost in misery. It didn't have to stay this way, she told herself. Whichever direction her life would take, she had to seize control again. She watched the sunrise and dug her fingernails into her hair and scratched her scalp. It was driving her crazy.

She'd had a super-short haircut when she was a kid. Age nine, she thought. She'd hated it at the time, but she'd gotten lots of compliments, and people said it made her eyes and her face more striking. What those people didn't know was that there'd been a lice breakout at her school. Her mother had washed her hair over and over with that special shampoo and had finally dragged her to the beauty salon and had them cut it. The long tresses had fallen as if weightless, silently curling into themselves as they hit the tile floor.

Sandra hadn't thought about that haircut in a long time and had completely forgotten the reason for it until this morning. Now the old memory fell into place with the mindless grace of that long-ago hair coiling onto the floor where it landed.

She could solve this one problem, at least.

She located the scissors in a bag in the trunk and went to the park's ladies' room. She ran her fingers through the length of her thick hair, dark like her father's. Trent had liked her hair long. She'd talked about cutting it. He'd been upset, had made her promise not to. Keeping it long meant a great deal to Trent. It meant a lot more to him than cutting it had meant to her, and she'd given up the idea.

She lifted the scissors and held them in front of the mirror, flexing the fingerholds so that the blades snicked open and closed over and over. She ran the fingers of her free hand through her hair again, pulling it out and away from her face. The scissors seemed to drive themselves. The cool blades pressed up near her scalp and slid back together. Sandra gasped. By the dim yellow light above the restroom mirror, the hair fell, dark, almost alien, and as silent as that childhood haircut, into the sink.

The gasp didn't repeat. This felt appropriate. The cut was inelegant, and she kept tweaking at it, snipping, trying to even it up, until finally there wasn't much left.

Sandra pressed her fingers against her scalp, pushing and massaging. She closed her eyes and felt such lightness, weightlessness, it was almost unbearable. She opened her eyes, and all she could see were those eyes, so dark, exactly like her mother's, staring right back at her. She was no Audrey Hepburn, no Jaimie Alexander, and frankly their short cuts had had more hair than was now on her head. She was just Sandra, and now she had no hair, and it was no one's business but hers.

She gathered up the butchered hair and dropped it into the trash, brushing at the orphan strands as they clung to her fingers.

Her being felt lighter, but her scalp still itched. She bent over the sink and ran the water over her scalp, rubbing and massaging and grateful that the faucet was the old-fashioned kind that kept running until it was physically turned off.

When she was done, she tried not to linger at the mirror, not ready to deal with regret. Really, why did park restrooms need mirrors anyway? The glimpse she caught from the corner of her eye was enough. Punk or Goth or something like that. Not a model, not an actress. If her eyes looked bigger, so did the purple patches under them. They reminded her of the ones she'd seen on her mother's face that last day.

She looked away and pushed past the door, wanting fresh air. At least the itching had stopped.

Sandra was back in a park, but this one was far enough out of town that she didn't have to share it with the homeless, yet not so far that the trip burned a lot of gas. She was crossing the picnic area, heading to the ladies' room, when the phone rang. Her aunt? Her mom?

Frantic, she almost fumbled the phone. "Hello?"

"Sandra? That you?"

"Yes, it's me." Suddenly breathless, she stepped into the ladies' room and checked the stalls. She was alone.

"This is your Aunt Barbara, dear. How are you doing? I got your voice mail. There was some kind of delivery delay. Did you get mine? No? Well, I'm flying out to Florida in two days. Why don't you drive out to the cottage? We can visit tonight and tomorrow, and then you can drive me to the airport the next morning to catch the flight."

"I didn't get your message." Sandra's voice was shaky. She'd practically buried Barbara . . . at least the idea of her calling. Her uneasy sense of reality quaked.

"You OK, dear? You sound funny." Barbara cleared her throat. "Now if the timing's not good for you . . ."

The thought of seeing her aunt was almost overwhelming. Somehow the world had moved on without Sandra. Barbara said a neighbor could bring her into town if that worked better for Sandra's schedule.

Her schedule? Her nerves were shot. As she rushed to answer, she turned and saw herself in the mirror. Really saw herself. As if looking through her aunt's eyes.

How much money did she have left? Enough to pay for a hotel room for two nights and a tank of gas? She stared in that bathroom mirror at her haunted face, the shadows dark beneath her eyes, the hollow look, and knew she couldn't pretend at this level. Two nights in a hotel, hot showers, and a decent bed would go a long way to bringing her back so that she could face her aunt.

"Actually, if you could get that ride to town, that would be great. We could meet near the airport and have a short visit before I take you the rest of the way."

Aunt Barbara agreed. They set a time and meeting place, and she rambled on for another few minutes before they said good-bye. The last of the conversation was a blur to Sandra.

The one upside to the sad, miserable story was that if Trent had been following her, somehow tracking her at her mom's house, then he must have lost the trail by now. Maybe, in the end, the trauma was worth it.

No, it wasn't.

Less than two weeks ago, Sandra had wanted to punish her mother, had wanted her to know her feelings were hurt, that she had let her down. Sandra had also wanted to avoid her aunt's questions and criticism. Pride? Resentment? Had it been worth it? No. Her reflection in the restroom mirror frightened her. Less than two weeks adrift on her own, and she was at the lowest point of her life—one of Trent's points of failure? This was more like a cascade of failures. On her own, she was doomed to fail. There was nothing to be done, no lessons learned, only a dark time to be packed away into the darkest corner of her mind and forgotten. That she could do.

She pressed her hands against the smudged mirror, almost touching the dark bruises under her eyes, seeing the dirt under her fingernails. She was thirty and had failed so badly, she didn't know if she could find her way back.

Chapter Three

Sandra saw Aunt Barbara standing on the sidewalk outside of the fast-food place at the intersection of Nine Mile Road and Airport Drive. Her aunt's friend could have driven her the final mile to the airport, but Barbara wanted to see Sandra in person, however briefly, to give her the key and share instructions. More than that, her aunt probably wanted to reassure herself that Sandra was capable of keeping her promises. Well, Sandra could and would. She might be a failure on multiple levels, but she could manage house-sitting and a dog.

Her aunt gripped the handle of her black upright suitcase with one hand while her other was shading her eyes as she scanned the area. A large leather tote bag with lots of bling hung from her shoulder, and she was wearing jeans, cowboy boots, and a purple and orange sweater vest. As Sandra pulled into the parking lot, her aunt leaned forward, squinting at the car. Barbara's long curly hair, now all gray, blew across her face, and she pushed it away.

Sandra rolled down the car window and waved. Her aunt's posture relaxed.

So far, so good, thought Sandra. Two nights of civilization had had amazing restorative powers, though it had cost most of her remaining cash. A manicure, shampoo and conditioner—all that good stuff. It meant as much as, or more than, the tangible value it actually delivered. It meant, among other things, that the planet still turned and was steady in its orbit, and all was as it should be. It might not be totally true, but it gave one permission to believe.

Sandra parked her car at her aunt's sandaled feet, swung the door wide, and stepped out.

"Hi, there. Ready for your trip?" Sandra flashed a bright smile, determined to keep the tone light, social, and impersonal.

"Am I ready?" Barbara echoed, her voice high and a little shrill. "I've been ready. I was worried you wouldn't show. I was racking my brain trying to figure out what I'd do if you didn't."

"I'm here, so no worries." Sandra hugged her aunt, then took the suitcase. "In fact, I think I'm a little early."

"I wasn't sure I'd recognize you after so long."

Sandra awkwardly lifted the suitcase onto the narrow backseat, but she managed. Better that than to open the trunk and expose the truth of her entire self-worth to her aunt.

Barbara paused, seeing the nicked paint and the dented fender. "That's your dad's old car, isn't it?"

"Yes, ma'am. It doesn't look great, but it runs fine." Sandra opened the passenger door and held it for her.

"So long as it works. That's the main thing, certainly." She patted Sandra's arm as she climbed into the car. "It's not a short drive out to my place. Can't risk you not making it there. What would happen to Honey?"

Her aunt's voice was playing "Chopsticks" on her nerves. And yet, something was stirring in the back of her brain. A familiarity she'd forgotten.

As Sandra slid into the driver's seat, Aunt Barbara looked at her gravely. "You remember the way to Cub Creek?"

The lines around Aunt Barbara's eyes and mouth were deeper than Sandra remembered. Her skin was pale and looked fragile and dry.

"Of course I remember." Sandra paused before backing out the car and touched her aunt's arm. "Did you eat breakfast?"

Aunt Barbara shook her head. "I'm too excited for food. I've never flown before, you know. I've never even left Virginia."

"Try to get something at the airport, OK? Go through security and to your gate. They'll have shops there with pastries and such." Something her mom had often said popped into her head. "You need your energy."

Barbara took Sandra's hand and pressed something into her palm.

"The key. Don't lose it. But if you do, there's a spare under the fake rock by the shed in the backyard." She closed Sandra's fingers around

73

the key. "Now, as soon as you drop me off, go straight to the house. Don't change your mind or get distracted. Honey is home alone." She stared intently as if to underscore the meaning. Apparently satisfied Sandra understood, Barbara sat back in her seat and pulled the seat belt across to latch it.

"All set, then. You look well, Sandra." Barbara coughed. "No, you don't. I wish I could be one of those polite people who say the right things instead of blurting out the truth. You look awful. What did you do to your hair?"

Sandra ran her fingers through the close-cropped, uneven edges. "I cut it myself. You don't like it?"

Barbara snorted softly. "You're trained to cut hair?"

"No."

"Didn't think so. You're skinny, too. When'd you get so thin?"

Her aunt was right. Sandra knew how she looked. Then again, Aunt Barbara wasn't looking so hot herself, not with those straggly eyebrows and that full, frizzy, old-hippie hair. How could sisters be so different?

"You don't do drugs, do you?" Aunt Barbara asked.

Sandra stared, her mouth gaping, until her lips managed to form the word *no*.

Aunt Barbara patted her arm. "Glad to hear

it," she said and nodded. "You need a good rest, that's all, and you'll get it at Cub Creek."

"Cub Creek?" Sandra tried to lighten the tension by joking. "I hope there's a roof and walls, too."

Barbara's expression went blank, then the lines in her face rerouted, and she laughed. Her laughter was high and musical. "You've been there, so you know perfectly well there's a house. What you are is a So Silly. That's what our mama used to call us girls. She'd call us So Sillies. It was from an old fairy tale, I believe."

Sandra took a deep breath and let it go. She forced a smile, trying to respond to her aunt in kind, and it paid off as her own tension seemed to ease. "Heaven knows I need a rest. Get yourself some rest, too, and have fun. Mom's looking forward to your visit."

"Too bad you couldn't come to the house a few days early. We could've enjoyed a visit. I've been curious as to what you've been up to. And of course, all that business with your husband. Marriage isn't easy, I know. Or rather, so I hear." She waved her hand. "Never having been married, I guess I wouldn't know, not personally, but I can certainly see what's what. More importantly, I could've helped you settle in. Shown you around. You haven't been to my house in . . . I don't know how long. You could've driven me directly to the airport from there."

"Sorry I couldn't make it work," Sandra answered, not exactly truthful but not wanting to go into detail about her lost two weeks. Her dismal failure. But her aunt hardly paused.

"Fred didn't mind taking me. He comes into work this way every day." She sighed. "I'm looking forward to seeing Meg, if I can survive the airport and the plane. If she'd waited, I could've driven down with her and helped with the driving, and Honey could've come, but no . . ." Aunt Barbara gripped her tote bag in a white-knuckled clutch. Her hands trembled. "I'm not as young as I used to be."

Sandra glanced over at her and noted the wide eyes, round and dark, and her aunt's constantly moving hands, the agitated fingers.

The DEPARTURES sign was ahead. Sandra turned the other way.

"Where are we going?" Barbara asked.

Instead of heading to the drop-off curb, Sandra drove to the hourly parking deck. "I'll walk you to the ticketing counter. It'll give us a few more minutes to visit."

Her aunt smiled, and her eyes brightened. "You have a kind heart despite what you've been through. You always were such a sweet child."

A sweet child. Those words echoed in Sandra's head as she parked and retrieved the suitcase from the backseat. They walked through the parking deck and the elevators to cross over to the terminal, Sandra pulling the suitcase and Aunt Barbara holding her niece's arm. The physical contact seemed familiar somehow. Maybe she remembered more of those early days out at the homeplace than she'd realized.

Barbara said, "I've left cash for you in an envelope in the bookcase behind the *Treasury of Knitting*."

"For me?"

"For emergencies or whatever. The bills should be taken care of already, but one never knows. Anything can happen in a couple of months." Her aunt's words flowed without pause. "I left groceries, and you'll find meals in the freezer. The post office is supposed to be holding the mail, but if you will, please check the mailbox anyway, once a week or so, just in case." She pointed her finger as if the mailbox, or maybe the house, were right in front of them. "You should take my room. It's the best mattress and the coziest room, but make yourself at home and choose whichever you want. And Honey . . . I know you've never met her, but she's a sweetheart. A bit timid, but that's from being in a shelter and who knows where else before that. She's been with me for several years now, and her true personality has blossomed. Blossomed. A loving dog and smart as all get-out. I hate to leave her." She stopped, choking up a bit. She pressed a finger to her eye, cleared her throat, and continued. "But she's no youngster, and the heat, you know, in Florida . . . And how could she fly? The vet thinks she's about ten. Not so old, but definitely not young, especially having had such a hard life." Barbara smiled. "She'll be fine in your care. Are you sure two months won't be a problem?"

As her aunt had said, a lot could happen in a couple of months. For now, that sounded fine. Sandra nodded. "No problem."

Reassured, Barbara looked out the window but was silent for only a moment. "This is a fine day. Should be good for flying, don't you think? A nice day for Honey, too. I didn't want to leave her cooped up, so she's enjoying the garden. It's fenced, you know." She lowered her voice. "Soon after she came to live with me, she took off. Ran off into the woods. I couldn't sleep for fear she'd end up on the state road . . . if you know what I mean." Barbara gave a quick shudder. "She came back the next day, but I didn't want to go through that again, so I had the fence put up."

In the end, Sandra escorted her aunt to the ticketing counter and through the terminal to security, but from that point Barbara had to manage on her own. She patted Sandra's arm. "I'm glad you'll be taking care of my house. Honey will be in good hands with you."

Sandra read doubt in her eyes regardless of the encouraging words. And no wonder. Aunt Barbara knew enough about Sandra's past to have reason to doubt. But it didn't matter. Sandra's ears were ringing with the constant torrent of chatter. Keeping up a good front had exhausted her, but she'd gotten the job done, and her aunt would soon be on the way to Florida.

In the end, the most important lesson Sandra had learned over the last couple of years, and especially over the last month, was that life was mostly about survival. Anything else was a bonus. Trent hadn't been wrong about everything.

The interstate was easy. Sandra had driven I-64 many times. Beyond Short Pump, the trees dominated both sides of the highway, concealing most of the rolling, wooded landscape. Sandra liked the quiet the country promised and the prospect of peace, too. The right kind of boredom. Though she hadn't ventured out to Aunt Barbara's house since before she left for college—it felt like a lifetime ago—she knew the way. She left the interstate at the Cross County Road exit and followed the state road until she reached the turnoff for Shoemaker Road on the right, but she started slowing down a lot sooner, warned first by an old blue house on the left that she'd totally forgotten about, and then the rows of old mailboxes in a wooden frame opposite the turnoff. When she turned onto Shoemaker Road, the asphalt ended.

She recalled the road being in better condition.

She slowed way down to avoid the deeper ruts and tall clumps of weeds. An area of forest created a buffer between the state road and the creek. Beyond the trees, the road sloped down to meet the creek where it crossed via a wooden plank bridge. The bridge over Cub Creek was smaller than she remembered. The planks were gray and warped, and several were broken. She paused before driving over it. But it was the way in or out, so clearly the bridge was still usable. Had, in fact, been used that morning, she reassured herself.

Beyond Cub Creek, the land rose again. On the right, the land opened up. It had once been farmed. She remembered corn. But that was long ago. The woods, wild and unkempt, continued along the left-hand side and came right up close to the drainage ditch.

Her tires were new. She'd spent a nice bit of change on them, and she didn't want to risk wrecking them or the car's undercarriage, so she took her time maneuvering the ruts and wallows and weeds. In a clearing on the left, she passed the broken-down one-room schoolhouse and, suddenly flooded with memories, she was tempted to pause, but she'd save reminiscing for later. She was going to be hanging out at Aunt Barbara's house for a while. For now, she had a date with a dog and needed a bathroom.

Despite herself, she paused to acknowledge her

memories of this place. They'd come out here often when she was a child. A kid's memory was different. Size-wise and shiny-wise, too. The adult brain provided a different experience. But if her aunt's house wasn't quite as her child's memory billed it, it was a roof over her head and private. Other than a pillow and bed, and the opportunity to rest, alone and not looking over her shoulder, Sandra didn't need much. As for the dog . . . she wasn't a fan, but how much trouble could one old dog be?

The dirt road ended in front of the house, with the house on her left, facing the road and a long, fallow field on the opposite side. The house was large. Perhaps not as large as her child's eyes remembered, but much larger than a cottage, as her aunt had called it. Mostly Sandra remembered the porch that spanned the front of the house. That had been her particular space when they visited. In recent years, Aunt Barbara had let vines run up the left side of the two-storied house. They were a riot of leaves, not all green. Lots of sticks and dead leaves were caught in there, and who knew how many insects were living in that greenery?

She felt twiggy legs creepy-crawling on her arms, her ankles, and up her back, and she tried to shake the sensation.

The wood siding was painted white. It was dirty, and the color was faded, but the structure looked sound. The blue shutters needed repair and painting. Several were missing slats, and some were slightly askew.

It was an old house, but if the doors locked and the plumbing worked, she'd be fine.

An old sedan was parked on the left side of the house. Her aunt hadn't mentioned it, but it was surely hers. The woods came up close to the driveway, and a few branches, high above, arched over and reached toward the house. Sandra pulled up and parked behind the car. There was plenty of room.

The driveway had been graveled once upon a time, but what little gravel was left was embedded in the hard blue-gray dirt. There were a few rain puddles. It had been a rainy spring in Richmond, too, with more expected. But the air smelled fresh. She stopped, closed her eyes, and breathed in deeply.

Nothing hurt. Not her lungs. Not her head. Grateful, she touched her scalp and ruffled her hair. No itch.

Around her, the trees were leafing out. The new green leaves were bright.

Who cared about old shutters and dingy paint? It was the bones that mattered. Her mom or someone in her past had said something like that. It was funny to hear it, almost as if it were being whispered in her ear, while she stood there dreamy-eyed in the driveway puddles, staring at the house.

She opened the trunk and grabbed the small suitcase and the plastic laundry basket, and then carried them up to the porch.

A porch swing hung at one end and a wicker chair was at the other. Both needed cleaning. A blue bench was situated next to the door, and empty terra-cotta planters were shoved beneath it and stacked beside it. Metal chimes with blue ceramic insets hung from the porch roof near the steps. Sandra put her baggage on the bench and dug Aunt Barbara's key from her jeans pocket.

Birds trilled nearby, loud in the silence. It struck her that there was no barking. But Honey was out back in the garden. Maybe sleeping. Sandra turned the key and had to give the knob and door a little extra shake before it opened.

The interior smelled old, and the light inside was dim. She stopped at the threshold. The curtains and shades were closed. She sneezed. Being in someone else's house, without the person who owned it, felt like trespassing.

It didn't matter. Sandra grabbed her basket with the purse on top and her other stuff on the bench, and then went back inside, pulling the door closed behind her and jiggling it to be sure it latched.

Still no barking. Honey must be napping, probably cozy in the sun. At least she wasn't complaining.

Maybe it was because Barbara was old and

lived alone in the middle of the woods, but she'd let the house get out of hand. Her aunt was obviously a hobby lover. From the porch to the living room and the foyer stairs, the entire area that she could see from this vantage point spoke of hobbies interrupted. She moved farther into the living room. On the floor beside a well-used stuffed chair, a half-knitted garment was wrapped around a thin skein. The needles were stuck into the midst, and it crowned a mound of countless other knitting projects piled on the floor. More projects filled the space between the chair and bookcase. Some of the yarn had spilled out onto the floor beyond the area of the piles. A tripping hazard. Stacks of magazines and pages torn from magazines occupied the coffee table. Sandra gave them a quick look. Recipes. Knitting patterns. There were more stacked in front of the windows.

She didn't remember it looking like this. All she remembered was that the house had been stuffy and dark. She laughed softly. That much was still true. The foyer was dark, and the living room was in shadow, but other than the sense of intruding in someone else's life, it wasn't creepy. Or peaceful, either. It simply mirrored her mood—discouraged and used up. Adrift. How sad was it to think such thoughts of oneself at thirty?

Books were stacked in corners, and knickknacks were everywhere. There were no plates with half-eaten food, thank goodness, and generally, the place looked fairly clean, but it was oh-so-very dusty. No point in worrying over it. She could manage around the current state for the time she'd be here.

She needed a rest, maybe a hideout, too, and she'd found it here in the midst of someone else's clutter. She wanted to feel grateful, but the goodwill she'd felt outside evaporated as her chest tightened.

Her lungs contracted, and her ribs hurt. She sat carefully, gingerly in the knitting chair and then leaned forward, dropping her face to her arms, breathing deeply. Long. Slow. In and out. It was a panic attack, nothing more. In and out. As her breathing eased, she sat upright and put her head back against the chair, waiting for the last of the tension to ease out of her chest.

She fell asleep, though not intentionally, and awoke with a jolt.

Honey.

How long had she slept? Minutes, that was all.

Still no barking. It struck her as very wrong. What kind of dog didn't bark when their person came home? Barbara said Honey was old. Maybe Honey was deaf, too.

Sandra hurried into the dining room, to the French doors, but her aunt had stacked boxes and books against them, and the boxes had sagged against the drapes, creating a significant drag. The drapery rod looked very iffy. Sandra went to the kitchen and unlocked the door. It was stuck, but an extra yank got it open.

The kitchen extended beyond the rest of the house so that the door was in a side wall and the view from it was of the length of the back of the house. It opened directly into a disaster of a garden, where the fencing and the overgrown bushes and riotous weeds intermingled.

Was this where the dog was supposed to be hanging out? Poor Honey.

The fenced-in garden was as out of sorts as the house. Weeds and wild grasses had overtaken everything, had woven greedy strands up through the legs of the black metal patio table and chairs. The old-fashioned wire fence was attached to corner stakes that canted this way and that. The thick bushes did as much or more as the stakes to keep the wire in place.

Sandra stumbled over a rock on her way to reach the gate at the back. It was open. In fact, it looked like the gate had come unlatched when the fence had parted on the far side.

There was no dog anywhere in sight.

Chapter Four

"Honey?" She yelled louder. "Honey!"

Take care of my house. Take care of my dog. I trust you, Sandra, her aunt had said. And she heard her mom's voice saying, *And there's an old dog. No trouble at all.*

She ran out through the gate and across the yard calling for Aunt Barbara's dog. There was a large, open grassy area beyond the fence and gate, and then the woods with two paths heading into the trees.

"Honey!"

Sandra stood there, hitting her fists against her thighs. What should she do? Call the police?

No. She crossed her arms and tried to calm down. She looked at the ground and thought it through. A dog had run off, and she would come back. Dogs did stuff like that. Hadn't Barbara said Honey had done that before and returned the next day? Maybe she'd chased a rabbit or followed some interesting scents.

She surveyed the yard. The fire pit in the backyard wasn't tall enough to hide more than a tiny puppy. Farther back, in the corner, was the old shed. Sandra walked around the shed, checking behind a board and other junk propped against the side and back. No dog.

At the edge of the woods, she hesitated. Was she going in there? Who was she kidding? She wasn't a country girl. There were ticks and snakes in there. Mom had warned her many times about the dangers in the woods when telling her she must stay on the porch and in the yard.

The dog would come home when it got hungry.

Indecision nagged at her as she walked back to the house. She called one last time, "Honey?" and left the gate open.

Honey would be back. There was no point in phoning her aunt. In fact, Aunt Barbara's plane was probably still in the air on its way to Florida. It would be wrong to worry her over nothing.

In the house, unable to relax, Sandra looked through the kitchen cupboards and the fridge. Milk. Eggs. Bread. Barbara had left the basics and more. Sandra peeked in the freezer. Frozen packages. Looked like meat loaf and a casserole. Maybe lasagna. Her aunt must have done a lot of cooking preparing for this visit. Sandra certainly wouldn't starve, and she wouldn't need to drive the many miles to a grocery store anytime soon.

She stood at the kitchen window hoping to see Honey, tail wagging and loping home. A watched pot never boils, right? That was something else her mother used to say. Sandra went back through the living room to the foyer, sneezing as she went. Dust and more dust.

Her belongings still sat at the foot of the stairs.

She should carry them up and figure out which room, which bed, to use. Or maybe sort out the dirty clothes and carry them to the laundry room first. But it was hard to move on with the next logical tasks when the first, most important one was still hanging out there unresolved.

A noise. Through the front door, she heard it. Almost a brushing sound. A creaking board.

"Honey," she whispered.

She fought the lock and the sticking latch in her haste to open the front door, but the reward was a dog lying there on the porch in a dwindling patch of sun. She had longish, silky black and white hair, with a touch of brown on one ear. Relief washed over Sandra.

True, she didn't have much use for dogs, but the loss of this one would be a failure, her fault or not, and she didn't want to start off that way.

"Honey," Sandra said, stepping carefully onto the porch, stooping, and holding out her hand.

The dog sniffed the offered hand and seemed content. She panted a bit and gave a short bark.

Huge relief. The dog was not only home, but she bore no resemblance to Leo whatsoever.

"I knew you'd return home." Sandra stood and patted her thigh. "Come in, girl."

Honey cocked her head, her brown eyes moist and curious, then stood and trotted inside, heading for the kitchen.

Sandra sighed in relief again. In validation.

She'd done the right thing by not calling her aunt, and now Honey was home safe and sound.

She followed the dog into the kitchen and checked the bowls. There was water in one bowl, and Honey was lapping at it. Dry food, too. All was well. They were back on track.

Now she could carry her stuff upstairs with an easier conscience. That awful prospect of calling Aunt Barbara, of trying to explain the missing dog to her aunt and mother, was gone. Maybe that twinge of guilt, too, that her dislike of dogs had somehow caused the problem. Ridiculous, but that's how it was. Now she was free to get on with things. She headed toward the stairs, tossing a stray skein of yarn into the corner pile as she passed Aunt Barbara's knitting chair, hitting the top perfectly. "Score," she said, and raised her fist in celebration.

Upstairs, Sandra stood in the doorway of her aunt's bedroom. It was a study in chaos. The bed was hastily made. Clothes were draped over a chair and the foot of the bed. It was all far too personal and rather thoughtless, since Barbara had advised her niece to sleep in here. But that wasn't the worst . . .

She walked forward, almost mesmerized, into her aunt's bedroom.

The worst was the wall mural. Painted flora filled the wall in thick, childlike swathes of green and blue. Tropical plants. A palm tree? A view of sand and ocean? Greens and blues predominated with some brighter colors thrown in here and there. Brown was interspersed throughout and poorly done, lending a jarring note to the scene. Was that a conifer? So maybe not a tropical theme?

Assuming she could fall asleep with that painted wall, wild and waiting, just beyond her closed eyelids, she wouldn't risk waking to it in the middle of the night, perhaps lit by moonlight. Not a chance.

There was a fireplace in the corner. The opening was blocked with painted tiles.

Back in the hallway, standing at the closed door to the room opposite, she tried the knob.

This room was larger than Aunt Barbara's but nearly empty. A bed. A chest of drawers. A clothing cupboard. Not much more. Nothing personal or decorative. None of the clutter that reigned elsewhere in the house. It opened onto its own bathroom, which was shabby but usable. The windows were grimy. One overlooked the backyard, and one was on the side wall near the corner fireplace. It backed up to the one in Barbara's room and used the same chimney, but this fireplace wasn't blocked.

Mrs. Shoemaker's room. Sandra's grandmother. But she'd never called her that. Even Sandra's dad had referred to her as Mrs. Shoemaker.

She remembered the room as cavernous and dark and hot, but that memory was from many years ago, from when she was a child. It looked and felt very different now. She breathed.

Had she been holding her breath? Sandra hadn't realized she was anxious about the room until this moment when she felt relief.

It no longer seemed cavernous, but it was larger than the other bedroom. The bed was placed nearer the bathroom. The empty area near the fireplace looked like it was intended as a sitting area. Sandra lifted the navy-and-white brocaded bedspread and checked the sheets. No signs of unwanted inhabitants.

She walked to the head of the bed and peeked under the mattress. She moved the sheet aside and examined the mattress seams. Seemed clean. It would do.

Before committing, she looked in the other rooms. A bathroom in the hallway. Powder and lotions and sundry bottles covered the flat surfaces of the sink. The bath decor was pink and fluffy and looked relatively modern. This was surely the bathroom her aunt used.

She moved on down the hall to another bedroom. It had a twin bed, not properly made and covered in a jumble of stuff. The smell of oil paint and thinner permeated the air. An easel was leaning against the wall with a painted-up table next to it. The tabletop was littered with half-squeezed tubes and dirty brushes. She'd known her aunt dabbled in painting, so this wasn't a mystery, but given the wall mural, it was still something of a wonder.

There were three doors left. One was directly opposite the painting room and would overlook the back. But it was chock-full—a mini Mount Everest of furniture and junk. She closed the door. At the end of the hallway, two doors flanked the gable window. Both of those were intended for storage and were full. Having watched reality shows on television, Sandra figured her aunt probably had a small fortune in antiques and memorabilia stashed away in these three upstairs rooms.

The almost-empty room it was, then. She'd been in that room once, and it hadn't been anywhere near empty back then. She'd been a child and was playing out on the porch when she'd heard her name called. She'd gone inside but didn't see her mom or aunt in the living room or kitchen, so she wandered upstairs. The room had been filled with huge dark furniture, heavy draperies, and pictures in massive wooden frames on the wall. And butterflies? Was that a real memory? Orange butterflies? A woman was in the bed, buried deep under blankets. It had been a short visit. Her mom had found her and dragged her out, scolding and shushing her.

Sandra emptied the laundry basket onto the bed

and unzipped her backpack. She put the toiletries into the bathroom. The bathroom was long and narrow and many decades out of fashion, but the toilet flushed, and the water ran clear. So far so good.

Most of her clothing would go back downstairs to the washing machine. Barely an armful. Not much laundry. Not much to wear, either.

Sandra opened the top drawers of the bureau. Empty. Musty smelling. She had a tiny bottle of lavender oil with a few drops left and dabbed it into the corners of the drawer before putting her clean clothing inside. She took the little money she had left and tucked it under her clothing.

Honey hadn't followed her upstairs. Sandra went back to the hallway and looked down the stairs. The dog had stayed in the foyer. She was napping, pressed up close to the front door.

This suited Sandra fine. She was glad Honey had returned, but if she kept her distance, that would be even better.

Sandra's phone was in her pocket. She pulled it out and dialed her mother's number. No answer. She'd try again later. Next task was to toss the laundry in the washing machine next to the kitchen, but not to wash yet.

Honey barely stirred as she walked past.

Sandra wasn't hungry, but she hadn't eaten today, so hungry or not she had to eat. She made the easy choice and scrambled some eggs. No peanut butter. She didn't want to taste, see, or smell peanut butter again anytime soon.

During the afternoon, Honey stood at the front door making little chuffing noises, which Sandra interpreted as wanting "out." Each time Sandra grabbed the leash and escorted Honey outside to do her business, the dog gave her odd looks, but Sandra wasn't taking any chances.

"I'll fix the fence tomorrow, Honey. For today, we're sticking close together."

This was one downside of dog ownership. At least a cat would use a litter box. Honey did her business, and they went back inside.

While she still had the security of daylight, Sandra unzipped her jeans and shed her blouse. She dropped the clothes on the tile floor and stepped into the shower. It was one of those old curtain contraptions over a freestanding claw-foot tub, and the fabric was awkward and wanted to cling to her skin, but she let the hot water stream down and over her. She'd showered that morning at the hotel, but she felt like the misery of the last weeks, maybe the last couple of years, had adhered to her skin like a stain.

This water was different. Not really home, but almost. No water could rinse away everything, but this was a start. A breath of freedom. A moment, a hint of being a real person again. This shower, old and annoying as it was, felt right. Maybe it was the well water. Maybe it was packed with healing minerals. Nice thought, true or not.

Sandra put on pajamas, tossed the clothing she'd worn today into the machine with the rest of her laundry, and started the wash.

She didn't fool herself. So much of life was made up of impressions and memories, interpreted by emotion, including the negative. Almost none of it was absolute, nor was the future. She could do this. She could rearrange her life if she was determined to do so and maybe improve her destiny. She didn't know how she would do it, but she believed it was possible.

In the evening, when Sandra snapped on Honey's leash and they went out onto the porch, Honey grew more insistent, pulling ahead into the dark night.

The steps were damp. Sandra regretted not putting on her shoes because damp steps promised wet and itchy grass. In fact, she'd have been smarter to borrow a robe from her aunt, because her own thin T-shirt and pajama pants weren't much defense against the chill.

They had some elevation out here. Not like the mountains, but the Blue Ridge wasn't far.

She shivered as the leash played out. Honey moved across the grass, hardly taking time to sniff as she went. Finally, the leash stretched to its limit, and Honey strained against it, pulling it taut, clearly not concerned with Sandra's plans.

Sandra stepped down to the stone paver at the base of the steps and refused to go farther. Honey angled over toward the bushes as far as she could. The moon was large and bright, and with Honey in that denser shadow, Sandra could barely make out the movement as Honey squatted to do her business. When Sandra tugged on the leash to hurry her up, Honey uttered a low-throated growl.

"Sorry," Sandra said, and relaxed the leash as much as she could. She wasn't sure that sound could come from such a gentle-seeming dog. Surely not. She held her breath, listening, but when the leash pulled tight again, she said, "Honey?"

Honey made a chuffing noise and added a few short barks.

"Enough." Unnerved, Sandra tugged on the leash and stepped back onto the steps, forcing Honey out of the shadows. She came, seeming reluctant, but then stopped to turn back and bark again, and that finished Sandra. She ran up the steps to the porch, pulling the dog along with her. Sandra closed the door, then unleashed Honey and peered out around the edge of the front room window curtain.

She searched the darkness with her eyes, half expecting to see a man's tall form in the moonlight. She'd known he was in Richmond watching her, and she was sure she'd sense him if he was here. She'd lost him with the car misdirection her mom had suggested. Trent wasn't here. He thought she was in Florida.

Honey could've been fussing over nothing. Maybe a mouse or possum in the bushes. And now, having made Sandra uneasy, the dog was already in the kitchen and lapping at the water for a last drink before bed.

"Come on, girl." Sandra flipped on the outside light and decided to leave the kitchen light burning, too. She wasn't afraid, but a little nervous, thanks to Honey.

Her cell phone rang. Where had she left it? On the counter. She grabbed it.

"Mom?"

"Hi, Sandra. Barbara's here. She's worried because we haven't heard from you. But she made it, no problem, and it sounds like you did, too."

Sandra was standing in front of the bookcase. One shelf was filled with photo frames. One showed her mom and Barbara, arms entwined, with their brother, Cliff, standing a few inches away. "Yes. All's well."

"We've been out to eat and introducing her around and settling in."

Sandra waited for a moment in case her mother wanted to add more. She reached out to straighten a frame with a photo of Barbara and Honey, then looked at the room crammed with junk and dust and thought of her family, together in the Florida sunshine without her. When the silence had stretched sufficiently between them, she responded. "Good. Sounds like fun. How's Dad?"

This time her mother paused. She sighed. "He keeps mentioning going home, and I remind him we're on vacation. Sooner or later, he'll stop asking."

What could Sandra say to that? Nothing.

"What I mean is, this will become home to him."

Home. It was more than a house. At least he and Mom were together. Sandra sat and leaned her head back against the chair.

"Your Aunt Barbara wants to talk to you."

"Sandra?" her aunt said.

"Hi. I'm glad you made it safely. I hope the flight was easy."

"Easy because you helped it get off to a good start, sweetie, and your momma was here to meet me at this end. Your daddy looks so good, Sandra. This place agrees with him, I'd say, so don't you worry."

"I'm glad."

"Is the house OK? How's Honey?"

"All's well. Honey is fine." Thank goodness. "She misses you, but she's eating and all that, so she's good."

"A good arrangement, I think. Don't you? I'm

having a lovely time with your mother. And you have a place to rest and recover for a few weeks. Thanks for helping me out, dear, and don't forget the envelope in the bookcase."

"Will do, Aunt Barbara."

"Keep your chin up, dear, and don't worry about anything. Here's your momma."

Mom came back on the phone, and she sounded civil, and her words seemed carefully chosen. "So, everything good there? Do you have what you need? Are you . . . do you feel . . . secure?"

What she needed? Security? In this tumbled, jumbled house in the middle of nowhere? She thought so, but it was hard to know what "good" meant.

"I'm fine. It's very peaceful here."

"All right, then."

"Good night, Mom. Give Dad my love."

Barbara had sounded happy. How nice for her and Mother, visiting and partying and stuff. Sandra would've enjoyed sunbathing on a sandy beach and relaxing and reading to the sound of waves, instead of the last two weeks of hard decisions and failed choices.

She stood at the top of the stairs. Down below, Honey was stretched out next to the front door again, apparently gloomy and missing Barbara. Sandra called to her softly, but Honey lifted her face and looked up for only a second before dropping her muzzle back to her paws.

It was a matter of time. Honey would get used to her.

Sandra paused in the bedroom. Aunt Barbara had lived in this house all her life. With her parents and brother first, then more recently on her own. As far as Sandra knew, no one had ever bothered her or the house. Had never had a break-in. But Sandra wasn't Aunt Barbara. Her luck hadn't been as reliable. And something had bothered Honey. Something in the dark.

In the end, she went back down to the kitchen. Honey looked up hopefully as she walked past. Sandra said, "Still just me, girl." She took a sharp knife from the kitchen. She carried it upstairs and put it between the mattress and box spring, near the edge.

When she finally slipped into bed, the mattress was soft and dipped in the middle, but it wasn't squeaky, and it beat the car floorboard hands down. It was a joy to either curl up or hog the bed as she chose and not worry about what she'd spend tomorrow. Tonight, she dropped her defenses in favor of rest.

In the morning, after yet another trip outside with Honey on the leash, Sandra fixed some toast and tea. She nibbled at the toast while she searched through the kitchen drawers and in the lower cabinets for wire or twine. She found none but did find wire cutters mixed in with twist ties, so that was a plus. She took a wire coat hanger from the closet and went out to the garden.

A garden? Maybe long ago. Never a large garden, and the black metal table and its chairs occupied an area that was sort of bricked in, as if a patio had been started but not finished.

Honey whined at the door when Sandra shut her inside.

"Not yet, girl. Let me get this fence fixed first."

The dog was so well behaved, so patient. She sat at the door, her nose to the glass, watching Sandra and fussing when Sandra moved out of sight. The dog was anxious, but Sandra understood why. Honey was missing Barbara.

The area was too small for a dog run and seemed to have one purpose now—as a dog toilet. But Sandra had survived Trent, and she could overcome dog poop. She picked her way carefully across the bricks, tall weeds, and grass runners. She went directly to the gap where the fence had parted and squatted to examine the break. She wouldn't kneel because of the fecal matter, and the ground was damp, too. Instead, she crouched. It was awkward, but this should be a quick job.

Sandra stripped the cardboard tube from the hanger and flexed the two metal ends. It would need to span the gap vertically for a few inches. It would be a patch job, but it needed to hold for only a couple of months, until it became Barbara's problem again. Sandra was pretty sure it was the unlatched gate that had been the actual means of escape. Stabilizing this section of fence should fix the gate. Plus, she might rig a piece of wire, like a safety pin, to keep the latch secured. While she was appreciating her own cleverness, the wire cutter slipped and fell, disappearing into the grass.

Keeping a hand on one end of the wire patch, Sandra released the other end so she could feel for the wire cutter in the weeds. The end popped free, and she nearly lost her grip. Frustrated, she lost her balance, landing on her butt in that mix of grasses and almost-mud she'd been so intent on avoiding. Cursing, she retrieved the wire cutter and righted herself, and then set back to work with a will. She would do this. She would beat this thing.

She worked the wire again, fitting the ends through the open spaces almost like a running stitch, but the wire was tougher to bend than she'd expected. Never mind the wire cutter. She was going to need more hangers.

Sandra scratched her face and remembered her fingers were muddy as she felt the grit transfer. She rose and reached for the nearest bush to steady herself and looked directly into a face.

A man was standing only feet away on the other side of the bush, and inside the house Honey began barking and howling like a crazed berserker.

Chapter Five

"Sorry to bother you," the stranger said.

Sandra stumbled backward. In that first, startled moment, she saw light-brown hair, brown eyes, that he was tall . . . maybe forty years old. She tried to ask, "Who are you?" but didn't get all the words spoken. Honey's barking alarmed her. Honey was shut inside. She was protective, but how could the dog help her? She couldn't. Honey's racket was overwhelming, and the man looked toward the house. His eyes narrowed as he frowned.

"Is Barbara home?" he asked.

Was he asking her if she was here alone? She held the clippers like a weapon.

He raised his hands. "I'm sorry I startled you. It's OK. I'm Colton Bennett, Barbara's neighbor."

There were no other houses in sight and no other people around.

"I live in that direction. Down that path." He pointed back toward the woods and the shed.

Sandra rushed the words out as she was backing away. "I can't talk right now. I'll let Barbara know you stopped by." She turned and hurried toward the house. The blood was rushing in her ears so loudly she could hardly hear herself speak. From the corner of her eye, she saw him moving around the fence, approaching the gate.

She rushed to the kitchen door, got inside, and locked it—not easy since Honey was determined to get out—then ran for her phone, but when she grabbed it and turned back toward the kitchen door, she didn't see him. She went to the window. He wasn't out there.

She double-checked the door. Yes, locked. She raced to the front of the house. Honey was running back and forth, panting, from the back door to the front door, to Sandra and to the front door again. Sandra felt light-headed. She put a hand against the foyer wall and the other on her chest. She reminded herself to breathe.

There was a knock on the front door. The man called out, "Can we talk, please?"

Oh, crap. She leaned against the wall and slid partway down it. Honey panted in her face.

His voice sounded calm and apologetic. He knew her aunt. A neighbor, he'd said. Nothing about him, except his presence here, should have been cause for alarm. The man had looked reasonable. Sandra wanted reasonableness. Mostly she wanted him gone.

"Look, it's important. I'll wait in the yard, OK?"

Honey whined loudly and bumped her head against Sandra's leg. She reached down to scratch her. "It's all right, girl. I can do this. I lost my head for a minute, that's all. He doesn't seem dangerous. But then, they never do, do they?"

Sandra yelled to the man, "Just a minute."

She pushed away from the wall, smoothed her cropped hair, and squared her shoulders.

"Honey, you're my backup. Let's send this guy on his way."

The stranger wasn't on the porch. She could see that much through the window. After a deep breath in and a slow breath out, she flipped the lock. She intended to open the door and slip through quickly, keeping her hand on the knob. If he made a move for the porch, she'd jump back inside. But she never got the chance. As soon as the door opened a few inches, she was knocked off her feet.

By Honey. As the dog raced past her to reach the stranger.

In joyous abandon, Honey tried to jump up and lick his face, but she wasn't tall enough and hit him at the shoulders. The man knelt and gave her the chance to greet him with a swipe on the cheek, then stood and commanded her to sit. She did, but it was iffy as to how long she could restrain herself.

Traitor dog.

Clearly, Honey knew this man. He'd said he was a neighbor, after all, but this seemed a total failure of loyalty.

"Good girl, Sammy."

Sandra frowned. "Her name's Honey. I thought you knew my aunt?"

"Her name is Sammy. She's my dog. Rather, my

son's dog. She didn't come home yesterday. He's been worried. Could hardly sleep last night."

Sandra opened her mouth, then closed it. She walked over to the vine growing by the porch rail as an excuse to turn her back to him. *Think. Think.* Trouble was, she couldn't conjure up any scenario in which it made sense that Honey wasn't this man's dog.

Not Honey. Sammy.

Sandra turned back toward him. "But that means my aunt's dog is missing. I thought this was Honey. Where is Honey?"

She ran into the house and grabbed a small, unframed photo from the bookshelf and returned to the porch. The picture showed Barbara and her dog sitting on a blanket. Sandra looked at Honey-Sammy and back at the photo.

The man said, "They are similar."

Sandra shook her head. "Somewhat, but the dog in the photo doesn't have brown on her ear, and the black-and-white markings are a little different. I didn't look closely before." She was talking more to herself than to him. "Why would I? The dog was here on my aunt's porch."

"No hard feelings. I can see you didn't do this on purpose. The dogs are similar." At the sound of him speaking her name, the dog moved closer to him, and he reached out to scratch her head. "She's a good girl. Sammy and Honey are friends."

She sat on the blue bench and gripped the

armrest. "Now what? Where is my aunt's dog? What happened to her?"

The man moved nearer to her. Honey—rather, Sammy—moved closer to sit at Sandra's feet. "She's around. She's probably out visiting in the area. She'll come home."

Sandra didn't believe it. Honey would've returned yesterday. She would've shown up for supper. If not at the back door, then certainly, as Sammy had done, to this porch.

"Last night I told Aunt Barbara that Honey was here and fine. How am I going to tell her that her dog is missing?"

He didn't answer right away. When he did, she felt the sympathy. "Maybe you shouldn't. Maybe you should check around first. Like, the shelters? You might find her right away."

Shelters. Maybe. Oh, no. What if Honey had been adopted or claimed by someone? What if she was already on the list to be euthanized?

"What if I'm already too late? What if they put her down?" Sandra jumped to her feet.

"No way. It's only been twenty-four hours. Call them, starting with the nearest. Quick and easy to check."

"How? No one has phone directories anymore."

"Use your computer. Google them."

"I don't have one."

"No problem. It's easy enough to search on your phone."

"I have a phone, but it doesn't . . . it can't . . . it doesn't have that capability."

This time the pause was longer. Sandra noticed his lashes, his profile. He had nice features, pleasantly strong but not too sharp. She looked away. She knew better than to judge by appearance.

"Do you have pen and paper? We'll do the search on my phone, and you can write down the numbers."

"Pen and paper. I'll be right back." She dashed inside. *Where would Aunt Barbara keep such things?* She yanked open the kitchen drawer and pushed the junk around for the second time that day. *No. On the end table with the skeins of yarn unraveled and cascading over the edge? No, again. In the dining room on the buffet? Yes, bingo.*

Sandra sat again on the bench outside and held the pencil and paper at the ready. "Sorry it took so long. I'm not familiar with where Aunt Barbara keeps things."

He chuckled. "No worries. Your Aunt Barbara keeps lots of things, which, no doubt, adds to the challenge."

He ran his finger across his phone screen, scrolling, and she experienced a moment of phone envy. Hers was very basic. But it was enough, she reminded herself. It met her needs.

"There are a few animal shelters and some pet

rescues, but most of them are for specific types of dogs, not dogs like Honey." He glanced up. "Like greyhounds or other special breeds. But there are animal shelters in Mineral and Goochland. Neither is real close, but my bet would be on one of those." He held up his phone. "So you can give them a quick call right away. Here are the numbers. Write them down. Say you're looking for a dog that looks like this and her name is Honey and so on. Do you know whether she was wearing a collar or . . . ?" His voice trailed off.

Sandra looked at him, staring.

"You don't know?"

She wanted to go hide in a dark corner or do something equally shameful and cowardly. It wasn't him. He was being kind, and he had a nice-looking face. No, it wasn't about him. It was her. She'd been given two tasks in exchange for a roof and a place to rest—watch over her aunt's house and her dog. The house was still standing. Sandra could say that much after twenty-four hours onsite. Actually, there was a third task. It was to take care of herself, too, to recover so she wouldn't be this burden-person, this person who had to sleep in her car or beg her mother for money or other help. She was too old for this. She'd made a mistake. But then she'd made it a second time and lost the goodwill and sympathy of her friends and family.

Now was the time to move forward, and first on the list was to find her aunt's dog.

This man, this neighbor she'd treated so poorly, dialed his phone.

"The shelter in Mineral," he said as he pushed the "Dial" button and put the phone to his ear. "Hi, I'm looking for a lost dog. Lives in Louisa. A few miles from Mineral. Near where that new subdivision is going in? Yes, there." He listened for a moment and then said, "Medium hair, black and white markings. Female named Honey. Border collie. Age?" He looked at Sandra.

"My aunt thinks Honey is about ten."

He continued into the phone. "She's an older dog, about ten years old. She's been missing since yesterday." Another pause. "No? Thanks for checking. Hold on." He turned and asked, "What phone number should she call if Honey shows up?"

She gave him her number. "Tell them my name is Sandra Hurst." After he hung up, she asked, "What's that about a subdivision?"

"Through the woods as the crow flies. Near where I live. It's small as subdivisions go, so the houses are big and expensive, but the construction shouldn't bother you given the location." He put his phone in his pocket. "So no luck at the shelter, but at least they have your name and number. Meanwhile, it might not hurt to check out the construction site. A few of the homes already have families, and maybe someone thought she was a stray." He smiled. "I'm over there every day. I'm in construction. I'll check around the jobsite. If she hasn't come home by tomorrow, what about making posters?" He held up the photo. "Do you have any way of making copies?"

"No. Maybe I could find an office supply store. Or a library would have a copier."

"My son will help. He can make a copy of the picture, write up a flier, and print out a few. He's good with a computer."

"Are you sure?"

"He'll be proud to help Barbara and Honey. Mind if I take the photo with me?"

"No, of course not. I appreciate it. I don't know my way around here at all. It would be a big help." She added, "I grew up in Richmond, but I've been away for a while."

He didn't ask more questions, so she gave him credit for courtesy. They stood, and he extended his hand.

As they shook, she said, "Thank you very much, and I'm sorrier than I can say for the confusion over Honey. I mean Sammy. My aunt said Honey would be in the fenced area when I arrived, and she wasn't. So when I found the dog lounging on the porch, I was so relieved I didn't notice the differences in the picture. I hardly looked at it. I'm sorry for the worry I caused you and your son."

"Aaron is my son's name, and no harm done. I'm glad we met. I'll be back with posters tomorrow. Hopefully they won't be needed." He withdrew a business card from his pocket and handed it to her. "You can reach me here if Honey comes home."

He headed toward the woods with the dog trotting closely at his side.

Sammy. Not Honey.

She waited for him to round the corner of the house before descending the steps, and then followed. As she reached the back corner, she saw him take the right-hand path. Within moments, he had disappeared into the woods.

Sandra quickened her pace, then paused again as she reached the edge of the woods.

Was Honey in here somewhere among the trees, lost in the forest? If she were near, surely Colton and Sammy walking through the woods would draw her out more quickly than a strange woman she'd never met.

Oh, Honey. Where are you?

The house seemed empty without Honey. Or without Sammy, rather. Sandra had never had a pet. Her mother wouldn't allow animals in the house and said it was cruel to pen them up outside. Sandra believed it was her convoluted way of saying, "No pets." Trent owned Leo. She'd shared living quarters with that dog for several years, but never by any stretch of the imagination did she ever consider Leo a pet. He was merely another means by which Trent set traps for her. His points of failure. There were many. She suspected he added to them as he saw fit. Being a survivor was an important point, as well as saying you are as weak as your weakest link. Trent also cited one about valuing the opinions of others, that trying to live up to the good opinion of others was a fool's task and deserved the heartbreak it was bound to bring.

Sandra had met Trent's father once, and he hadn't seemed evil, but he was a hard man and had had a hard life. Whatever wisdom he'd tried to pass on to his son must have been twisted and stained in the transfer.

The loss of Honey wasn't her fault, and she hadn't failed anyone. It was just a dog anyway. But Aunt Barbara was going to be devastated by the loss of her pet, and Sandra didn't want to be the point of failure that caused her pain.

It turned out that a dog sleeping by the front door did make a difference. Sandra knew it was true because that second night, alone, she felt uneasy. She pretended everything was cool, that the evening was normal, but suddenly the house was too overwhelmingly junky, the room she had chosen was too bare, and those painted vines and trees in Aunt Barbara's room were extremely vivid, even as a memory. Sandra had a swift vision of them growing, their tendrils creeping around the walls of Barbara's bedroom until they reached the doorway, and then sending shoots forward to grip the doorframe and probe the hall.

She shivered and got out of bed. She crossed the hallway and closed Barbara's door, and then went downstairs. She searched the pantry for a snack and found cookies. She put a few on a plate and carried it, along with a glass of lemonade, upstairs and set them on the nightstand.

New problem. Was she going to sit here in bed, staring at the dingy walls of this nearly empty room while she nibbled and sipped? No.

Back downstairs again, she found a book out of the numerous ones Barbara was hoarding. Not the knitting treasury, thank you, nor any of the heavy encyclopedias, and definitely not a hot romance. She was done with romance and men and the crap they called love. But here was a dusty blue volume of American history, fat but not huge. A friendly size. It looked reasonably certain to put her to sleep fairly quickly.

She rearranged the pillows and settled in again.

The book was actually rather quirky. It was amusing and informative and wasn't doing the sleep trick at all, especially when the author, Mr. Woodward, got going on King Henry VIII and his daughter, Elizabeth. A lone woman, queen or not, had done what her predecessors couldn't and had balanced England's budget. The author's description of her didn't paint a flattering word portrait, but he clearly admired her skill and vision.

Sandra flipped back to the flyleaf. Copyright 1936 by W. E. Woodward. Inside the cover was written the name *Clifford Shoemaker* and the year *1940*. It had to be her grandfather's writing, since the date would've been before her uncle had been born. There were lots of books downstairs. She might enjoy thumbing through more of them. Somehow it surprised her to realize that the Shoemakers had been readers.

Finally, about midnight, Sandra put the book aside. She made a trip to the bathroom, then stopped at the window on the way back to bed.

The moon was huge and so bright she could pick out every bush and distinguish twigs and leaves lying on the lawn. Among the trees, the shadows were deep, and the line between moonlit landscape and intense shadow was stark, almost magical.

It would have been nice if the pole light near the shed worked. She might have to call Aunt Barbara to ask where the switch was located.

Only days ago, the shadows at the commuter lots and parks, sometimes even in daylight, seemed threatening—the genesis or lair of possible nightmares—especially toward the end, until Barbara had finally called. One's eyes began to see things that the brain had not perceived before. Vague threats sometimes, but real people did lurk in the shadows in the woods near the commuter lots, and most definitely in the park restrooms. Even walking through the mall when you had no money to spend made you feel marked. A fraud. Someone who was where she didn't belong. But not here. This felt like . . . well, not home, but not foreign, either.

This was the Shoemaker homeplace. This was where Mom and her siblings grew up. It was impossible to imagine her mother as a pigtailed, dirty-faced kid. No mud pies for Meg Shoemaker, Sandra was sure. Meg had gone off to college, majored in business, and had had a career in banking before meeting and marrying James Lovett, and then they became parents—Mom and Dad as far as Sandra was concerned. Barbara had never moved away. Never married. Nor had Cliff. Barbara and Cliff had stayed here with their parents and had cared for them until death took them, and then had grown old here themselves, until Cliff died two years ago.

Sandra understood somewhat. It wasn't about being trapped in the past or where you lived, but rather choosing to stay somewhere safe and familiar where you were loved and needed. Had her aunt and uncle wanted to move on with separate lives? Sometimes the home you knew was the best place imaginable. You already knew what unhappiness or sadness dwelled there. The familiar was often better than the unpleasant surprises the world held in store for the more adventurous.

Her memory of Uncle Cliff was vivid. He was a tall, large man, yet quiet and gentle. He didn't smile much, but when he did, it was a shy smile. Mom and Dad drove out here a lot when she was a child. She remembered being told to be quiet because her grandmother was sick upstairs. Sandra had her Barbie dolls and a case full of clothing and accessories. Beneath the clothing were her coloring books and crayons. Sometimes she brought her special doll, Felicity, but Felicity didn't go into the case. She was more like a friend who came along to keep Sandra company. She would set it all up at one end of the porch, the opposite end from the swing and between the wicker chair and the railing. She created her world. Mostly, she felt forgotten by the adults, and she was OK with that. She never felt the least inclination to explore the woods or the house. This was her safe place, about four by four feet, and she had her friends, Barbie and Midge and Ken and the others.

Uncle Cliff would show up, wandering out to the porch through the screen door that tended to slam, or, more often, he would emerge from the woods having trod paths she couldn't see. Mom would've punished her if she'd wandered away and caused an uproar like a big search or such. The porch was her territory. Sometimes her uncle would carry a twisted brown paper bag in one hand. He held it down by his side. She never saw what was actually in the bag, but she recognized the shape. He rarely spoke more than a few words to her, but he always nodded pleasantly, and his thick eyebrows would arch, as if in surprise. He might say, "Where'd you come from, Cassie?" and laugh like it was the funniest joke, then keep on to wherever he was going. There was always a smell about him, a distinctive odor that she hadn't recognized until many years later. Cheap wine and beer. But she liked his laugh.

He didn't get along with Sandra's parents. It was something about him not living up to his responsibilities. Those were words overheard on a day when the windows were open and no one remembered the little girl sitting on the end of the porch with her dolls, quiet in her pretend world, waiting to be told when it was time to leave. The squeak of the swing's chain if someone walked by, a breeze that set the trees to swaying overhead, their leaves brushing and singing their own song, those were the voices she heard most often out at the homeplace.

She remembered it mostly as a strange but peaceful time.

Now she was an adult, and it was time to sleep. The night was half along already. She last checked the clock at three a.m. and must have fallen asleep shortly thereafter. Considering the day and everything that had happened with the dog and Barbara's neighbor, Sandra wasn't surprised Trent visited her dreams.

He didn't look like Trent, but rather he appeared as a yellow grizzly. The golden yellow fur coat glowed, and as he rose to his hind legs, the thick fur moved in the wind. He waved his paws, displaying long, curved claws, and growled and threatened. He wouldn't hurt her, Sandra knew, at least not with a punch or a slap, but she cowered anyway, knowing he'd shred her intellect and ego into bloody strips one word, one patronizing smirk, at a time.

She was glad to wake up that morning. To see the glimmer of dawn was a blessing, a rescue. She didn't attempt to go back to sleep because the bear might still be wandering in the neighborhood of that sleeping state.

The day stretched long and empty ahead of her. How would she fill it?

Looking for Honey.

Had Honey come home? Suddenly hopeful, Sandra jumped out of bed and raced down the steps. She opened the front door. No dog. She went to the kitchen and opened the back door. No dog. So early in the day, and she was already discouraged.

Sandra fixed coffee and took it upstairs to sip

while she got washed and dressed. The aroma alone was a help. She decided to view the day as full of potential.

In front of the mirror, she tried to fluff up her hair with her fingers. Not much she could do with it until it grew out. She'd have to wet it to get rid of the morning bedhead effect.

Her hair would grow. Didn't everyone say that after a bad cut?

Sandra's wardrobe was pathetic, so she settled for a clean pair of jeans and a plain T-shirt. Despite the disturbed sleep, she counted her blessings. Hot water, a roof over her head, privacy and security (at least of the premises), and food in the kitchen, with no one to give orders or ask questions. She felt like a princess in a castle, even if it was full of junk and dust.

Sandra cooked some eggs for breakfast. Colton Bennett had said he'd bring posters, so she waited. Always waiting—not assuming—never forcing. She needed activities. Her lack of a to-do list was the result of being in someone else's house.

Her aunt's yarn was beside the chair, under the chair, and dangling from the bookcase.

Enough.

Sandra tidied the yarn projects and stacked them in a yarn bag she found behind the chair. She gathered more loose skeins and tucked those into plastic grocery bags she found in the pantry. From there she decided to get rid of the junk mail left lying around. She gathered the fliers and envelopes, being careful not to trash anything worth keeping. Things were starting to look better, but then Sandra stopped abruptly. How does one clean up someone else's mess without those actions declaring it was a mess to begin with? Rude. She was a guest, after all.

She stood in the dining room. Her arms felt twitchy. Muscle memory? From when she had a house? A home and a place for everything and had enjoyed managing it? At least for a while. Until Trent learned to twist that, too.

Suddenly deflated, Sandra pulled out a chair and sat at her aunt's dining room table.

A year into their first marriage, she'd wanted to join her friends for a girls' weekend. Trent had known many of her friends from college. After all, that's where she'd met him. He was a little older, and he worked as an engineer in a firm that built bridges and other highway-related construction. His employer was paying for him to take the courses he needed to complete his degree. That's how she'd met him, in an English class. He'd spent a lot of time on campus with her, especially in the evenings, and had met her friends, and many of them had ended up being her bridesmaids.

Tammy had called to invite her to the girls'

weekend. "We're going to the lake. My parents' place."

Sandra was excited about seeing her old friends. Trent wasn't.

"But Trent, you know them. They're great gals. They're my friends. This is about a weekend at the lake."

"You're a married woman now. They're still college students. Their responsibilities, their focus is different."

"They are my friends. They were in our wedding."

"We haven't seen them since." He shook his head. "Save yourself the heartbreak."

"There's no heartbreak, Trent. They are in school, they're busy, and I'm not there. We don't live close, so it's hard to get together. This would be so much fun."

"More fun than staying home with me?"

"Trent. Be reasonable."

"Do whatever you want, Sandra. I guess I can understand, but I think you'll see I'm right. You'll be sorry you went."

She went.

It wasn't wild or crazy. Her friends were sweet, funny gals, and they did a lot of laughing. It was good to get away. She hadn't realized the tension had been building with Trent until she was removed from it. She returned home from the long weekend with renewed energy and was genuinely happy to see him. She was barely in the house when Trent said, "Grab a spoon for me, will you?"

When she opened the drawer, she saw the difference immediately. She looked at Trent. He broke into a full grin and came to stand next to her.

"Do you like it?"

She stammered, "Wh-what's going on? Where's my silverware?"

"I bought new. Got rid of that old stuff. It was junk. You like it?"

"Where is it? Tammy gave it to us as a wedding gift."

Trent frowned. He moved closer until his chest was almost touching her shoulder. His extra inches towered over her.

"Does it matter? It was stained. I got you this really nice set—the knives, forks, spoons. It has all the serving pieces. See?" He picked up the gravy ladle and waved it near her face. "I told the clerk I was living dangerously, that you might not like the pattern." He chuckled. "She said I can bring it back if you want to choose your own."

"Trent, where's my silverware?"

"I tossed it. Trashed it."

She moved toward the trash can. He stopped her with a hand on her arm.

"It's too late. The trash already went to the dump. I made a special trip over there because

I did some other clearing out, too." He gave her a thin smile, dropped his hand, and lowered his voice. "That's the thanks I get? I try to do something nice to surprise you. That was a long, lonely weekend with you gone." He thumped his hand on the counter. "Fine. Teaches me a lesson. I won't be so thoughtful next time. Besides, don't blame me. If you'd been here, it wouldn't have happened, right? If you don't like the new utensils, the box is in the garage. Pack it up and return it. Regardless, the old stuff is gone."

He gestured at Leo. "Come on, boy." He let the door slam behind him and the dog. Trent tossed the ball as he walked down the porch steps, and the pit bull mix chased it, his muscles rippling under short hair, and clamped his unforgiving jaws on the ball.

Sandra had loved her silverware. It wasn't silver, and it wasn't top-of-the-line stainless, but when she set the table or washed the implements, she wasn't seeing cheap flatware. Instead, she was remembering her friend and the fun they'd had in high school and college. Everyone liked Tammy. Being in her company was like wearing a seal of approval, and the people who liked her liked you.

Memories could soothe a lot of what was wrong in one's life. Sometimes a good memory helped a person believe that life could be good again.

The knives, forks, and spoons now in the

drawer had a nice enough pattern and were better quality, but Sandra had loved that other set.

She was angry and hurt. She called her mother.

"What's wrong, Sandra? Didn't you have a good time at the lake? You went, right? You sound upset."

"I did go. It was great, but Trent got angry."

"I thought you said he was OK with it."

"He said he was. But Mom, he bought new silverware. He threw away the utensils that Tammy gave us. Took them to the dump. I can't get them back."

"I don't understand. New silverware? Don't you like the pattern?"

"That's not the point, Mom. He did it to punish me because I went. He knew how I felt about that silverware."

"They're knives, forks, and spoons, Sandra."

"It was a gift from my friend. Trent didn't even ask. He smiled when he told me."

"Let me make sure I understand. You went away for the weekend with your friends, and while you were gone your husband missed you and bought new silverware to surprise you."

"Yes." It sounded different when her mom said it like that.

"Sandra, I think you should just say thank you."

"He should've asked first, Mom."

"I agree, but he's a man, and men don't think that way."

Sandra breathed. She tried to concentrate on breathing and nothing else. The intermittent pain in her side was trying to come back.

"Sandra? Are you there?"

"I'm here, Mom." There was no point in explaining it again. Repetition wasn't going to make her mother understand, but overreaction or not, it didn't change the truth. Trent had gotten the new silverware because of the choice she'd made to leave for the weekend. He'd trespassed into her space, her kitchen, and had taken a wedding gift from a dear friend, and then he'd made sure it was irrevocably gone to punish her. Sandra heard in her mother's words and the tone of her voice that she believed Sandra was the problem. It had been only silverware, and cheap at that.

It was early in their first marriage, and so long ago now, but it still hurt, especially as it proved to be one of the first of many such incidents to come.

Sandra pushed up from Aunt Barbara's dining room table. Was there any similarity to what she was doing to her aunt's belongings? She didn't think so.

She walked over to the sofa. She was tired and that tightness in her chest was back. She was going to lie down, to . . . She stopped.

No, she wasn't. This chaos was far different from a set of silverware.

She had to do what she had to do.

In the dining room, Sandra moved the sagging boxes away from the French doors. She pushed them under the dining room table and then opened the drapes. The drapery rod was iffy but holding. She sneezed and sneezed. The sunlight was nice, but it highlighted the dust.

The house was full of chaos, tripping threats, and dust—multiple potential health hazards. She was actually doing her aunt a favor.

She unhooked the drapes and tried to bundle them up to contain the dust. She took them outside, made sure of the wind direction, and then shook them. An old clothesline was strung by the shed. She threw the drapery panels over the line and left them there to air.

Back in the house, she sorted the magazines on the dining room table while keeping watch on the garden and the yard, in case Honey put in an appearance. That's how she happened to see the boy approaching. A blond-headed boy limped across the backyard holding a large manila envelope. He was maybe ten and wearing jeans and a collared knit shirt. He stopped to watch the drapes on the line flap and billow with the breeze.

Sandra knew nothing about children, especially boys. He angled toward the side of the house. Sandra went to the front door and stepped out onto the porch as he came into view.

"Are you Miss Barbara's niece?" he asked.

"I am. You must be Aaron."

"Yes, ma'am." He nodded. His manners showed in his posture as well as his words. "Have you heard from the authorities or the animal shelters about Honey?"

"Nothing."

"If you don't mind me suggesting, you should hang up these posters near the main road and then over by the new subdivision. Plus, there are several gas stations and convenience stores along the road."

Sandra came to the edge of the porch and looked down at Aaron. "First, I'd like to apologize for keeping Sammy captive. It was unintentional, I promise you. She wanted to leave, and I didn't understand. I realize now she wanted to go home to you."

The boy shrugged and smiled. "No problem. Dad explained what happened. I was worried, but she's fine. I'm glad she was safe." He held out the posters. "Would you like to take a look?"

"Sure." Sandra accepted the posters and sat on the steps.

Aaron joined her. She pretended not to notice his awkward progress up the steps or his careful movement as he twisted to sit on the step.

The picture on the poster was slightly grainy because it had been enlarged from a photo that wasn't sharp to begin with, but Honey's face and coloring would be recognizable to anyone who saw her.

"These are great. How will I hang them? Tape? Nails?"

"Depends on where. I'd start with the gas stations on the main road and down to Interstate 64."

"Do you think she'd go that far?"

"Honey might not, but people coming through this area do, and they might see her and remember her. Hang some in the businesses in Mineral and down in Goochland."

The task felt so big. This boy's composure made her ashamed to be so inadequate. She tried to rally. She sat taller and smiled. "I appreciate your help."

"No problem. Dad said you didn't have a computer." He pointed to the posters. "I'm pretty good with it. If you need anything else, let me know."

"Aaron," she said.

"Yes, ma'am?"

"You are a lifesaver. I could never have done such a wonderful job myself. Thank you."

"My pleasure, ma'am. Glad I can help."

It was up to her now. Aaron had brought the posters, offered advice, and limped away. Sandra had offered him a ride home. He assured her he could manage fine.

Yesterday, Colton had called the shelters and the local police, and they had her number, but she couldn't sit around waiting. She would call them all again. What if she annoyed them? Like with the temp agencies? That might not help her cause.

What about showing up in person? Too bad she didn't have a more appealing, engaging personality. Aaron was a cute, personable kid and much more of a heart-wringer. Maybe his father would loan him out? She laughed. Shame on her for thinking that way, but honestly she was only half-kidding.

She called each listing one by one. As she dialed and spoke, she started in the house and then migrated to the porch and out to the yard. As each call was answered, she explained who she was and why she was calling, and they said, "Hold," and then came back to report there was no sign of Honey.

Thirty minutes' worth of phone calls didn't seem good enough. She could try harder. She had to, because at some point she would have to explain to her aunt and mother about Honey and what she did to try to find her and bring her home.

She needed to go to these places personally. Make it real. Hang posters where it was allowed. She'd go in the morning. She glimpsed her reflection in the china hutch glass, and then took a second look. Not good. The hair could be a quirky, eccentric kind of style-maker thing, but the clothes?

Aunt Barbara. She and her aunt weren't so very different in size. Style? Yes, very different, but surely she had a few things in her dresser and closet that were more understated than that purple and orange sweater vest.

In the short time that the front door had been closed, the room already smelled musty. Sandra opened a window a few inches. The air was cool, but pleasantly so. Spring. The forsythia bushes were green and fully leaved, having already dropped their yellow blossoms. When the hardwoods started pushing out their leaves, spring was well under way.

Her car was still parked at the side of the house. Gas, or the cost of it, was a consideration for tomorrow's plan. You had to drive forever to get anywhere out here. Suddenly, Aunt Barbara's cash popped into her head. Behind the *Treasury of Knitting*, hadn't she said?

Sandra found the thick volume at eye level in the bookcase. She pulled it out, felt around behind the books on either side, and found the envelope.

For unexpected bills, she'd said.

Like gas, maybe?

The long white envelope was sealed. Sandra opened the flap. Cash, for sure.

About $300 in fifties and two hundreds. *Nice.*

Sandra slid out the note. Barbara had written a long note, but the gist was that the utilities were on auto-pay, and there shouldn't be anything else needing payment, but in case of emergency with the house or with Honey . . . and a request to start her car from time to time to keep the battery charged. She felt behind the books again and found the car key.

Really, Aunt Barbara? But she'd done well otherwise, and, yes, Sandra called this an emergency. It was all about Honey.

She took a fifty-dollar bill, tucked it deep into her jeans pocket, and returned the rest to its hiding place.

Now on to Aunt Barbara's closet.

It was barely noon, and Sandra was already listless and feeling at loose ends. It was awful pawing through someone else's clothing, and that mural felt like it was watching her, judging her, in Barbara's absence.

She'd found sweatpants and stretch yoga pants and a couple of casual tops that would augment her wardrobe. A nightgown and pajama pants, too. She tidied her aunt's bed and laid the clothing on the bedspread. She had her job-interview outfit, and while she wasn't planning to dress up to that degree, pairing a nice blouse from the interview outfit with her jeans would be fine for the shelter visits. Too bad her aunt and she didn't wear the same size shoes. That said, she'd found a pair of green galoshes in the kitchen. With a thick pair of socks, courtesy of her aunt, she could probably make use of those outside.

Sandra sat in the dining room eating a cheese sandwich for lunch and stared at the garden. Not a garden. A dog run. And not much of a dog run with no dog. She stretched her fingers and hands. They'd knotted into fists. She needed action. If this were her place, if the decision was up to her, she knew where she'd start . . . but it wasn't hers, and she had no right to make substantial decisions without consulting her aunt. Aunt Barbara hadn't left the money for home improvements.

But maybe a cleanup? That old shed must hold a rake and shovel. The sun was shining. The light dappled the new leaves of the oak and created shadow patterns on the green grass that danced with the breeze. It was an inviting scene. Trent hadn't liked her to do yard work. He wanted to keep it simple; nothing that a lawn mower couldn't take care of.

She stretched her arms out to her sides and felt the muscles ease in her back. She needed exercise. Fresh air.

In the garden, the air wasn't fresh. In fact, it smelled like old, damp manure, so the kitchen door and French doors had to stay closed. Her aunt hadn't bothered with a pooper-scooper or otherwise picking up after Honey. But that could be fixed. Sandra could clean up the area. It would be nice to be able to open the dining room doors and combat the dusty, musty air inside the house.

If the shed was locked, she was out of luck.

It wasn't. The door opened awkwardly, and she hoped it wouldn't fall off the hinges before she could get it closed again. It was jammed with implements and old crates and all manner of "where else are we going to put it?" stuff.

The dirty, rusty jumble was intimidating. *Tomorrow,* she told herself. After she visited the shelters in the morning and had hung the posters, she'd tackle this. She'd find the tools she needed and get to work on the erstwhile garden and make it more bearable for people and friendlier for Honey.

The to-do list for tomorrow was building in her head, and it felt good. All except for the most glaring, most important task: finding Honey.

She walked into the woods, following the left-hand path and calling Honey's name. No response. Birds flitted around and above her, and a few surprised squirrels scampered away.

Sandra stood and listened. Any number and variety of animals roamed these woods. Her mother had taught her to stay out of these woods, to stay on the porch and be quiet. This felt like it should be dangerous somehow, but it wasn't. It was peaceful.

She had been young when her grandmother died, and they hadn't come out here often after that. When her mom had come out here, she didn't bring Sandra. To be fair, Sandra hadn't wanted to come, and Mom hadn't insisted.

She stood there feeling the peace and thinking about how people are influenced by those they love and trust. Mom never liked the woods. As her daughter, Sandra hadn't questioned her mom's opinion on it.

The path before her was a faint two-wheel track that vanished over a low hill ahead. Wooden wagon wheels had probably passed this way long ago. Sandra walked a little farther, and beyond a downed tree blocking the path, she saw the creek. It had to be Cub Creek. She was surprised to recall an image from many years ago—a small plaque attached to the house, near the porch. It was probably hidden under the ivy now. The Shoemakers had named the house and the farm "Cub Creek" after this very watercourse, this dark water.

How many miles did the creek run? How many properties did it border or cross as it flowed through Louisa County? The Shoemaker homeplace was only one of many. How many lives had been touched by its waters through the years?

The path was damp, and where it was bare, it was muddy from the recent rain. Sandra turned back to retrace her steps.

When she returned to the house, she pushed aside the ivy and located the bronze plaque. CUB

CREEK was engraved on it, and the date below the name was 1867.

How had the family let the nameplate get lost like that? Her mother, Barbara, Cliff . . .

So many forgotten things. No one could keep track of everything, let alone an aging woman managing by herself in a very old house. No one could do it all on her own.

Sandra went into the kitchen. She found rags and sponges and cleaning products under the sink. She cleared the counters, tossing questionable items into the trash and putting appliances and keepsakes and utensils on the kitchen table. Barbara's table was an amazing wood plank affair that looked like reclaimed barn wood, but reconditioned and finished. It weighed a ton, as she discovered when she tried to shift it.

She washed the stained, ancient Formica counter-top and the pine cabinet doors from top to bottom. She scoured the stove top and inside the microwave oven. She got down on her hands and knee and scrubbed the faded linoleum floor. It had looked clean but was really only broom clean, and the water was dark gray. Now it shone. Sandra was exhausted, but at least she had something to show for it, and that made all the difference.

A small bonus was that she'd found an orphaned light switch hidden behind the blender. She flipped it, hoping nothing would blow up, and through the kitchen window she saw the pole light was lit. Bingo.

That afternoon, she brewed iced tea on the stove top. She found lemons in the fridge. After washing and cutting them up, she put them into a glass pitcher full of ice and water to steep. She was craving brownies. How long had it been since she'd craved any kind of food? It felt like progress. Unfortunately, she didn't have brownie mix or the fixings to make them from scratch, but that went on the grocery list for her next trip to civilization.

She poured the cooling tea over a glass of ice cubes. Old-style ice cubes, twisted out of a tray, and she remembered to refill the trays and return them to the freezer. Then she went out to the porch with her book and iced tea. She pulled the bench closer to the railing so she could prop up her feet.

The porch chimes made their music, and they were nice enough, but they belonged to Aunt Barbara, and it was like listening to someone else's noise, not her own. A small annoyance, but one she could change. She reached up and took the chimes from the hook and carefully laid them on the porch floor next to the house.

Sweet peace and quiet. She took her seat again and settled in.

Mr. Woodward's history book was amusing,

but the air was too perfect, and she was soaking up the outdoors more than what was written on the page. Trees waved in the breeze on either side of the house, and their leaves rustled like voices speaking, perhaps a story being told, but in a secret language that human ears couldn't decipher. She put back her head and closed her eyes, not understanding the story but soothed by the cadence. If she looked to her right, and if time travel were possible, she might see herself as a child, her toys surrounding her, with the adults inside, the rise and fall of their conversation creating a cadence of their own. Across the yard and the dirt road was the fallow field. Beyond that, the woods began again. On the far side of that field was the family cemetery. She'd never walked out there. Never been allowed. It was the forbidden land of snakes and ticks and other creepy-crawlies, per her mother.

She heard a vehicle in the distance. The state road was a ways away, but on such a quiet day, if the vehicle was loud enough and the breeze had the right heading, she supposed the sound could travel this far.

Her uncle was on her mind. Maybe because he seemed so absent from this place after spending his entire life here. Their last real conversation had happened the day her grandmother died, and it had made an indelible impression on her. Sandra was very young at the time. Seven, maybe? Mom had had red, wet eyes that morning, and they'd piled into the car to drive out to the homeplace, so Sandra knew on a day of such seriousness that she'd be on the porch. She took her favorite dolls and her coloring books with her. She didn't mind. She understood *important,* and she understood obedience.

Uncle Cliff had come out of the house, and the porch door slammed shut. He jumped as if he was surprised by the sound. She looked up at him from where she and her doll were coloring at the end of the porch. He held out his hand and said, "Let's take a walk, Cassandra."

She nodded, situated her doll on the bench, and then accepted his hand. His hand was big and warm. They walked along the dirt road as if they'd taken this stroll every day of their lives.

The wind rippled through the goldenrod growing by the roadside. It made *swoosh-swoosh* sounds that she could hear because she was walking with Uncle Cliff and not Mom. He stopped, and she followed his gaze to where a hawk sat on a branch above their heads. Not more than twenty feet away. After a quick look from one eyeball, the hawk ignored them and resumed its own watch of its kingdom. They moved on.

Uncle Cliff stopped at the old, ramshackle one-room schoolhouse.

"Did you go to school here?" she asked.

He hummed. "Me? Started there, but after the

first year, we got assigned to the new school. Our parents went here for sure. Last generation to sit in those desks all the way through. Building stood up pretty good for a long time, but once it was out of use, it couldn't last." He looked down at her. "Weather and all, you know? Stuff can't hold from the center for long. You can fight it, but ultimately it's a waste of effort."

She had no idea what he was talking about, but she liked the sound of his voice, soft and gravelly and with mystery in it. There was beauty even in the derelict building. Its door broken, the roof sagged into the one room, the porch planks sprung. She heard a watery noise, too. The creek ran back there behind the building and clumps of trees.

"You don't go in there, you understand? It could fall on your head, and no one would find you."

Sandra nodded. She wondered whether the children who'd studied in this building were sad or happy that it was so badly broken. Likely, since they were grown-ups now, they never thought of it one way or the other except as something to remember—like memories of friends and teachers. She didn't have many friends, but she liked her teachers a lot.

A noise grew. Uncle Cliff and Sandra turned to see a vehicle driving up the road toward the house, leaving dust clouds behind it. It was a van, long, lean, and dark. Not a regular van. More like a station wagon.

"Hearse," Uncle Cliff said. "Don't look, Cassie."

She tightened her hand around his. "Why not?"

"They said to get you away from the house so you wouldn't see."

"See what?"

He sounded almost surprised. "Miz Shoemaker died. They didn't tell you, I guess. You're too young to be exposed to all that. Death."

Sandra must've looked confused because he added, "Your grandma."

Her grandmother was the reason she always had to stay downstairs or out on the porch, and be quiet.

"I know," he muttered to himself. "She's been sick a long time. You hardly knew her."

"Why us?"

"Us?"

"Why'd we have to leave? Where's Momma and Daddy and Aunt Barbara?"

Uncle Cliff took a seat on the corner of the porch. Enough of the boards supporting the walls and roof remained so that, hopefully, he was safe as long as the roof didn't decide on a whim to avalanche the rest of the way down.

"Come here," he said, and patted the porch.

She sat next to him, a little excited, as if she were daring that roof to move. Momma wouldn't be happy about this.

"See here." He took a stick and drew a shape in the dirt. He raised the stick and waited.

"It's a square," she said, proud to give the right answer.

"Yep. Now this." He drew a circle within the square.

The circle was perfect in its roundness and was situated with a couple of inches to spare inside the borders of the square.

He stabbed the stick several times in the center of the circle. "What's that, Miss Cassie? Can you guess?"

He called her Cassandra or sometimes Cassie. They all did back then.

"A circle."

"Inside the circle, I mean. That's your auntie, your momma, and your daddy."

"What about us?"

He poked the stick inside the right angles of the corners of the square. "Us." Then he tossed the stick into the nearby brush. He rocked back and forth in a couple of quick movements with his hands braced on his thighs. "That's us in the corners. The center is where the strength is. But what's outside of the center don't fit in the circle."

"Me, too?"

"You tell me, Cassandra. Where do you fit in?" He coughed, cleared his throat, and spit.

For a flash of a moment, she caught the clarity of her uncle's whiskers, the unshaven face, the soft jaw and ragged hair. The odor of alcohol was there but faint, perhaps because it was early in the day. She didn't know. It was part of Uncle Cliff, nothing more. Then the moment of sharpness faded, and they were only two people sitting on the edge of a broken porch of a dilapidated schoolhouse waiting for the black vehicle to drive back the other way so they could return to the house. Sandra giggled.

"What's funny?" He perked up a bit.

"We aren't in their circle. They are in our square." It sounded like nonsense but right nonetheless.

He shook his head. "You're wrong and right at the same time."

He seemed sad. Her joke hadn't cheered him up, so she let him be. They sat in silence. After the van had passed, heading back to the state road, they let the dust settle for a few minutes and then set out for the house to see what the rest of the family was up to.

As they walked, she took his hand and asked, "Where would you rather be, Uncle Cliff? In the square or the circle?"

"Cassandra, unfortunately, I don't think we are born with a choice."

Her present had been hijacked by that memory. It took her on a side trip into the past with her uncle, leaving behind the old history book on her lap. She was surprised to find the book still open on her legs, her hands resting on the pages.

She hadn't done this much reminiscing in years. Maybe ever. She hadn't thought of Uncle Cliff in recent times, except for when he died early in her second marriage. She and Trent were living in Arizona. Mom said not to come back for the funeral, and Sandra didn't. It was too expensive, and her life had become too complicated.

She stood, setting the book in the chair. The white-painted handrail slipped beneath her fingers as she descended. The long dirt road called to her, and she decided to revisit history in person. Funny how, all these years later, she knew what Uncle Cliff had meant. It was true then, and, for her, nothing had changed.

They weren't in the circle. The family circle. The family and friends circle, even. They existed in the barely tolerated fringes. They couldn't be in the circle because they couldn't fit. Fitting in—that was the key. She'd known that for a long time, but she'd never understood why it had to be that way. For Uncle Cliff? Maybe it was the drinking. The family hadn't approved of his weakness, his inability to toe the line and live up to his responsibilities. But Sandra-Cassandra? Cassandra had been a cute, smart little kid who was on the fringe long before she had the chance to become a person in her own right, and when she did, she, Sandra, finally fell off the diagram map altogether.

Looking back, she didn't think it was them—the other adults. Uncle Cliff had made it sound like it was a family decision to treat them as if they were different. She wasn't sure about that now. Some people didn't fit in, and some people didn't want to. She'd been too young to make that kind of distinction at the time, and there was a part of her that had empathized with her uncle, bonded to him. She'd recognized his brokenness. It was one thing to be different and embrace it. It was something else to cast blame and drink it away as her uncle had. And years later, she'd married a man who was, to all appearances, successful and confident, and yet he, too, was very broken. He'd fooled everyone into believing he was a highly rated, well-respected engineer. They'd been together several years before she'd figured out that he wasn't much more than a clerk who, every time he came close to actually achieving the respect he wanted, alienated his boss and coworkers and had to start looking for a new job.

Different. Broken.

She was, too. How had she ever thought she could fix anyone? Or their marriage?

The road was dirty and rutted. She'd barely started down it when a tread mark caught her eye. It wasn't much, but it was captured in the dirt because of the rain they'd had during the night.

Only the one tread mark, so she couldn't

estimate the size of the vehicle, but it seemed large. Maybe a truck? The road ended here, so the driver must've turned in the grassier area right in front of the house. Perhaps a stranger who thought he or she could cut through somehow? Or maybe someone selling something?

Standing there, thinking, she heard a distant motor. An approaching vehicle. For a crazy moment, she almost thought she'd see that old, dusty black hearse, but it wasn't, of course. That was long ago. This was a pickup truck, one of those big ones, dark green, moving slowly along, negotiating the dips and bumps. Somehow she knew who it would be. Colton Bennett.

A skinny arm shot out through the passenger-side window and waved. Aaron. Sandra moved to the side of the road, the driver's side, as they pulled forward.

Colton rolled down the window. "Want to take a ride?"

Chapter Six

Sandra put up a hand to shade her eyes. "Ride? Where to?"

"Hang some posters."

"You've already done so much."

He frowned and pressed his lips together as if considering her words before he reshaped them into a smile. "I'd help Barbara if she was here and dealing with this. Besides, Aaron thinks you don't know your way around here. He's worried you might get lost. Then who'll find Honey?"

Aaron was up on his knees so he could see past his dad through the window. He waved, and she waved back.

"I was planning to visit the shelters and local authorities tomorrow and then hang the posters."

"Let's do it now. There's plenty of afternoon left."

Sandra looked down at her clothing and spread her hands. "I'm definitely not dressed for that."

"You look great. Change if you want. We'll wait. But you look nice. This is the country, after all, and we're talking about animal shelters."

She glanced down again. A T-shirt, but she could see that's what Colton and Aaron were wearing. Her jeans weren't too wrinkled. She was wearing sandals.

"Thanks. Let me get my purse and the posters, and I'll be right back out." She was moving before the period hit the end of the sentence. She stopped and looked back. "This is very nice of you two. I appreciate it."

She grabbed her purse, phone, and umbrella, and then dashed back out to the truck.

Colton drove slowly down Shoemaker Road. Sandra and Aaron kept a sharp watch, looking back and forth along the road for any sign of Honey. When they passed the schoolhouse on the right, Sandra caught her breath. The memories were so fresh she couldn't help herself. But once they were on the state road, she sat back and tried to relax.

"We'll head to the county line first," Colton said. "The Goochland shelter is right there. Animals picked up in the area, regardless of county, often end up there."

He smiled, and suddenly the proximity, the unwarranted friendliness, made her anxious. He was pleasant and attractive, but he was a stranger. She felt uncomfortable with him in the truck. Or rather, she didn't.

That was the problem. She was uncomfortable because she wasn't. *Or maybe,* she thought as they drove along and Aaron rivaled Aunt Barbara's ability to chatter, *it's because of the boy.* She and Aaron had absolutely nothing in common, aside from their humanity, and yet she saw herself in him. In his smile? In his eagerness to be liked? What exactly she saw, she didn't know. It certainly wasn't the talkative part of him. But she felt an affinity nonetheless.

Aaron had printed out a map of Louisa County, Goochland County, and the surrounding areas. Obviously, it couldn't be detailed at that level, but he had carefully marked the locations of the various shelters. He leaned forward between the seats and tried to hold the paper so Sandra could see it.

"See here." He tapped the paper then pushed it at her to take it.

"What am I looking at, Aaron?"

"Are you wearing your seat belt?" Colton asked.

Aaron disappeared, and a quick click was audible. "I am. I wanted to show Miss Hurst where the shelters are."

"I'm driving, Aaron. I've got the navigation covered. Besides, we can't get to all of them today. We'll visit the closest ones."

There were county-run facilities in both Goochland and Louisa, as well as specialized rescue shelters in the regional area. Aaron was right. There were a number of them, but they were spread across central Virginia, so Colton was right, too, and they couldn't visit them all this afternoon. She was happy to have Colton and Aaron chart the itinerary, but as they drew closer to the first shelter, the feeling of not getting enough air in her lungs, a feeling of suffocation, kept trying to roll over her. If it had been only Colton, she might've told him she was feeling ill and to turn around and take her back to the house. But for Aaron . . . His belief and determination kept her trying to relax past the point where it was practical to return without it looking too odd.

She lowered the window a bit and tried to discreetly point her nose toward the air rushing in. She didn't miss the irony. Apparently she shared that need with every dog ever born during the age of the automobile.

If she'd driven herself, she would've been engaged and distracted. More likely, if she'd had to rely on herself, she would've found reasons not to go. Had Aaron suspected that?

"Are you OK?" Aaron asked.

She twisted in her seat to see him. "I am. I'm fine. Just . . ."

"Worried about Honey?"

"Yes. That's it."

"Me, too. I was worried about Sammy. After she came home yesterday, we kept her in the house and on the leash. She's still in the run, but she wants out. Dad said she's probably missing Honey. They hang out together a lot."

"Probably so." Small talk. She could do this if she tried. "Sammy. Is that short for Samantha?"

He nodded. "How'd you know?"

She smiled. "A good guess."

"Almost there," Colton announced.

"Miss Hurst," Aaron said, "would you like a bottle of water? We have some in the cooler."

"Thank you. That would be lovely." Holding the bottle helped. Not really cold, but cool. She wrapped her hands around it. "Why don't you call me Sandra? We're friends, right?"

"May I, Dad?" He was a genuinely courteous young man. "Is that like a nickname? Like Sammy for Samantha? When Miss Barbara talks about you, sometimes she calls you Cassandra."

"She talks about me? All good, I hope?"

"She was looking forward to seeing you again. It had been a while, she said."

"It's been a long while. I've been away, lived other places over the years." She was speaking to Aaron while keeping a discreet eye on Colton. What had Aunt Barbara actually said? How much did he know about her?

"No one calls me Cassandra anymore, except maybe my father, and that's only because . . . only occasionally. My aunt has been calling me Sandra for years, so I'm surprised to hear she said Cassandra." She shrugged. "It was my grandmother's name. Old-fashioned. When I was a kid I felt different, you know? A little teasing, nothing much, but one of my teachers suggested I try Sandra, and I did."

Aaron nodded. "Yeah. Sometimes it's not good to stand out or be different."

"Everyone is different. Only fools want to spring from a cookie cutter," Colton said.

"I'd like a cookie." Aaron laughed. "Chocolate chip, please."

"Smart aleck." Colton grinned. "We're here."

The building was trim and neat on the outside. She needed to go inside and speak with whomever was running the show and ask if she could hang a poster. It was simple enough.

She climbed out of the truck. Colton hovered near Aaron, but not obviously, as the boy exited the truck. Aaron favored the leg with the limp, but he managed.

The interior looked a lot like a vet's office, but no animals were waiting to be seen by a doctor and there were no anxious owners hugging dog leashes or cats in carriers waiting their turn.

Sandra explained her mission. The woman smiled at Aaron. Having him along was a bonus. She smiled more than once at Colton, too.

"Mrs. Hurst," the woman said as she noted Sandra's information and added to the contact info she already had. "Mr. Hurst, did you want to leave your cell number, too?"

They all exchanged looks, and Aaron laughed.

Sandra smiled. "They're my neighbors."

"Oh, you look like you belong together. You're lucky to have such nice neighbors."

As they left, Sandra asked, "Should we have looked in the kennels?"

Colton opened the truck door for her. "She said they didn't have a dog like that, and she'd know. I think we can trust her, and now they have the picture and both our phone numbers, so we're covered."

They climbed into his pickup.

In Mineral, they made a quick stop at the vet's office.

Colton said, "It's worth a check."

They went inside and asked if anyone had brought in a border collie for treatment.

Sandra said, "I've lost a dog. Black and white. Her name is Honey."

The woman at the counter said no one had brought in a "found" dog recently or a border collie. They left names and phone numbers and continued on.

The county operation in Mineral was busier and noisier than the other. There were a couple of doors from the reception area to the kennels. The door on the left had been propped open a few inches. From what she could see, kennels lined the corridor. Some of the dogs were barking. Had they heard the voices in the reception area? She had trouble turning away. Colton and Aaron were speaking to the woman at the desk. Sandra caught bits and pieces of their conversation as if from a distance.

"No, I haven't seen this animal. I came on duty this morning. I can check the log."

While the woman skimmed through the records, she continued speaking to the guys, and snippets lodged in Sandra's brain.

"We're always full, and there are always more coming. Old hunting dogs, new puppies someone found in a barn, animals that get dropped off in the country because someone in the city can't keep them . . . No, I don't see that anyone logged in a border collie. I hope she's wearing a collar or has a chip. We always look."

"How long do you keep them?" Colton asked.

"Not as long as we'd like. As I said, they keep coming. Fostering is a huge help, and volunteers are welcome. If you want a pet or are interested in fostering some animals, let us know."

Sandra opened the door wider and moved past it into the kennel area.

Concrete and fence wire. Cages. No, not cages. These were called kennels, and they were clean. She kept repeating under her breath, "It's clean. There's food and water. Safety. Never mind anything else."

But the acrid smell of bleach and antiseptic mixed with the earthier smell of the animals and, as she walked, the dark eyes followed her. The hopeful, the scared, the trapped, the abused. Every wounded animal . . .

She put her hand to her chest. Her lungs were tight. Light-headed, she leaned against one of the kennels. She closed her eyes and kept them shut, and tried to concentrate on her breathing.

Among the other dogs barking, one barked close to her. She opened her eyes. A dog was near her feet. A small white dog. His eyes were wary but with a glint of willingness to accept . . . whatever . . . to be wanted and loved.

Abandoned. Unwanted. Fear and grief had a smell, and it swirled in the air around her. She held her breath rather than breathe it in.

Half-blind, she felt the wire of the kennel cages pass beneath her fingers as she headed for the door at the far end. As she fell against it, it opened. Outside, she leaned against the exterior wall, slowly sliding down the wall until she was crouched, her arms resting on her knees, her face in her hands. She concentrated on herself, shutting out the rest.

Abandoned. Unwanted. The fringe.

She and Uncle Cliff were the fringe. The out-casts. As were these animals.

Don't think about the animals. Don't think about Uncle Cliff.

But Honey. Where was Honey?

"Are you sick?"

It was Colton's voice.

"Aaron, you wait inside. Miss Sandra and I will be in in a minute."

Colton touched her shoulder. "What's wrong?"

Raising her face from her arms, she said, "I'm OK. I need a minute."

Aaron, still there with them, said, "I guess this made you more worried about Honey. I know it feels sad here sometimes." He too put his hand on her shoulder.

She was already struggling to breathe, and now his kindness nearly reduced her to tears. The truth was, this wasn't about Honey. This was about her and how she felt. But she couldn't say that aloud.

She wheezed. Heaven knew they'd think she had asthma. The last ragged breath made it all the way into her lungs. She put her head back. The block wall was hard and bumpy behind her head, but the contact steadied her.

Her voice was hoarse. "I'm sorry for falling apart." She put a hand to her forehead. "They are so needy. I can't help them. I can't help anyone."

"Can you breathe now?" Colton asked.

His tone had changed. She looked at him. He was frowning. She couldn't read the change beyond that frown.

She nodded. "Better."

He grasped her arm. "Let me help you up."

"I don't want to go back inside."

"Well, that's good, because we're already in the parking lot, and the door locked behind us."

She looked. Really looked. They had exited into the parking area and were near Colton's truck. She shook her head and touched his arm. "I'm sorry for the drama."

"No problem," he said.

But to Sandra, it didn't feel like "no problem," and she wished she'd never come.

When they reached the truck, Aaron was holding a fresh water bottle out to her. She accepted it and twisted the cap off and drank a good bit of it.

"Thanks for the water, Aaron. That helped a lot."

Colton was staring at her.

"I'm fine now, really." She put a hand on her chest and coughed lightly. "A touch of asthma." It wasn't, she knew that, but it sounded good for the moment, certainly better than saying she was a coward and had had a panic attack.

"Maybe we'll skip the other shelters today," Colton said. She didn't object, and he added, "They're pretty far away anyway. Honey isn't likely to have gone that far."

She nodded. It was silent in the truck as they drove, retracing the miles back to the house, until Aaron spoke up. "There"—he pointed—"for a poster."

After a quick glance at Sandra, Colton slowed, then pulled off the road and into the parking lot of a convenience store–gas station combo. The building was modern, all metal and plastic, and the pumps were operational.

"We'll be right back," Colton said.

He meant she could wait in the car, but Sandra eased out of the seat and held onto the door until she was safely on her feet. She followed Colton inside, and Aaron was right beside her.

Aaron took the lead. He spoke to the man at the register. Such an earnest child. So serious. *One of those who was born old,* Sandra thought. The store was small but neatly stocked. The tall man behind the counter waved at a bulletin board on the wall. He was old and thin, making his hands seem overlarge. Sandra looked down at her sandals and the floor tile.

"Thank you, sir," Aaron said.

Colton added, "If anybody mentions seeing a dog . . ."

"You got it. I'll call the number on the paper." He looked beyond Colton to Sandra. "That the lady missing the dog?"

Sandra looked up and nodded. She tried to appear normal. She was grateful. After all, each of these people, including the old man, was willing to help.

Colton cast a quick back and forth. "That's Barbara Shoemaker's niece. She's the one looking."

"Oh, yeah? Miss Barbara said she was going out of town." He looked at Sandra again as if he couldn't see her right. "Cliff and I were buddies. I asked Miss Barbara out on a date long, long time ago. Turned me down, she did." He laughed. "The Shoemakers set themselves apart. And Miss . . . Sandra? You have that look."

"What look?" She tried to sound pleasant.

He was a friend of the family, or so it seemed. Courtesy was called for.

"The eyes. You got the Shoemaker eyes."

She didn't know what to say to that. She had eyes. Two of them. Both brown. She stammered, "I-I don't know much about the Shoemakers. Aunt Barbara, of course. And Uncle Cliff. As to any other Shoemakers, I don't know. My mom and dad lived in the city."

"Sure, I remember. Your mama was Miss Meg. I recall her. Not your daddy, though. Didn't know him." He smiled. A nice smile, though he was missing a tooth or two. "Well, you stay in these parts long enough, you'll run into some." He laughed again. "Mostly, they're harmless. The Shoemakers, I mean." After another laugh, he added, "That's a joke, Miss."

He cleared his throat. "So you lost Miss Barbara's dog, did you?" He shrugged. "Happens. Dogs run away and come back as they see fit. Lots of room to run around at the old Shoemaker place anyway, as I recall it. I haven't been out that way in a long time. Not since Cliff was buried, for sure." He stopped and faced the window. "That was real sad about your uncle. Sorry for your loss. I was honored to be there for his burial." He nodded toward Sandra. "Don't you worry too much. If the dog ain't been hit by a vehicle on the highway, she'll turn up."

The thought of Honey as roadkill caused fire to

race from her gut straight up along her esophagus. She thought she was on fire inside.

A hand found hers. She looked down. Aaron.

"Thanks, Mr. George," he said. "I'm sure Honey's fine, but we do want to help her find her way home." He gave Sandra's hand an extra squeeze.

Inside, she whimpered. She hoped the sound hadn't made its way through to the outside.

When they settled back into the truck, Colton said, "I'll hang some other posters around. I drive around the area a lot anyway. I think maybe we've done enough today."

Sandra nodded wordlessly.

Aaron was pale. Her fault. He was still pale when they returned to the house. A real person would've invited them to stay for iced tea or lemonade as a thank-you for their help and kindness. Sandra slid out of the cab of the truck and walked away. She did turn back and wave, but a heavy cloud had settled over her, and simple niceties were beyond her.

It was more than the loss of Honey and those animals that no one had bothered to claim. It was all capped by that last moment—the understanding that that man, Mr. George, had been at her uncle's funeral. The one that was family only, and where she hadn't been needed.

Her feelings were hurt all over again, and yet there was a tiny spot in her heart that was glad. It might have been a small, quiet gathering, but she was glad her uncle had had a friend to see him off.

She tried to eat an early supper, but she wasn't hungry. She stood at the French doors. There it was, the overgrown garden and the broken-down fencing, and her imagination populated it with the eyes of those hungry dogs. Not hungry for food. Hungry to forget they'd been forgotten and unwanted. Hungry to live in a new present where they were cherished and appreciated.

Aunt Barbara had stashed a pair of yellow rubber gloves and a gardening spade under the sink. Sandra donned the gloves to pull a few weeds. She could do that much without having to dig through the shed.

The frequent rain had kept the wet manure odor ripe and pungent. The weeds and grasses were itchy. If nothing else, this dirt was heavily fertilized. As she was digging at a clump of weeds, a gnat repeatedly tried to use her face as a landing pad. It was impossible to deal with a gnat while wearing thick rubber gloves.

She yanked off the gloves and tossed them aside in frustration. This was an impossible task. Better to nuke the area.

Sandra went out through the gate and walked the perimeter of the yard calling Honey's name as loudly as she could, not caring who heard.

Anyone close enough to hear was trespassing anyway. Her pulse began to thrum in her temples, but it felt good to release some tension by yelling.

"Honey!" she shouted as she ventured down one of the paths. "Honey!"

She stood and listened but heard nothing except birds and squirrels and a light breeze ruffling the new leaves.

Sandra tried the other path, again calling out. This time, she heard something more. Something heavier was coming and brushing against the lower branches. Honey? Could it be? She froze. It might be a bear or a coyote.

No, it wasn't Honey. Sandra recognized Sammy as she trotted closer. The dog paused out of reach.

"Where's your family, Sammy?" Sandra knelt and extended her hand.

Sammy moved closer. She allowed Sandra to scratch around her ears. "They let you out on your own again? I'm glad you came to visit. Honey still isn't home."

The dog's paws and underside were muddy. "Where have you been, girl?"

Sammy barked and ran past her toward the house. She stopped at the garden and looked back.

Sandra caught up. "She isn't here, Sammy."

Sammy stood, her tail wagging, staring at Sandra. Sandra went inside and filled a bowl at the tap, but when she brought it outside, the dog was gone. Sandra picked up her aunt's gloves and spade. The day was nearly done and so was she.

She'd been here two full days and still no Honey. She should call Barbara. There was nothing her aunt could do from Florida, but she deserved to know.

One more day. Would it hurt to wait? Maybe their visit to the shelter would yield results tomorrow.

Sandra started the water running in the tub, and while it was filling, she opened the windows to allow in fresh air. She found some bath salts in the other bathroom, and she dumped them into the steaming water along with a few drops of lavender.

She wasn't a smart person, and she wasn't a survivor, but an important lesson she'd learned was that one tragedy wasn't improved by another or by self-denial. A person had better enjoy what they could today, despite what ailed them, because it might be worse tomorrow.

Sandra woke shortly after midnight and lay there in the dark.

She hadn't been this rested in years. She'd gone to bed early, exhausted by the emotional day and relaxed by the lavender salts bath. Her reward was to awaken for no reason and know she wasn't going back to sleep right away. And the dreams. Haunted for the last two nights by Trent and Uncle Cliff, tonight it was dogs and dogs and more dogs and their big, wet, begging eyes. But not a nightmare. The dream had seemed more . . . informational. She didn't know what to do with the information. She left the bed and went to the window overlooking the backyard. She parted the curtains. The moon was still bright and mostly full.

Maybe a snack? She'd barely touched supper.

Navigating the stairs in the dark was made more interesting by the items Aunt Barbara had left on them. Moving this stuff was going on the to-do list for tomorrow. Rather, later today.

The kitchen was half-lit by the moon. Honey's garden looked different, almost alien, and certainly wild and unkempt. A poor comparison to the holding pens she'd seen at the shelters. Those pens were modern and reasonably clean. In that case, it was the occupants that made them seem so tragic. In this case . . . Sandra moved to the door and looked out through the glass . . . In this case, the absence of the dog was the tragedy.

Sandra pressed her face to the glass. She could believe with all her heart and with everything in her being that Honey would come home. And that belief would get her exactly nothing and nowhere.

When would she dredge up the courage to tell her aunt?

It bubbled up—hot anger at the stupid broken-down fence that was her aunt's fault and the loss of the dog on Sandra's watch. Correction—discovered as missing on her watch. The dog may have run off before Aunt Barbara made it to the main road. But it was typical that Sandra would take the fall for it.

The moonlight glinted on the mended wire. She could see the repair was already coming apart.

She stomped outside, flinging the screened door wide, and nearly stretched its hinges beyond recovery. Sandra was already across the garden and yanking the fence wire back together when she realized sharp things were pricking at her tender soles. She was barefoot. Disgusting.

Irate, she wrapped her fingers around the fence and pulled, stepping backward and yanking. Something popped, and suddenly the whole side sprung loose. Her heel hit the corner of a half-buried brick, and she stumbled. A corner pole followed her momentum. She regained her balance and then realized she was yelling. Not polite, reasonable yelling but words that sounded a lot like *enough, enough, enough.* She tripped again and fell. The yelling had stopped. She disentangled her foot from the wire and sat there, exhausted.

What had she done? She'd pitched a hissy fit worthy of a two-year-old in the moonlit night in the dog's garden. Yes, she had, and she was suitably humiliated and disgusted.

Her hands and pajamas were filthy. She plucked

at her muddy pants, doubtful they'd ever come clean, and she laughed. It was a small, uncertain, uneasy sound, but it was something, and she felt better than she had in a very long time.

Chapter Seven

Sandra stood, glad and relieved that only the moon could see her face, which was surely bright red with embarrassment. She brushed her hands clear of debris. She shook her clothing to shed the dirt and bits of grass. Sandra was past thinking of the smell of the dog garden, of the nastiness. She stepped over the bunched fencing and the corner stake, crossed what was left of the open space, took hold of the doorknob, and went back inside, gently pulling the door closed behind her.

No one needed to know about this unfortunate event. Simply, in the sane light of day, she would fix it. The fence had needed repairs anyway. She would also call her aunt in the morning and tell her the bad news about Honey.

At two a.m., she ditched her pajamas in the laundry room and showered to remove the smell of wet dirt and manure from her body. She then went to her aunt's bedroom, leaving the lights off and steadfastly keeping her eyes averted from the mural, and looked in the most likely drawer for pajamas. Maybe the right place for storing certain items was genetic, because she hit the drawer right the first time. It was the second drawer in the bureau.

The blinds were open at the front window, and

Sandra used the filtered moonlight to negotiate the pajama legs and the ribbon ties at the waist of the pants. She was doing pretty well, too, when, from the corner of her eye, she saw a light moving outside.

One leg in and one leg out, she stopped and peered through the blind slats.

A light. A flashlight. Held about waist high by someone walking around. Looked male and grown.

She struggled to put her other leg into the pajama pants, and when she looked again, he was heading down the dirt road and fading into the darkness.

Part of her wanted to chase after him. Part of her was glad he was going. Was there any chance he'd seen her doing her crazy business outside in the garden? She didn't think so.

Was it Colton? Maybe Sammy hadn't come home? Colton might not have wanted to disturb her at this hour by calling or knocking on the door.

That made sense. She felt reassured and decided the next best step was to put on the pajama top. If the man returned, she'd handle it better if she were dressed.

She crept downstairs and looked out the windows. No sign of anyone. She slipped on her sandals and went outside, cautiously, and stayed in the shadows of the porch.

The insects were humming. The night sounds seemed right. Distantly, she heard a motor. It sounded a lot like Colton's truck, going the other way.

Maybe he'd left his truck down the road so as not to wake her.

Thoughtful, of course. Unnerving, too. It would have been better to give her a head's up. She'd ask him about it the next time she saw him.

Funny how she automatically assumed she would see him again. She double-checked the locks and returned to bed.

Thunder rumbled in the distance as she tried to find sleep. The rough shock of lightning breaking the dark didn't startle her. It reassured her in a cozy way. The rain hit hard. No one would be out in that by choice. A storm like that was as effective as a dog sleeping by the front door.

In the morning, after breakfast and after making her round of calls to the shelters and police station, Sandra stepped carefully through the garden mud and went to the shed. The grass was soaked, but her feet were dry because, mindful of the rain and mud, she'd grabbed her aunt's socks and galoshes.

She eased open the shed door. An old plastic egg-carton crate was in the front. It was filled with brown glass bottles. Next to the crate were some wooden tent pegs and some sort of long tool. She found an old metal rake. The business end of the rake, the tines section, had been nailed onto the wooden pole, and though it rattled, it would work. A claw-shaped tool would be effective for breaking up the soil and freeing the weeds. She could use that for sure. She continued to pull out stuff and set it on the grass. Fence stakes. No wire. But how expensive could that be? She had the money Aunt Barbara left. Would her aunt ask for an accounting? Probably not. But regardless, she'd said it was for the house and expenses. Did that instruction include nonessential renovations? Hard to know for sure, but looking at the mess she'd made of the fencing last night, this project was now necessary.

If Colton did come back with his truck, perhaps he would help her get new fence material.

She began working outside the kitchen door and used a screwdriver to loosen the bricks. She broke a fingernail trying to pry one up. The weeds came out in clumps. Within thirty minutes, she was perspiring, a little breathless, and feeling strain on her back. The mud, despite her care, was getting on her jeans and shirt. She changed position to ease her back, then stood to pull the crumpled wire and stake back out of the way, or she tried, but there was nowhere for it to go, especially with those overgrown bushes forming a perimeter. She tugged at the gate, but the posts holding it in place were stubborn, so she returned to working the fencing loose from the other corner stake. She had to pull the fencing outward because those bushes were in the way, but it did give her more latitude to pull back the growing tangle of wire. She tossed the stakes aside to land where they would.

When she stopped to assess her progress, she saw none. In fact, it looked worse. Her heart took a dip. What had she done?

No doubts allowed. After all, there were no witnesses. She had plenty of time to fix it before Barbara returned from Florida.

She took the metal rake and used the tines to loosen the bricks, but the weeds were tougher than she was. She knelt and tried the weed puller. Soon her knees were hurting. Her arms, too.

Skinny wasn't necessarily good. It was more about how one got there, and she had gotten to this state through near starvation and malnutrition, because stress had stolen her appetite, and she'd been eating junk food for comfort.

Feeling overwhelmed, she reached up to scratch her face, and the dirt got into her eye, and something felt like it was crawling up her leg beneath her jeans. She sat back in disgust. She was a wimp.

"Sandra?"

She jumped a mile. The tool she'd been using went flying.

Colton knelt beside her. "Are you OK?"

When she nodded, he moved back and said, "What's happening here?"

"This is unacceptable," she said, shaking her head.

"What?"

"This." She waved her arms. "Honey deserves better."

He looked around. "Is she back? Did she come home?"

It was sweet he was so happy about the prospect of Honey being found.

"Not yet, but she will. She will return, and this garden is going to be clean and properly fenced for her safety and a heck of a lot better than before."

Colton knelt beside her again, placing his knee on a brick to avoid the muck. "Sandra, what happened to the fence?"

His tone was gentle, his voice soft. She looked away, almost ashamed.

"It was an accident." She brushed at the dirt on her arm and made it worse. "The first part was an accident."

"Your hands . . ." He reached across to take her hand and turned it over, examining it. The scrapes, the broken nail, the minor cuts—all were smeared with black dirt.

She pulled her hand away and held it close. "It doesn't matter how it happened. Honey deserves better, and I intend to see that she gets it."

"Sounds like a plan." He nodded. "You're going to need a new bale of wire."

She stared straight ahead. "Can we use your truck?"

"Oh, so you're assuming I'm going to help?" he said with a sly smile.

"Yes." She added with a sly smile of her own, "Aaron will insist."

"He doesn't need to. I'm all in."

She felt immediate relief. There was no way she could do this alone.

"But there are decisions to make," he added.

Decisions? Choices? Those weren't her forte.

"Where do you want the perimeter? Where do you want the gate?"

"The gate's stuck right where it is. The hinges, the posts—they won't budge. Can't we work with where it is?"

"If that's what you want."

It wasn't, but she wasn't thinking in terms of what she wanted. Instead, she had to consider what she could manage both physically and financially. Plus, it wasn't her property. But if she was going all in, then shouldn't she aim high?

"I need to price it out first. I have a limited budget."

"All the more reason to figure out exactly what you want. Think big at the start. You can always scale back."

That sounded reasonable.

"What if I started the fence at the corner of the house that way? And then"—she rose and stepped over a few yards—"brought it back to here and moved the gate to this location?"

He examined the setting. She knew he was calculating the possibilities. He'd said he was a contractor, hadn't he? So he must know what he was talking about.

Colton mentioned the number of square feet and bales of fencing needed. "It's more like fencing a small backyard than a dog run."

"You're right," she said. "I'm taking it too far. I don't want to pull out my aunt's bushes. So, really, it doesn't make sense to do all this."

"Well, now, hold up. Don't talk yourself out of it so fast. Check with Barbara if you want to, but I can't see her being unhappy about the improvement."

"Nor can I, but it's still her property."

"Have you talked to her yet?"

Sandra drew in a deep breath. "About Honey? No. This is the third full day Honey's been missing."

"And no word?" He already knew the answer, of course.

"I've called them each day. Nothing."

He looked around the garden. "Why don't I get some pricing info? In fact, I might be able to scare up some of what we need for the project. I have contacts in construction."

"My budget is very limited. Even aside from the materials, I'll need help, and it costs money to hire people. Barbara left me some funds but not all that much, and without her approval . . ."

"Mind if I bring Aaron back after lunch? We can talk more about it then."

"Sure." Sandra walked with him to the front, where his truck was parked. "I don't know why you're being so kind. You don't owe me anything."

He smiled. A slow smile that grew. "Barbara's a good friend." He climbed into the truck but then leaned out the window. "See you in a couple of hours."

As he drove off, Sandra realized she hadn't asked him about Sammy or whether he'd found her last night. Or, for that matter, why he'd shown up here this morning.

She returned to the garden, picked up the tools, and tried to tidy the work area, and then went inside and showered. Standing in front of the bathroom mirror, she thought she looked different somehow.

Sandra touched her face, her shoulders. Her collarbone still stuck out, and her face was too thin, making her cheekbones and jaw more pronounced. Her eyes looked huge. The Shoemaker eyes? She smiled at that silliness, and it made an amazing change in her face. She touched the mirror. Was that how she looked when she smiled at Colton? At other people?

But she was no model. Such features, combined with the cropped hair, looked odd. Wrong for regular people like herself.

Still, there was a brightness to her eyes that she hadn't seen in a while. Maybe she was standing a little taller, too. She trailed her fingers down the length of her throat. She hadn't been aware of slumping. Deliberately, she put her shoulders back. She thought maybe that helped lift up the rest of her worn appearance. Mom had told her a gal could carry off almost any look, no matter how ill considered, if she wore it like she meant it.

Sandra borrowed a blouse from Aunt Barbara. The jeans she'd worn yesterday weren't great, but they'd do. While she waited, she called the shelters and local police again. They recognized her name now, but there was still no sign of Honey.

She lingered, staring at the screen on her phone. She should call Barbara. *One more day,* she told herself. *One more day.* She felt her tension ease, but the sense of time running out wouldn't go away. This was no more than a postponement. Meanwhile, she needed to clear the assorted stuff from the stairs before she tripped and hurt herself.

Sandra picked up a sweater from the second step, well-worn shoes from the third, and grabbed a couple of skeins of blue yarn from the next. But now there was a new question. Where would she put this and the rest? The dining room was jammed with boxes, and the living room was full of its own assorted stuff. So not downstairs. Upstairs? In Barbara's room? No.

There was one room with some space. Other than her own, of course.

She climbed the stairs and walked down the hallway. She worked a hand out from under the stuff she was carrying and was able to turn the doorknob.

The easel and cart looked pushed aside, abandoned. The half-squeezed tubes of oil paint looked dried-up and dusty, as did the paint dabs on the palette. Surely her aunt wouldn't mind if she used this room for storage, too.

Sandra used her hip to push aside the cart so she could reach the bed. She intended to drop the armload of Barbara's stuff there, but her foot caught on something, and she fell instead, landing on the already jumbled mattress.

She started to sit up, and the tickle began in her chest, almost like a faint pain, and then she started laughing. The discomfort kept growing until the tears started, then she fell back onto the bed and into the pile of stuff. She laughed harder until finally she was gulping, and she began to calm down. She was a So Silly, just like Aunt Barbara had said.

She wiped the tears from her eyes. What had she found so hilarious? Something had tickled her long-lost funny bone. Was it one more room being used for storage? The question of whether her aunt would mind? Or her own slapstick descent into the mess?

Somebody needed to seriously rethink what was worth keeping and holding onto and what wasn't.

It was early afternoon when Colton and Aaron arrived. Aaron held a metal clipboard. Repairmen sometimes carried those, and Aaron meant business. After a courteous hello, he set to work measuring with a long yellow tape measure. He noted numbers and made comments on a pad of graphing paper. Sammy trailed in his shadow, his faithful helper.

Sandra looked at Colton, and he smiled back at her.

"Need help with that, Aaron?" She stepped forward.

"Well, if you don't mind . . . could you hold the end of the measuring tape? There at the corner?" Beyond helping him get a few measurements, he needed no other assistance. "I'll have final numbers for you shortly."

So very grave and serious. He was too young for that.

"How about some lemonade?"

He nodded. "Thank you, but not until I'm finished with the layout."

"Yes, that'd be great," Colton said.

As she returned with two glasses and a bowl of water for Sammy, Colton appeared from around the corner carrying some canvas folding chairs. "I'm sure your aunt has some of these, but no need to go searching when I have mine handy."

They picked a nearby shady spot and sipped their drinks while Aaron worked. Sandra noticed Colton was wearing jeans but had changed his T-shirt for a collared button-down shirt. Plaid. Thin blue lines on a cream background.

"I like your shirt."

He looked down as if he'd forgotten what he was wearing. "This?" He shrugged. "Nothing special, but thanks."

She nodded toward Aaron. "He's very industrious. And very serious."

"He's a good kid. He likes projects."

"Does he get that from you?"

"Maybe by association." He must have seen her confused expression because he dropped his voice. "He's not my son. Not biologically. Feels like my son, though."

"I assumed . . ." She let the words trail off.

"He's been with me for a couple of years now. His mother and I were involved. She got sick and made me his guardian. I assumed it was temporary, that if she didn't make it other family would come for him, people who knew about raising kids. Grandparents, aunts and uncles . . . She said there weren't any around. I thought she meant no relatives lived in the area, but apparently she meant there weren't any at all."

"Wow."

Colton stared across the distance at Aaron. "He had an accident last year. Became a daredevil for a while. The therapist said it was a response to losing his mother. I don't know, but he hurt his leg when he tried to impress some kids with skateboard skills he didn't have. The doctor said he'd heal. He's been checked, and the doctors say there's no physical problem, nothing to account for the limp. They think it's psychological, probably tied to his mother, with her getting sick and passing."

"How did she die?"

Colton ran his fingers roughly through his hair. His voice dropped to almost a whisper. "Heroin."

"Oh. I'm so sorry."

"She was clean, and then she wasn't. Calling it 'getting sick' is a euphemism, I know, but it's simpler. She went to get treatment and left him with me." He shook his head. "She arranged the documents for the guardianship and everything before she went. I did what she asked.

"She seemed better when she came back. She was good for two days, and I thought she and Aaron would be moving on, but I was worried about him. By then, we'd spent a lot of time together. Anyway, she went missing. They found her downtown. Too late."

Colton leaned forward and looked down at the grass. "He changed. Became moody. Had some problems in school. Got hurt. After he'd supposedly recovered from his injuries, he was still limping. We tried physical therapy, but Aaron didn't deal well with it. In my opinion, anyway." He looked up. "I know—who am I to overrule doctors and psychologists? But I am his guardian." He shrugged. "So I made the decision to give him time. He's homeschooled, and I have tutors work with him. He's smart. Smarter than me, that's for sure."

Sandra was amazed. "I had no idea. I assumed you were father and son. He calls you 'Dad.' What a wonderful thing you've done for him."

"No. It's been wonderful for me. It settled me. Single guys aren't supposed to like the idea of settling down, right? I was wild." He looked at her again. "Did lots I'm not proud of. His mother was wild, too. When I found out about the drugs, I told her to leave. She asked for time to get clean. What was I supposed to do? Kick out the woman and her little kid? To go where? She was already living in my house. But I couldn't accept the drug use. I did what I could and gave her the chance to get clean, but I don't deserve any credit for it. Like I said, no fake modesty here—I never thought he'd still be on my hands." He took a long sip of lemonade. "When I agreed to be his guardian, I didn't have much time to think it through. I'm glad. I might've made decisions I would've regretted for the rest of my life."

Such honesty. It overwhelmed her. Her eyes burned. She coughed to clear her throat. She wanted to speak but was glad she couldn't right away because she didn't know what to say.

"Is something wrong?" he asked.

"No. I was thinking."

He looked curious. "Thinking about what?"

"That planning doesn't really pay, does it? It seems like we're luckier sometimes if we don't get what we thought we wanted."

"That's often true."

"Hey, I remembered something I wanted to ask you."

He looked curious again.

"Nothing big or serious, but last night someone was walking through the front yard with a flashlight. I thought it might be you looking for Sammy. It unnerved me a bit, seeing that flashlight bobbing along."

"Wasn't me." He looked around. "I can't imagine what anyone would be doing out here at night except maybe walking through."

"Well, no harm was done. I assumed whoever it was didn't want to disturb me or alarm me by knocking on the door after dark. He walked down the road, and then I heard a motor. I thought of your truck. I was going to say you should call whenever. Don't worry about the time if you need to speak with me, but if it wasn't you . . ." She shrugged.

"It was probably someone cutting through on their way to the main road."

"On foot? Then why the motor? Sounded like a truck."

He shook his head. "I don't have an answer, but whoever it was probably never thought they were disturbing anyone."

"Yeah, probably."

He added, "That works both ways, you know."

"What does?"

"You're welcome to call at any hour. If you need anything."

"Thanks." She smiled as she asked, "Why did you come over this morning?"

"Oh, that." He grinned. "Your umbrella. I was going to drop it off. You left it in the truck yesterday. It's still there. Don't let me drive off with it again." He called over to Aaron. "Are you almost done?"

"Yeah, Dad."

Colton turned back to face Sandra. "I'll be back in a day or two with an estimate on the project." She must've inhaled audibly because he added, "No worries. I understand about the budget."

• • •

The day had started out so iffy after a crazy night, but sunshine and a visit from Colton had changed it to a day of promise. She wasn't fixing her attention on Colton like a daydreaming schoolgirl, but she was grateful to him for more than his offer of help. To see that she could feel this way again, still be open to friendship and love after a decade with Trent, was so amazing, she could almost cry. Instead, she wanted to hold it close. To think about future possibilities. Life after Trent. It was out there waiting for her.

When Colton and Aaron drove away, it was still afternoon. Blue sky, a distant ridge of clouds on the horizon, and the air provided an interesting mix of warm and chill. Sandra went outside to the porch but grabbed a lightweight jacket and tied the arms around her waist, in case. She liked the porch and the open view in front of it, thanks to the fallow field across the road. Long fallow. She remembered a corn crop there long, long ago. The forest was a solid bank of dark green beyond the field, and woods stood on either side of her and the house. From this vantage point, she couldn't see the Blue Ridge, but that chill in the air made her think of the mountains, and that gave her comfort. Perhaps in the sense of place it offered. Storms were forecast, though, and this afternoon's chill was about to be displaced by warmer air.

The goose bumps on her arms predicted a sudden, imminent weather change.

She leaned against the porch railing. If this were her place, her home, the first thing she'd do would be to fill in the worst of the ruts and trim back the growth in the high places. Improve the approach—and the experience of the approach. She'd pull down those vines and plant azaleas and rhodos. That's what Dad had called them back when he cared about such things. Rhodos.

She must be feeling like a person again, rested and fed and secure, otherwise she wouldn't be standing here letting her thoughts linger over vines and fixing dirt roads.

It felt, smelled, and tasted a lot like hope, but hope might be premature.

Honey. If she was sick, she could be lying out there somewhere. In the cornfield. In the woods. If a car had hit her, she'd be lying beside one of the winding roads.

Tomorrow she'd get an early start. How lost could she get? There were only so many roads in the county. She was going to drive up and down every road she could find. It had been several days now, and she had to find Honey. Wherever she was, she might be running out of time.

Sandra rested her face against the post and closed her eyes.

On impulse, she pushed away from the porch rail, opened her eyes, and yelled as loudly as she could, "Honey! Come home!" That got her exactly nothing. Until the weeds in the old cornfield stirred. "Honey?"

Some birds took flight.

Hope to discouragement in a split second.

Sandra descended the steps and crossed the grassy area of the front yard, stopping where the dirt road began. A shallow drainage ditch ran between the road and field, and it nourished a thick natural fence of sticker bushes and saplings and poison oak and ivy, probably. Maybe a little sumac. She couldn't recognize it and wasn't interested in acquiring the ability—or the need for the ability. But the heavy rain during the night still filled the ditch and puddled on the road. And in the unstable air and growing bank of clouds, there was the promise of more.

"Honey?"

No response. She walked a few yards along the edge of the road, keeping to the higher ground, stopping and listening along the way, and occasionally calling Honey's name, more out of stubborn persistence than with hope.

The clouds that had been hovering on the horizon were moving in, surprisingly quickly. Winds aloft? That sounded like a weather phrase she'd heard somewhere. Watching the bank of clouds roll in and eat up the blue sky, she wasn't conscious of her footing and caught the edge of a puddle. Her poor sandals were taking a beating.

What had happened to the dozens of pairs of shoes she'd left behind in Martinsville? Were they still in her closet? Maybe Trent had made a bonfire with them.

As she walked, her thoughts were in Martinsville, rummaging in her shoe closet. She shook it off and called out Honey's name again. As she reached the old schoolhouse, thunder boomed. She stopped and stared at the sky. Dark, billowing clouds were overhead. The air tingled and had a greenish tint. A raindrop hit her nose. A big, fat one.

There was the porch and the corner where she'd sat with her uncle while they chatted about squares and circles and fitting in. The roof of the porch made a triangle of sorts, a dark cubby where she might shelter to avoid the imminent rain. If the roof held, it might work. If it chose today to cave in the rest of the way, she was in trouble.

The wall of rain moved like a solid force. The first drops hit hard. They hurt. She sprinted, heedless of puddles, hoping there was no hail to come. The jacket she'd tied around her waist loosened as she made that last great dash. It snagged on the wooden upright, hung there, and was drenched within moments as the wind blasted through and the rain sheeted down. Sandra was snug, or relatively so.

The building groaned and shifted when the

wind hit. Sandra curled up, hugging her knees, almost in an air bubble, as the rain solidified outside, in the open area around her dry place. The sound, and the sharp, pure smell of the pounding rain filled the air. She breathed in deeply, amazed she wasn't short of breath and nothing hurt despite the sprint. Despite the threat of the building possibly falling down around her, she felt OK, and that blew her away. She was marveling about feeling good when she heard the noise.

To be able to hear anything over this rain meant that it must be inside and nearby. She listened intently.

Something moved a few feet away. A muddy sound.

A whimper.

And she knew.

Chapter Eight

"Honey?"

In response, there was another whimper. A tiny noise.

Behind Sandra, the upright door frame still supported part of the front wall and roof and created a narrow opening. It was dark, especially with the heavy clouds overhead. She twisted to peer into the dim interior.

No sign of anything moving back there.

Danger, her brain whispered. The building creaked again, and she almost backed out of that now hellish space, but then the whimper, almost a whine, sounded again. A giving-up sound.

"Honey?" Sandra spoke more strongly this time.

Was that a bark in response? No, but definitely a noise.

The rain was heavy. She could wait until the storm passed, maybe investigate from the outside of the building. It would be very wet and muddy, but it would be safer.

She was already here, inside. She could hear drips within the structure, but it was relatively dry. It wouldn't hurt to look. She maneuvered her shoulders through the awkward triangle of the opening behind her. Once her shoulders and chest were clear, she twisted to work her hips through.

More than dim inside, it was dark due to the storm. She heard running water. It was a separate sound from the pounding rain. Cub Creek was well over its banks.

Sandra felt her way around an obstruction, and as she worked her body through the maze, her hand fell upon emptiness—a jagged opening where the floor had been.

"Honey?" she whispered.

This time there was a soft but definitive bark from below. Sandra heard the mud sound again, a sucking noise that made her think of sliding or of being stuck, like in the movies where someone steps into quicksand and can't pull free.

Her eyes had adjusted, or maybe the clouds had lightened, but now she could make out the boards around her and the dark area below. Additional light filtered in via the building's open foundation. It fell upon the animal's eyes, and they glowed for a brief moment before dimming again.

This had to be Honey. She wasn't moving. She was in deep trouble but not gone, not yet.

The floor was about two feet above ground level where the hole, like a dark pit of unknown depth, had been dug into the earth. Sandra pressed her chest and shoulders flat to the floor and reached down, her fingers stretching and searching. She repeated Honey's name over and over so she wouldn't think about reaching blindly into that dark, nasty hole, toward an animal she'd never met and who didn't know her.

The tips of her fingers brushed the living creature, but barely. She couldn't help the dog from up here. Sandra pulled her arm back and rose to her elbows.

"Honey," she said. "Hold tight. I know it's you, and I'll get you out of there."

She could run back to the house for her phone, but how long would it take for help to arrive? Honey had been trapped here, enduring several days of repeated storms and chilly nights. Or Sandra could ease through this opening and drop gently, softly, into that dark space. She visualized it. From inside the pit, she could push Honey up over the edge and onto the level ground. From there, it would be simple. At least the dog wouldn't be trapped in the mud and the fresh onslaught of rain runoff and creek water.

"I'm coming, Honey. Hold on."

Sandra crouched, kicked off her sandals, and rolled up the legs of her jeans despite the awkwardness of the cramped space. Rain still hit the tin roof, but the onslaught had lessened. Perhaps it was wishful thinking, but she also heard soft, labored breathing.

Sandra dropped her legs through the opening, avoiding the splintered edges. With one hand positioned on each side, she pushed up, straightened her body as her legs and butt lifted over the edge, and then descended. As her waist passed the level of the edge, she felt cold mud on her toes, then her feet, swallowing her ankles as she descended into it.

Sandra shivered. It was cold and clammy. If nothing else, Honey would be suffering from hypothermia.

Time to finish this.

As she eased herself down the remaining distance, she shifted from supporting herself by her forearms to her hands. The muscles in her arms trembled, and she knew she had passed the point of being able to pull herself back up into the building, and she nearly panicked. She was still descending into oozing mud, with no hard surface yet in contact.

Sandra tried to maneuver her legs to the side, seeking the edge of the muddy space. Her foot hit something solid. Maybe a board? She kept one foot on it, slanted though it was, and tried to shift her hands for a better grip on the broken boards above.

Splinters bit into her palms. She reacted instinctively and lost her grip. She knew she was going down and tried to control her landing. She didn't want to fall on Honey or do a face-plant in the mud.

Her hands landed on a solid yet soft, matted

body. Honey whined. Sandra felt Honey's muscles move as she tried to pull away but with little result.

Sandra settled on her knees, thankfully not continuing to slip deeper into the mud, at least as long as she didn't move much. She ran her hands lightly over the dog's body. Honey didn't seem to be in pain. Assuming she'd been here the whole time, Honey was suffering from food and water deprivation, but the biggest problem was probably hypothermia.

The light was brighter now beneath the building. If she could get her head back over the top of the pit, she'd be able to see what was around them.

Sandra assessed the situation as best she could in the low light. She was on her knees, and she sensed that the slope continued downward a bit farther. If she moved wrong and started sliding again, she'd find out for sure. The top of the pit was level with her forehead. If the ground had been dry, any good-size dog could've managed to scramble out. It was the mud that made it impossible.

And the water. The rain had stopped, yet a small stream continued to trickle in.

If she could leverage herself behind Honey and push the dog up by her flanks . . .

Sandra felt through the mud to find Honey's back end. She settled both hands under Honey's hips but could hardly budge her. Sandra put her hand on Honey's chest. Yes, her heart was still beating, but there was little warmth in her body.

If Honey couldn't help . . .

Sandra would simply try harder. "Aunt Barbara, if you only knew . . . ," she muttered. She dug her feet down into the stinking mud and tried to fit most of her body at the tail end of Honey's and envisioned pushing her up. It was slippery, but she could overcome gravity. She could do this.

Her feet, her legs, slid farther down. Honey slid another inch or two with her.

She would have to leave Honey to get help. Sandra tried to work herself up, to grip the top of the pit. She'd get herself clear, if she could, then run for her phone.

She heard an engine.

A truck. Colton's truck. But how would he know she was here? The engine rumbling stopped.

"Colton!" she shouted. Her voice hardly carried, lost in that muddy pit. She needed to move up higher. She needed to yell with force. This was their chance. A real chance. Colton would know what to do. Between them, they could make this rescue happen.

She dug her fingers over the edge and stretched toward the top. She was able to pull up, not enough to climb out, but she had a window that she needed to make good use of before the mud shifted and she lost the opportunity.

"Help!" she called again. The truck had pulled up near the building and parked by a clump of trees. A drier area. The door opened. She heard the truck door slam. She saw cowboy boots. The bottom of the truck was also visible. Black. Not green.

A stranger. Not her first choice, but she was willing to beg for any help. No matter what.

She opened her mouth to call out again. But something held her back. Even the reality of a dying dog couldn't hush the warning voice in her head.

"Somebody here?" the man yelled.

Sandra went still.

Trent.

Her jaw clamped shut. She pulled back, wishing the mud would swallow her. She couldn't think, couldn't allow herself to think, because the questions would start, followed by the swift realization that she had failed again.

He walked over to the porch and stopped. She remembered her jacket had snagged on the post.

"Last chance," he said. "Thought I heard someone call for help?"

Her tendons turned to mush. She lost her grip and slid back down into the muddy ooze. Her knee hit Honey, and Sandra remembered it wasn't about her.

"Here," she said. Not loudly.

"Hello?"

Sandra looked up at the floor above her head and shouted, "I'm here! I need help!"

"That you, Sandy?" His voice sounded clearer, closer. She imagined him kneeling, peering into the dark.

"It's me, Trent."

He moved around to the back of the building. It gave him a better view. She could see better, too, when she struggled back up a few inches.

"What are you doing under there? Are you in some sort of hole? You hurt?"

"I'm not hurt, but I need help. Do you have a rope or something?"

He was gone. She heard another slam. A tailgate.

Why was he here? Not exactly an angel sent to help. But accept his help, she must.

"Here, grab this."

Sandra pushed, and then pulled up again. Trent was several feet under the building, getting closer. He tossed the rope to her.

"Got it? Put your foot in the loop and hold on tight."

"I have it, but give me a minute to arrange it. I'll yell when it's time to pull," she said.

"I'll bet you've got an interesting story about how you ended up here."

She was thinking the same thing about

him—here despite all her efforts to lose him.

Sandra placed her foot in the loop, put one arm under Honey, and held the rope with her free hand. She drew in a deep breath.

"Pull, but take it slow and easy. I've got company in here."

"Company?"

"A dog. She's hurt."

"You're kidding. I haven't heard a bark. Sure she's not dead?"

"Slow and easy, please."

"Yes, ma'am. You know me. Whatever you want, I'm your man. But, Sandy, you're gonna owe me for this." He laughed.

Trent was tall. His shoulders were broad. He looked like the good guy in an old western. She never doubted that he could pull that rope with his bare hands and haul both herself and a nearly dead dog out of that mud. The problem wasn't whether he could—it was what it would cost her.

"OK, OK. Stop." She was covered in that gritty mess of mud. Being dragged hurt.

Trent dropped the rope and crawled toward them under the building, apparently oblivious of the mud. He pushed his fingers in Honey's side, poking at her. "She's not responding."

"Stop that," Sandra muttered, exhausted.

Trent grabbed the dog behind one foreleg and pulled her toward him. She kicked a paw and whimpered but didn't try to rise. When he had her closer to him, he grasped the other leg and got her the rest of the way out.

"Not dead. But not far from it." He lifted the dog's body as if it weighed nothing and walked away.

Sandra struggled from under the building. She reached the outside and stood carefully, resting one hand against the side for a moment. Feeling steadier, she looked down the length of her body. An hour ago, she'd been standing on the front porch admiring the day. Now . . .

Now she'd found Honey. That was the important thing to remember.

And Trent had found her.

He was at the truck. Honey wasn't moving.

She hurried over. Trent was at the back and was sliding Honey onto the truck bed. He reached up and unhooked the protective bed cover to get it out of the way.

He cast a quick look at Sandra. "Where to?"

Sandra experienced a moment of blankness as she fought the urgent need to turn away from him. She forced herself to meet his eyes. "The vet's office."

He gave her another look, this one longer, clearly referencing the mud. "Like that?"

"I'll ride in the back with Honey."

"Why? She won't make it anyway."

Honey chose that moment to lift her head an inch and raise one leg to paw the air weakly.

Sandra climbed onto the tailgate. There were some stuffed plastic bags in the way, and she shoved them back to make room.

Trent put one arm around her and hoisted her out of the truck bed. "Stay out of there. Follow me."

He dragged a canvas tarp from the backseat and spread the rough fabric across the passenger's side seat, back, and floorboard, and part of the driver's seat.

"Get in."

"I'm riding with Honey."

"I know. Get inside, Sandra."

Trent was displeased, but he was cooperating. For now. It didn't matter what he thought she owed him for his help. He had owed her far more, and then there was the question of how he'd come to be here. She clamped her jaws shut as he carried Honey from the truck bed around to where she sat. *One thing at a time,* she cautioned herself. She was close to feeling defeated. Honey was in rough shape. Not only might she have to tell Barbara that her dog had been missing, but that she was also dead. *Not dead yet,* Sandra reminded herself.

"Turn right when you reach the main road," she said, "and stay on it until the T intersection, then turn right. The vet's office is a few miles north." Then she settled back in her seat, wanting to relax but knowing it was beyond her.

How had he tracked her down?

She refocused on Honey. The mud was lathered, slathered, and caked in her coat. Her eyes opened a fraction. When Sandra held her hand on Honey's chest, she felt a vibration inside.

"You don't like dogs, Sandra." He said it almost as an invitation to disagree.

She held her breath when they crossed the wooden bridge over the creek. Her small car making it across was one thing. Trent's big truck was something else. But Colton had managed without difficulty, and his pickup wasn't that much smaller than Trent's. The creek water was high and rushing past but still well below the planks.

Even when she resumed breathing, silence didn't seem like a bad choice. Less room for error. She had to get through this. Stray raindrops hit the windshield as they drove along. The truck interior looked the same. Nothing out of place, ever, in Trent's life.

They reached the fork. "Turn here," she said.

"It's getting late. Hope the vet's in."

Sandra pressed her lips together, refusing to respond. She smoothed the filthy fur away from Honey's face. The dog was a mess and smelled. She did, too.

A sense of unreality crept in. One thing at a time. She'd been in tight spots before.

The tension in Honey's body shifted as the

dog lay across her lap. She hoped her own body warmth would help warm up Honey. She wanted to speak to Honey, to murmur reassurance, but not in front of Trent.

As they drove along, Trent shifted his hands on the steering wheel. She recognized the movement. Impatience.

"You haven't asked." He let the end of the sentence draw out.

She refused the invitation to engage.

He shrugged. "So why don't you tell me something? What's with the dog?"

Trent's voice, or perhaps it was her own tension, but something caused Honey to raise her head again. Sandra scratched the dirt under the dog's chin. "It's all right, girl."

"You never liked dogs."

"I never liked *your* dog." *Darn it.* She hadn't meant to get drawn in. She pressed her lips together. No more.

"That's why you left, isn't it? Over Leo? You said he snapped at you."

There was no law that said she had to talk to him. She caught her lower lip between her teeth. She caressed Honey's neck. Honey moved her head and peeked at Sandra again. She rested a paw on Sandra's arm.

Sandra's chest tightened, and her eyes stung. She couldn't cry here. She couldn't expose that weakness in front of Trent. Instinctively, she reached up to touch her eye and saw her hand in time. And her sleeves, her shirt, her pants . . . now she really felt like crying.

She hadn't been this dirty when she was homeless. What would the vet and his staff think?

OMG. She didn't have to check her pockets to know she had nothing. No ID. No cash. Not a credit card. Would they turn Honey away?

Her throat tried to close. Her chest tightened. She tried to relax, to envision what that looked like, felt like. She closed her eyes and discreetly tried to keep the air moving, to hold it in her lungs and fight the constriction. But discreet or not, with every breath, Sandra felt Trent's keen attention. He knew.

He saw her weakness. Like a laser, he could pinpoint her fear before she even knew it was building.

The vet's office was open. The lobby was lit, and the sign was turned to OPEN.

Trent came around to the passenger's side and gathered Honey in his arms. As he hovered over Sandra, touching her, she stayed emotionally in neutral. Trent seemed willing to keep this low-key and civil.

As he stepped back, Sandra slid out of the seat, and as she opened the door to the office, she called out, "We need help, please!"

Trent carried Honey inside, and the gal at the

desk rushed over—the same one who'd been here when she stopped by with Colton and Aaron.

The woman went to an interior door, opened it, and called out, "Doc Walker? We have an emergency!"

Chapter Nine

Trent rushed into the examining room with Honey in his arms, and Sandra was left standing in the entry, lost in a feeling of unreality. Having escaped the horror of being trapped in a muddy pit with a dying dog, to now being trapped in the vet's office with Trent, should be enough to cause anyone to break down, and yet, what else was she to do? Refuse his help? Again, it pricked at her. How had he found her? How had he come to be there? And why was Trent standing at the table with the doctor and the vet tech while she, Sandra, hovered in the reception area?

She heard words. Dehydrated . . . Possibly aspirated . . . They pulled her toward the action, but she didn't want to get in the way. She didn't want to be asked questions. She didn't know any answers.

A soft voice behind her caused her to jump. A hand touched her arm. The gal from the front desk asked, "Are you OK?" Sandra must've looked confused because the girl added, "You look like you've been through . . . a lot."

Sandra looked down at her clothing. The drying mud was shedding on the clean tile floor.

"I'm sorry for the mess."

"No, no worries at all," she said with a laugh. "When you're ready, would you let me know? We should fill out the paperwork."

There it was—the official financial stuff. Her stomach plummeted. "I'm sorry," she repeated. Sandra gave up on watching what was happening in the examining room and followed the receptionist back to the desk.

"I have money, but it's back at the house. I didn't have time to go home first. I hope you'll trust me for it."

The woman looked startled. "Again, no worries. I can see the situation. I'm glad you found your dog." She looked toward the room. "And in time, I think. It's a miracle."

A miracle. Sandra could use one. Honey, too. Was it a miracle or a sick joke? Maybe if the truck had belonged to someone other than Trent.

"You didn't give up, and it paid off."

"You remember us?"

The woman laughed gently as she shuffled a few papers onto a clipboard. "How could we not? We've been getting calls from you twice a day asking if we'd seen or heard anything of her. Plus that little boy of yours is so cute. He called a bunch of times, too. Did you know?"

Little boy of mine? Sandra almost corrected her and then realized it didn't matter.

"I thought the other guy was your husband, but I guess not. This is a different man." She looked toward the examining room door. "Not my business anyway."

Sandra nodded toward the room where Trent and Honey were. "He's . . . he's someone I used to know. He surprised me with a visit today."

"Like I said, none of my business. I apologize for being nosy." She handed the clipboard to Sandra. "Honestly, I hate asking you to do this. You must feel awful about your dog, and with all you've been through. I can't begin to imagine. Give me what information you can, and we'll finish it up later. Meanwhile, I'll see if I can get an update on her condition. Also, we have coffee in the back. Would you like some?"

"Thanks for your help. No thanks to the coffee." She stood, staring at the door to the examining room. She should be in there beside the table, hearing what the doc was saying. She should be there for Honey to see, for them to see that she, Sandra, was reliable, that she cared about her aunt's dog. But she felt collapsed inside. What more could she do for the dog anyway, other than what was already being done?

Sandra stayed at the counter. She was a walking mud ball. How could she sit in the chairs? As she filled out the form, her sleeve dragged. It was stiff and filthy. She pushed it up, out of the way, but her arm was filthy, too.

The receptionist returned with a cup of water and set it near Sandra's arm.

"He's giving her some fluids. She's responding well. He thinks she may have aspirated some of that mud. He'll probably keep her overnight. That's a guess, but we'll know for sure soon."

The vet decided to keep Honey overnight.

"Overall, she's responding well," Dr. Walker said.

Sandra was unconvinced. Honey was dirty, her coat matted, and her eyes looked inflamed. Her breathing seemed steady, if a little labored, and she attempted to rise as the vet's assistant cleaned the mud away from her muzzle and eyes.

"She's hydrating now. We'll try some food later, if all continues as I hope. I'm worried about her lungs, though." He rested his hand on her chest, then nodded. "If she feels like eating later and I don't see anything developing, then I'll feel very encouraged." He nodded again. "So Trent said you and the dog were stuck in a hole under an abandoned building?"

Sandra crossed her arms. It irritated her that he spoke Trent's name as if this were Trent's story instead of hers and Honey's.

"Yes. The old schoolhouse. It's on the dirt road to the Shoemaker house?"

He shook his head. "Not familiar with it, but I've seen the sign for Shoemaker Road, just past Apple Grove, right?"

"Yes. There was a deep hole under the building.

I don't know how Honey ended up in there, but she must've been trapped since I arrived on Monday. It was muddy enough and deep enough that she couldn't get out."

Dr. Walker said, "She was probably getting some water. A few days without food won't hurt a dog much as long as there's water." He held out his hand, and Honey placed her paw in it. She attempted to lift her head and managed a few inches. With his free hand, he smoothed back the fur on her forehead and gently eased her head back onto the table. "We'll clean her up, too."

"Thank you," Sandra tried to say, but she choked. The words barely squeaked out. She cleared her throat. "Thanks for giving her a chance."

The vet smiled. "You two should go home. Gayle will call you later with an update. You need to get that mud off yourself, too. Maybe get checked out by your doctor."

The door closed behind them. Trent opened the door to the truck and held it for her. He was the soul of courtesy and compassion.

She was going to do this? Really? Get in the truck with Trent? But she was filthy and had no money or shoes. How else was she going to get home?

They shared the first few miles in silence until Trent asked, "Am I allowed to talk to you?"

Sandra tried to keep her gaze straight ahead,

but from the corner of her eye, she saw his face was half-turned toward her. She clenched her fingers together in her lap.

He sighed. "Sandra. Be an adult, please."

"Please keep your eyes and attention on the road." She bit her lip. She knew better than to get drawn in.

He nodded. "No worries there. I've been a good driver all my life. Driving is easy. Marriage? That's different." He paused before adding, "I'd like to know what I did wrong. Why did you leave this time, Sandra? And without a word?" He waited again, but she refused to respond.

He continued. "You're mad because I came here after you. But what was I supposed to do, not knowing what was going on?" He tapped the steering wheel with the back of his ring. It made a faint staccato noise.

"I left you a note."

"There was no note. Unless you hid it somewhere. Because that's what you do, Sandy, you hide." He waited. "But not very well."

She couldn't help herself. "I left a note whether you want to admit it or not. I told you to leave me alone. How did you know where I was?"

"Where else would you go? Which, by the way, I at least had the courtesy and consideration to call your parents. That's more than you can say."

"That's not what I'm talking about. You know what I'm asking."

"I don't know anything. I wish you'd explain it to me."

How had he known she was here? Did she want to know badly enough to ask him again?

He turned onto Shoemaker Road.

Sandra sat up taller, determined. "Stop at the schoolhouse."

He frowned slightly but did as she asked. She put her hand on the door handle and swung it open.

"What are you doing?"

"I'm getting out here."

"I'll drive you to the house."

"No. This is far enough."

"You're being silly."

"Maybe, but I don't think so. I appreciate what you did today."

"Aren't you curious how I happened to be there? Aren't you glad I was there to help? Even if the help came from me?"

"I'm not curious, and thank you again. It doesn't matter how or why you found me. You are leaving now, and you aren't coming back." She slid out of the seat. Her bare feet landed on rocks hidden in the weeds. Inside she winced, but she kept her face impassive.

"Sandra."

"Thank you and go now while I still feel a little grateful. You aren't welcome here. You are trespassing. I'm going to stand right here until

213

you drive back down the road and leave this property."

"You know, I couldn't pin it down before, but with that haircut, you kind of have that Audrey Hepburn look. The short hair, the skinny arms and neck. Not her charm, unfortunately, and not her class. Why'd you cut it, Sandy?"

"Go now, Trent." She slammed the door and stepped into the middle of the road, staring toward the bridge and the state road.

He reversed in the open area in front of the schoolhouse, and, without another look, he drove away.

She told herself he'd left because she was adamant, because she'd accept nothing else, but her hands were shaking as she watched him head toward the state road and the rest of the world. She waited to see if he'd come back. He didn't. After a few minutes, she crawled into the building to retrieve her shoes. When she saw the opening in the floor and the dank, dark, muddy mess below it, she vomited, barely making it out of the building first. It felt like mud and fire coming up.

A few minutes passed before she got back to her feet. She had her sandals. There was no sign of the jacket.

She carried the shoes as she trudged to the house. The front door was unlocked, as she'd left it. She'd been gone a little longer than intended, to put it lightly. As much as she didn't want to wear her filthy clothes in the house, dropping dirt and debris as she went, she wasn't going to strip on the porch.

In the kitchen, she ditched her clothing and left it all on the floor in front of the washing machine. She'd wash them later after she'd hosed them down out back. She stood at the sink and drank water. Just water. Thirsty. She drank more water. Her stomach rumbled a warning, and she set aside the glass.

She found her phone on the table beside the knitting chair and snagged it as she headed to the stairs. She shut the bedroom door and locked it, then, for extra measure, pushed the dresser in front of it. She retrieved the knife from under her mattress and laid it on the floor between the tub and the wall, along with her phone. Sort of like the Old West gunslingers did with their weapons while bathing in the bathhouses. Always ready.

Her body shook while she waited for the water to run hot, and then kept going while she showered. When the worst of the mud had washed down the drain, she put the plug in the drain and sat there as the tub filled up. There was a part of her that thought she'd never feel warm again. She was going to stay in this tub until she did.

She may have dozed off. When the phone rang,

she sloshed the water so badly that it spilled over the high rim of the tub. She grabbed her phone.

"Sandra Hurst, please?"

"This is she."

"Hi, this is Gayle. I was calling with an update on Honey. She's doing well."

"Thank goodness." Sandra leaned over the edge of the tub, not willing to risk her phone falling in the bath. "Is she eating yet?"

"Not yet. But her body temp is good, and her heart sounds good now. The doc is still a little concerned about her lungs, but if she continues to improve, he'll release her tomorrow."

Gratitude and relief went hand in hand. Sandra laid her head back and unclenched her hand from the side of the tub. "Thank you so much. I can't begin to tell you how much I appreciate this. I'll be over tomorrow morning."

"Wait until we call you?"

"Of course. Will she be all right there overnight?" Now that relief was rolling in, so was worry about the expense.

"Sure. We have another overnighter on the schedule, so unless Honey takes a bad turn, it won't be a problem for the tech to keep an eye on her."

"Thank you again."

Sandra hung up, dropped the phone onto the bath mat, and slid down into the tub again. The water had cooled now. She'd had good news, but bad news could always be counted to find its way in. Hopefully Barbara had left enough money to cover Honey's medical bills.

What about the fence?

She grabbed a towel and climbed out of the tub. She was almost restored. And hungry. She checked the time on her phone. Only a couple of hours had passed. Could that be true? It was still well within the supper hour.

Aunt Barbara had left some steaks in the freezer. How long would it take to defrost one?

The clothing she'd worn today was out of the question. She would have to raid Aunt Barbara's closet yet again.

She chose a pair of sweatpants and a long T-shirt. The T-shirt had three-quarter sleeves, and she hiked them up her arms.

Sandra glanced at the living room bookcase as she walked through. Aunt Barbara's cash. She'd call her aunt and give her the news. It was past time for Barbara to know about Honey and—thank goodness—the news was good. Barbara also deserved to know how Sandra was spending her money. She called the cell number.

"Aunt Barbara? Hi, glad I got you. Are you still having fun in Florida?"

"Oh, yes. Margaret and I went to a putting green. She's determined to make me a golfer."

"Yes. She always enjoyed golfing with Dad." Did that sound like a criticism?

"He's doing real well, Sandra. I know you've been worried about him." She had a sweet but fretful nature.

"I have. I'm glad you're there to help."

"Happy to. You sound like you have something on your mind, Sandra."

"You have a good ear, Aunt Barbara. There's something I need to tell you."

"What?" she asked, her voice suddenly sharp.

"It's all good. I'm sure I should've told you right away, but I didn't want you to worry, and there wasn't anything you could have done about it."

"For heaven's sake, Sandra, you're scaring me. Are you OK? The house? What?"

"Everything is fine, or it will be. It's about Honey. It's a long, confusing story, but a few days ago, she got out of the fenced area. The gate was unlatched. I don't know how or why, but she was gone. I've been looking for her ever since."

"Oh, my. Oh, my."

"But I found her! It worked out."

"Thank goodness."

She wasn't doing this very well. It was like a step forward, two steps back kind of approach and not very effective. "I found her down by the old schoolhouse."

"There?"

A long silence ensued that Sandra didn't understand. Finally, Aunt Barbara continued, but she sounded far away. "We should've had it torn down years ago. I didn't realize it was so . . . dangerous."

"There's a big pit dug in the earth underneath. It had rained a lot, and I found her stuck in there, in the mud, but I got her out."

"Oh, oh, oh . . ."

"Honey is recovering from hypothermia. She's at the vet's tonight."

"Do you need me to come home? I can, right now. What do you mean trapped? You were both trapped? And the vet? Which vet? Why is she still there?"

"Take a deep breath. Everything's good now. It's Dr. Walker's office in Mineral. The vet is concerned she might have aspirated some mud. He's watching her in case she takes a turn, but right now she's doing well. She'll probably come home tomorrow."

"Oh, my goodness, Sandra. Certainly I never thought you'd be caught up in all that."

"I should've called you sooner, but I wanted to call with happy news, and thank goodness I can."

"I'm so sorry I left things in such a state that this could've happened. I remember when those awful Minton boys were digging holes everywhere. Roger Minton and his cousin were building forts or traps or something. Once they built a dam and caused the creek to flood. Your Uncle Cliff complained they were messing around at the old schoolhouse. I told their parents. But that's neither here nor there. Suppose you had been injured while rescuing her? Horrible. I'll tell Meg I have to leave now."

"No!" The word sounded more explosive than intended. She didn't want Barbara to come home. If she did, there'd be no reason for Sandra to stay on. "Really, it's fine. I'll keep you informed about Honey, but she's doing well. I wanted you to know because I'll have to use the cash you left to pay the vet."

"Oh, that. Oh, goodness."

"Thanks for leaving the money. That was good thinking." Sandra was trying to be reassuring and uplifting.

It wasn't enough for Aunt Barbara.

"I'll give them a call," she said.

Sandra wanted to say no, but she bit her lip. She didn't want them to tell Aunt Barbara that Honey had been missing since the first day. That would make Sandra sound like a liar. "No need," she said. "They're probably closed for the day anyway. I'll keep you posted."

"Thank goodness you were there, Sandra. What on earth would I have done if she'd disappeared while I was home? I can't walk that far anymore, and I don't like to walk that way anyhow." She coughed, and when she spoke again, her voice was perkier. "Your mama surely knows that by now, though she's determined to rejuvenate me.

220

I'm so glad you were there to handle it, and I hope it hasn't been too hard on you."

"No, ma'am. I'm good. I'm thankful I could call you and tell you it's all over now and that there's a happy ending." She added, "One more thing?"

"What, dear?"

"I had to borrow some of your clothing. I hope you don't mind."

"Of course not, my dear. Take whatever you need."

They disconnected. Sandra sank onto the sofa in relief. Done, and with a good ending. She bounced back to her feet. She was hungry. Famished. She walked into the kitchen and debated whether she should defrost that steak in the microwave or choose something else. She paused at the kitchen door. The garden was a mess, and she was responsible for that.

Colton said he'd be back with an estimate. And Aaron had put so much effort into measuring and planning. What would she tell them?

Maybe the vet wouldn't cost as much as she feared. Maybe she could still afford the fence materials, at least for a small area.

She also had to tell Colton and Aaron that she'd found Honey. At least that much.

Sandra left the microwave to work its defrosting magic on the steak and went back to the living room. She picked up her phone and the slip of paper with Colton's number. She stepped out to the porch. An evening chill was settling in as the sun set, but it felt refreshing.

Tell him about Honey, she told herself. *Don't spoil this conversation with money stuff.* She would tell him they needed to discuss it but leave it at that for tonight.

She dialed his number. It rang, and as she waited, a breeze kicked up, and something on the porch banister caught her eye. She stepped down a few steps for a closer look.

Colton's voice mail answered, but Sandra couldn't speak. She flipped the phone closed.

Her jacket was hanging on the post.

And it hadn't gotten there on its own.

Chapter Ten

The jacket was an "I could've but didn't" message courtesy of Trent.

He could have done whatever he wanted, but this time, he hadn't.

Sandra's mind raced. She had watched him drive away. He must've returned while she was bathing.

Sandra was acutely aware that her choices, her actions, would determine his next step, and the result would be her fault. That's how Trent operated. She'd been caught in his game many times before.

The yard was empty, as was the dirt road. Trent was gone now. She hoped.

She took her jacket from the post. As she went back into the house, the phone rang. *Colton,* she thought. But no, it wasn't Colton.

"Sandra, how are you? What is Barbara telling me about Honey?"

"Hi, Mom. Nice to talk to you, too." Sandra closed the front door and locked it.

"Sorry. Barbara is going on and on, all but distraught, and I need to know what actually happened."

"Exactly what I told her. The dog went missing."

She paused in front of the bookcase shelf where the photographs were arranged. She tweaked the position of Barbara and Honey's photo. "I looked all over and couldn't find her. She was down at the old schoolhouse. Rather, under it. There's a very large hole under it, a muddy pit, and the dog couldn't get out on her own." Sandra touched the photo of her mother and Barbara posing in front of a bank of blooming azaleas. "Why is it always my fault?"

"I didn't say it was."

"The dog got out of the fence through no fault of mine. The fencing is a disaster, by the way. Please don't tell Aunt Barbara I said that. I'm trying to fix it for her."

"I didn't say it was your fault, but your aunt goes on and on sometimes. Should she come home?"

"No, everything is fine. The only concern is for Honey, and the vet is monitoring her overnight. If anything happens, I'll let her know immediately."

"Are you sure you can handle a sick dog?"

Sandra blew out a frustrated breath. She turned the photo to face the wall, then moved across the room, aggravated. She tossed a skein of yarn at the chair and wanted to kick something, but she was barefoot and didn't.

Mom added, "I knew something was wrong when we weren't hearing from you."

"I've been here less than a week."

"When things go wrong for you, you go underground. You go quiet."

"I might as well, for all the good it ever did me to confide in you."

"You're in your thirties."

"Barely thirty."

"Exactly. If you don't like something about your life, Sandra, then make better choices. Make better decisions, set goals, and stick with them. Don't allow others to derail you."

Heat raced through her. She tried to control it but couldn't. "One thing I know is that I did everything you and Dad ever asked of me, whether I wanted to or not. I did it for you two because I love you. Where did that get me?"

"Do you need money?"

Sandra paused, instantly deflated. "Is that a trick question? You know Aunt Barbara left cash."

"It's a simple, civil question. You might consider a reasonable response. You might also ask yourself who you're really angry with."

Sandra pressed her hand to her forehead. Angry? Maybe. Mostly what she was feeling was trapped. Should she tell her mother about Trent? But why? It would open up a new line of argument.

"Aunt Barbara's money will cover the vet, and my needs are simple."

"Goodnight, then."

"Wait, Mom. How's Dad? Is he settled in?

Are—" She almost asked her mother, the woman she'd snapped at, if she was doing OK. Sandra shook her head, this time in dismay at herself.

"He's actually doing well, and now that I'm rested from the move, I'm better at anticipating his needs and responding. He's enjoying himself, mostly. He keeps asking when we're going home. He can't remember eating breakfast ten minutes after he's up from the table, but he remembers home."

Sandra nodded. Home. "Do you have a day program for him down there?"

"Not yet. I don't want to throw too much at him all at once. It helps having Barbara here."

"Then I'm glad. I'd better go."

She hung up before something else could trigger her temper.

The poor steak, having spent extra time in the microwave, no longer appealed to her. Sandra slammed the microwave door on her supper and went back out to the porch, again staring at the empty yard and road. Would he come back?

The phone rang. Apprehension slammed into her. Her phone didn't have much going for it, but it had caller ID. She recognized the number as Colton's.

"Hi," she said.

"You called but didn't leave a message. Figured I'd call you back."

Funny. She felt a little lost as her tension began

to melt away. It was something about the warmth in his voice. It started in her chest and spread up and down and all around.

"Sandra? Are you there?"

"Yes, of course. I'm glad you called back." The change in mood was in her voice, and she couldn't hide it. "I have news, and I didn't want to leave it in a message." She paused for effect. "I found Honey."

The tear started in the wake of the warmth— the pressure in her cheeks and eyes, the sharp tug of her heart—and it rolled down the side of her face.

"You did? How is she?" he asked.

"She's good," Sandra said, laughing as she swiped at the moisture on her lashes and cheeks. "She's staying at the vet's tonight, but they said she's recovering well."

"Recovering? Wait." He spoke to someone. Surely Aaron, because there was a cheer in the background. "Can we come over? Aaron wants to hear the story as much as I do."

"Are you sure?" She wasn't accustomed to people asking to come over and share good moments with her. To celebrate. But before Colton could reevaluate, she said, "Of course, come over."

"Great. We can light up the fire pit. Be there shortly."

She stared at the phone. He'd disconnected and

would be here in minutes. She was wearing Aunt Barbara's sweatpants. She ran upstairs, and as she searched her drawers and closet for something a bit more attractive, a manila envelope came from somewhere and fell onto the floor. She picked it up and tossed it onto the bed. She'd figure out where it belonged later. For now, the clock was ticking.

She grabbed the yoga pants. Not great, but they'd do with a long T-shirt. Certainly better than the sweatpants. And miraculously, the last twinges of stiff muscles and aching joints left over from the rescue had vanished. She felt like a kid again.

At the fire pit, Colton arranged some logs and twigs and lit it up. Aaron was in his plaid pajamas, a jacket, and untied sneakers. He was busy, bent over a tray table, opening the bag of marshmallows, the package of chocolate, and the graham cracker box. They'd even brought wire hangers.

S'mores. Sandra had heard of them but never tasted one.

The fire pit flamed as the sun set. Night fell, and the fire pit turned golden. Colton looked up and smiled.

She was glad of the darkness that hid her blush.

"Miss Sandra?" Aaron asked. "Do you have an oven mitt?"

"I do, Aaron. In the drawer next to the stove."

"Is Honey really OK?" he asked for perhaps the tenth time since arriving.

"She is."

He nodded and went into the house, returning in a short minute.

Colton pulled the chairs closer, and Aaron handed her the clothes hanger with the marshmallow on its end.

"What do I do next? Hold it over the fire?"

Aaron and Colton exchanged looks.

"I've never done this before." She waved the wire hanger with its white blob on the end, but carefully so as not to shake it loose. "What happens after it toasts? How do I get it onto the crackers and chocolate?"

Aaron said, "After it's roasted and melty, hand the wire to me, and I'll do the rest."

"Got it." Sandra steadied it over the fire, and Aaron and Colton did the same.

"Now tell us," Aaron said.

"Where was she?" Colton asked.

A story, she reminded herself, should be entertaining, not necessarily fully and factually complete. Not all players needed to be mentioned.

"You'll never guess."

A star had popped out above the tree line. Star light, star bright . . .

"I went for a walk this afternoon," she began, taking Aaron and Colton through the sudden downpour, seeking shelter in the school, and hearing a bark.

Meanwhile, she handed the wire to Aaron, and he finessed the hot marshmallows onto each chocolate and cracker set up. He pressed down on the top cracker, and the marshmallow and chocolate lightly squeezed out the sides. No waste of chocolate was allowed.

Sandra stopped talking to take a bite. She closed her eyes. It was heavenly.

After licking some crumbs from her finger, she said, "So where did I leave off? Oh, right. I had crawled inside, and as the rain slackened, I heard a noise. A tiny noise."

"It was Honey," Aaron said.

Sandra nodded. "I was sure it must be, but it was a scary situation." She watched his eyes grow wider as she described the tight fit, the awkward maneuvering, and the sound of water and mud. "I'd left the phone at the house. You never have it when you need it, right?" She smiled and shrugged. "The sides of the pit were so muddy, Honey couldn't get out. She must've tried over and over. She was very weak when I found her."

"If she couldn't get out, how did you do it?"

An image of Trent flashed in her mind. And at that point, the story became fiction.

"There was a, uh"—she cleared her throat and shifted position—"a piece of board down in the bottom. I was able to get leverage by bracing my foot on that board and pushing her up and over. It took a few tries, but we got it done."

Aaron's second marshmallow caught fire. Colton reached forward and used his wire to clear the flaming sugar from Aaron's. Aaron layered the marshmallow and slabs of chocolate onto the crackers. He handed one to her and one to Colton.

"How did you get her to the vet's office?" Aaron asked.

"By vehicle, of course." She held the s'more to her nose. The chocolate smelled incredible with the marshmallow.

"But you were on foot, right?"

She nodded and finished chewing her bite. "Well, my car was parked here at the house." She shrugged and let the implication finish the answer. "The vet was great. He took her right away." Sandra sat back in the chair and finished off the delectable treat.

"Would you like another?" Aaron asked.

"I've had two already!" Sandra exclaimed.

"I have a question now," Colton said. Sandra tensed, fearing he'd found an inconsistency in her story. "How on earth is it that you've never had a s'more?"

She relaxed and laughed. "Oh, please."

"No, truly. How'd that happen?"

She shrugged. "My mother was very careful about sugar and chocolate and such. We didn't camp or anything. I never even went away to camp. Where would I have encountered them?"

Aaron and Colton exchanged those looks again.

"I've never gone fishing or hunting, either, so laugh away." She waved her hand at them.

"Where is Honey now?" Aaron asked.

"The vet said she was suffering from hypothermia. She must've been stuck there since the day I arrived. The last few days were chilly and very wet. Hence the mud."

"Lots of mud," Aaron said, "because Sammy kept coming home all muddy."

"She was probably checking on Honey," Colton added.

"All's well that ends well, right, Dad?"

"The vet was concerned she might've aspirated some of that mud. They think she'll be fine, but they wanted to watch her tonight, and I'll have to watch her closely for a few days. But she should be coming home tomorrow."

"Then we have work to do," Aaron said.

"We do." Some omissions mattered to no one but her. In this case, Sandra felt compelled to address them. "We need to scale back, though. With the vet bills, I need to keep the fence project cheap. I appreciate your help, and I hope you understand."

"No worries."

The conversation was general and inconsequential and a total pleasure. When they left, she walked them to Colton's truck. Aaron waved and said, "See you tomorrow!"

Sandra was relaxed and had not one iota of energy left in her, but it was a sweet exhaustion. She changed for bed and brushed her teeth and when she slept, she slept free of dreams. Even Trent didn't have the power to trouble her rest that night.

The green truck rolled around the side of the house and parked in the backyard. Colton and a stranger climbed out of the front. Sandra stepped out the back door to greet them.

Colton waved. He was wearing jeans, a gray T-shirt, and a grin. "This is John," he said. "He's here to give me a hand. Hope you don't mind."

John had black hair and a shy smile. He was taller and broader than Colton, but Colton was clearly in charge. The first thing they did was move Aunt Barbara's small metal table and chairs into the shade of the oak.

"We're going to clear out the rest of the old material—the fencing, the bricks, etcetera—before we dig out the dirt; then we'll put the bricks back in place. And I have a suggestion about that to discuss with you, too."

"About the expense . . ."

"No worries. The cost will be minimal. I have access to building materials that would otherwise go to waste." He pointed at the truck bed.

Sandra saw a bale of wire and some fence stakes.

"Those were left over from a job I did at my own house. They were in the way. I'm happy to get rid of them."

She crossed her arms. "I appreciate your kindness, but I meant what I said, and I can't afford obligations. I don't know how much the vet will charge, or Honey could take a turn for the worse, so I don't want to go broke over the fence. Honey must come first."

Colton removed his heavy work gloves, tucked them under his arm, and came close. He put his hands on her arms. "Trust me. And if it helps any, this is Aaron's project. His layouts, measurements, and estimates. This is a great school project for him. So, you see, it really isn't about you or me but about Aaron and Honey."

"Well, we don't want to be selfish, do we?" She practically choked out the words.

Colton smiled. "No, ma'am, we do not."

She left Colton and John digging out the dirt in the area framed by the bushes and the kitchen door. Aaron was situated in the shade refining the plans. She considered inviting him to go with her to the vet's office, but he was working hard over the clipboard and papers, and she remembered what Colton said about this being a school project. Sandra reminded Colton the back door was unlocked, everyone should help themselves to lemonade and tea, and that she'd be back shortly.

As she drove past the schoolhouse, her stomach gave a little flip. Honey. Mud. Trent.

The drive was uneventful, but her palms were growing damp as the miles fell away and the vet's office, and Honey, was getting closer. She patted her purse. She had the envelope with Aunt Barbara's cash stashed inside, the corner peeking out.

Reassured, she stole a deep breath, in and out quickly, before turning in to the parking lot. She grabbed her purse and went inside.

"Hi." It wasn't Gayle at the desk. "I'm here for Honey."

"Of course. Ms. Hurst, right?"

"How's she doing?"

"Very well. The doctor is very pleased. She's eating and drinking. Here he is now."

The vet told her to keep her quiet for a few days, to let her get active at her own pace. If she stopped eating or drinking or showed signs of breathing trouble or distress, Sandra was to call the office immediately.

"Thanks so much." Sandra looked back at the receptionist. "I need to take care of the bill."

The receptionist took another look at the computer screen. "It's all taken care of."

Taken care of.

"Who paid it?"

"Barbara Shoemaker. Your aunt, I believe? She told me you were house- and dog-sitting for her."

"Oh." How much had they told Barbara? Sandra's face felt hot. Liars never have an easy conscience. But she hadn't really lied. She'd omitted. It felt like a Trent trap. She looked around really quickly, as if thinking of him might conjure him.

She felt that downspin begin, that feeling of loss of control. Her chest tightened, and she gripped the edge of the counter, but then there was a bark and a furry body bumped her leg.

Honey. Sandra knelt beside her. "Hi, Honey girl. Nice to properly meet you. I doubt you remember me from yesterday, do you?" She scratched Honey's ears because it seemed the thing to do. She didn't like dogs, right? Despite herself, she put an arm around Honey and hugged her close. Honey licked her cheek, and Sandra felt a response in her heart.

Sandra rose, and the vet handed her the leash.

"Remember, call us right away if she worries you. Encourage her to drink, and don't let her loose. We don't want to risk her getting into trouble again too soon."

"I'll remember. Thank you."

Sandra opened the passenger door, and Honey took it in stages, first climbing onto the floor-board and then up to the seat. She moved like an old lady, but when she looked at Sandra and panted, Sandra was pretty sure Honey was smiling. Impulsively, Sandra leaned forward and put an arm around her neck and hugged her, patting her side.

"We're going to do just fine together, Miss Honey. You wait and see."

She shut Honey's door, taking care not to slam it, then got in the car.

"Down, girl," she said, stroking Honey's back and encouraging her to lay down.

Sandra reached across to pull the seat belt over the dog and fasten it. She didn't know if that was appropriate or not, and it looked awkward and foolish, but suppose . . . No. No supposes. *Pay attention to business,* she told herself. *Whether you go by Sandra or Cassandra, you don't have to worry about fitting into anyone else's circle. You have your own, and, suddenly, it's pretty darn sweet.*

Chapter Eleven

Sandra touched Honey's side a few times on the way home, and the dog seemed to take that as permission or encouragement and sat up in the seat again. She pressed her nose to the window. Joy and confusion radiated from Honey in alternating waves. Why not? There was bound to be some confusion. Sandra was a stranger.

Honey, missing, had been a big part of Sandra's life for the past week, but Honey expected to see Barbara, not a stranger. As the miles went by, the dog drooped a little, and by the time they turned onto the dirt road, Honey was lying down in the seat and panting instead of grinning. Sandra glanced at her, worrying. Secondary problems. One always heard how deadly they could be. Honey looked back at her, and Sandra saw the light in her eyes. They were bright, and maybe there was still a grin on that doggy face. When they turned onto Shoemaker Road, Honey sat up again and barked.

"Welcome home, Honey."

Sammy was the first to reach the car in the driveway, followed closely by Aaron and Colton. Sandra tried to help Honey out of the car, and she was moving, but slowly. Colton stepped forward and lifted her in his arms. She wasn't a

239

small dog, and she was fully conscious now, yet she seemed content to let him carry her. Sammy trotted faithfully at his heels, stretching to sniff at Honey's feet as she was carried around to the backyard. Sandra went straight inside the house, dropped off her purse, grabbed Honey's sleeping pillow, and carried it outside.

Honey and Sammy were lying in the sun, soaking up the noon rays. The pillow was apparently unnecessary when grass was available. Sandra put the bowl of water near them in the shade cast by the large oak tree. Honey gave Sandra a look and then closed her eyes and dozed. Sammy lay as still as Honey, but her eyes were alert. She was keeping watch. Those times Sammy had shown up here muddy . . . had she been trying to find help for her friend?

"She looks good, don't you think?" Aaron asked. He knelt and gave both dogs pats on the head. He rested his hand on her chest and waited. Apparently satisfied, he stepped back and returned to his chair.

Sandra sat in the chair next to Aaron. His plans were graphed and had lots of notations. Each bush was drawn in; each measurement was precise.

"Here." He pointed to the area within the bushes, closest to the back door. "This is where we'll put the bricks. If we can get a few more, it can be used as a real patio."

He pointed the tip of his pencil to an area

beyond the bushes but still next to the house. "This will stay grassy but will be within the fence. This is for Honey to do her business. And one thing I was considering . . . how about adding a layer of river rocks in a border about two feet deep along the foundation of the house? It would provide better drainage, I think."

"I have no idea. Don't get me wrong, it sounds like a good idea, but I don't really know anything about stuff like that. Should we ask your dad?"

She watched the two men shoveling dirt into a plastic tarp.

Why were they doing this? For a dog? For her?

"What does he do as a job, Aaron? He's a contractor, right? What does that mean?"

"He builds stuff. He's a general contractor. He makes the plans and coordinates all the workers and craftsmen for whatever is being built. He builds stuff himself, too."

"Stuff?"

"Sure. Houses or rooms or whatever the job is."

"He sounds very busy." Yet he had time for her, for this project. She was glad. She liked him. But building things was his profession, and he should be paid regardless of his talk about helping Barbara and so on.

"Sometimes he is, sometimes not, especially in the winter. It's very seasonal."

"Seasonal." He was ten, yet he sounded like a forty-year-old discussing the economic realities of outdoor occupations. She held back a grin. She wouldn't offend him for the world. "Thirsty? I have tea and lemon water."

"Dad's got his cooler in the truck. I'll grab a bottle of water." He put his work aside carefully, placing it on the seat of his chair when he stood. He went over to his dad and John. "Would you like some water?"

John nodded. Colton looked over at Sandra and called out, "Is there more tea?"

"Yes, of course." She was pleased. "I'll fetch it."

The two men had shoveled out the patio area. Colton said, "We'll fill that in with cleaner dirt. Hope you don't mind, but I've got a load of dirt coming over this afternoon."

"Dirt? How much does dirt cost?"

John looked up. Perhaps she was too loud, too shrill. She approached Colton and touched his arm to get his attention. She had to be honest with him.

Colton smiled. "It suits you, you know."

"What does?"

"The hair. Short and kind of jagged. I don't know what to call women's hairstyles, but it looks good on you. You've probably heard that a lot. I hope you don't mind me saying so."

"No, I don't." Her hand, of its own accord, reached up and fluffed her short locks. She tried to recapture that telltale hand by crossing her

242

arms. "But you're changing the subject. Don't think I can't see that."

His grin grew. The laugh lines at the corners of his eyes deepened. "You are determined. I can see that. Remember what I said about Aaron, and also about Barbara being my friend and wanting to help her out? I hope she'll be pleasantly surprised. Have you told her what we're doing?"

"No."

"Good. We'll surprise her. The dirt comes from the jobsite. It's got to go somewhere, and it's fine for me to take a load. Also, I want to suggest some blocks from another jobsite. The homeowner has a relatively new patio that they want updated again already. They're paying to have the existing stone hauled away. I'll haul it here, if that works for you."

"Seriously?"

He nodded.

With no prior notice to her brain, her arms flew around him, sweat and all, and hugged him. It was a fleeting hug because good sense intervened to save her from extended embarrassment.

"Thank you," she said, regaining her self-control and stepping back.

"You are welcome."

She remembered he'd asked for iced tea. Her iced tea.

"I'll be right back." She called over to John, "Would you like some tea?"

"No, ma'am. Got water." He waved the plastic bottle Aaron had brought to him.

Sandra nodded and headed inside to cool off. She held a damp cloth to her face. What was she thinking, flirting with a guy she hardly knew? For heaven's sake, what was she doing flirting with any guy at all?

She was still legally married. She needed to make her life work and resolve her issues before inviting anyone else into it.

She looked out the window and watched John and Colton drag the tarp away from the patio area. The last thing she needed was to jump from Trent into another relationship. On the other hand, she could use a good friend.

Could they be friends?

Someone had moved the dog pillow into the deeper shade. Honey had settled on it and was napping. Sammy was stretched out in the grass between Honey and Aaron. Sammy was clearly younger than Honey, and they were friends. Sandra was a little short of those right now.

Sandra delivered the tea. Colton downed it in one long gulp and then handed her the glass. He went back to work immediately, directing a truck into the backyard and backing up close to the space.

John came around the truck carrying a roll of black fabric. He unrolled it in the hole, and both men went back to work with shovels, moving the sand from the truck to fill in over the fabric. Sandra went back inside and watched as they added a layer of fine gravel. Then Colton knocked on the door.

"We have to go now. We'll be back tomorrow with the stone." He gestured at the work area. "We've covered it with a tarp. As much rain as we've had, it's better to be safe." He'd used the bricks to anchor the tarp. "Can you manage without the fence for a few days?"

"Oh, sure. I'll bring Honey inside now and keep her leashed when she's outside for the time being. When this project is done, it's going to be an amazing change for her." She looked at Aaron and the dogs enjoying the shade. "Is there anything I can do for Aaron? I want to show my gratitude. Is there anything he enjoys? Movies? Or board games?" She shrugged. "That sounds lame, but I hope you understand my intent."

Colton crossed his arms as he considered an answer. "Well, he's tired of my cooking. I don't want to assume you can cook. But if you can, he might like a meal prepared by someone who knows what she's doing."

"I'm no chef, but I have a few good dishes in my repertoire."

"Well, then, there you go. Perfect. And I'd rather eat someone else's cooking any day. Hope you don't mind—Aaron and I are a package set."

"What's a good time for you two?"

"How about next week? Maybe Friday?"

"It's a deal. Anything he really hates?"

"No kale or liver."

"Understood. Most kids don't like those."

"Ah, well, Aaron's not picky. I'm talking about myself." He grinned.

She smiled. "Friday evening, then."

"But we'll be back tomorrow afternoon with the stone, and I hope to get the fence staked out."

"Speaking of which, I found a tent stake in the shed. I thought maybe I'd hammer it into the ground under the oak for Honey's leash . . ."

"Happy to assist."

Sandra's phone rang. It was Aunt Barbara. Sandra put aside her book and answered.

Barbara said, "How is she? The vet's office said she was doing well when you picked her up. I'll bet being home has fixed her up the rest of the way."

"She's quiet but relaxed," Sandra assured her. "As the doctor ordered. He wants her to rest while she gets her strength back. She is delighted to be home. She misses you, but we are getting along fine. As a matter of fact, we're sitting here together, and her chin is on my leg."

"Can you put the phone to her ear so I can speak to her?"

"Of course." Sandra felt pretty silly about it, and Honey looked at her with a question in her eyes, but when Barbara started speaking, Honey barked twice.

"I think she's saying hello back to you." Sandra laughed.

"Thank you so much. I'm having such a lovely time with your mother here. I feel so light and carefree knowing you're taking care of things. I don't know when I've ever felt quite this way."

"Aunt Barbara, there's one thing I need to ask about."

"What's that, dear?"

"I was going to pay for the vet bill with the money you left."

"Well, I understand, and certainly that would've been fine, but I wanted to speak with the vet myself, and truly, dear, since I was already on the phone with them, it made sense to go ahead and pay. No reason to run you short. After all, you're going to be there for another month and a half. You've hardly arrived."

"I admit it feels longer."

"Do you need me to come back?"

This time she heard real reluctance in Barbara's tone. She reassured her aunt that she should stay down in Florida. "I'm fine. I'm making some repairs on the fence. Do you mind if I use some of the money for that? I don't want Honey running off on any further . . . adventures."

"Oh, goodness no. We most certainly do not want that. Do whatever you think best, dear."

After a pause, her voice dropped to a lower tone. "Your mama and daddy are doing well down here. But she worries, you know."

Sandra was expected to ask, so she did. "Worries about what?"

"You, my dear."

"Then she's wasting her time." Sandra cringed at her own change in tone. "I'm sorry. I know you mean well. What has she told you?"

"Your mom isn't one to talk about personal stuff, is she? But I can tell. I wish you'd talk to her. Set her mind at ease."

"She's probably worried about Dad and recovering from the move. I don't want to sound harsh, but sometimes people have problems, Aunt Barbara. Sometimes their own problems and sometimes with each other. It's not really anyone's fault. It's just how it is." No way was she going into details with her aunt. If Mom wanted to, then that was her choice. "I'm doing great. Really."

After a long pause, Aunt Barbara said she understood. Of course, she didn't. But she and her sister and her sister's husband all had one another. Sandra was the odd one out.

They said good night, and she was pleased overall. She'd gotten her aunt's approval for the garden improvement project without spoiling Colton's surprise. Pretty good deal.

As for being the odd one out, she was feeling

better about that. Maybe it wasn't such a bad place to be, after all, especially once she got past the hurt feelings.

Sandra walked Honey outside. Because of the hole Colton and John had dug by the back door, they went out through the front, much as she did that first night here with Sammy. Honey stopped at the top of the stairs and didn't want to go down. She sniffed at the night and whined.

"Really, Honey? You can do this." She scratched her head in encouragement.

Honey moved like her joints ached. Coming back up the steps was a little better. When they made it back inside, Sandra pushed at the dog's sides and patted her hips, but there was no indication of pain. Sandra held Honey's muzzle and looked into her eyes and nostrils. As if she'd know what doggy congestion looked like? *Sigh.*

As far as she could see, Honey seemed fine. A little slow. An older dog who was still getting back her health.

Sandra locked the door and turned on the front porch light and the pole light back by the shed.

It was a slow trip up the stairs, but Honey was intent. She wanted to go upstairs. Honey went down the hallway and turned directly into Barbara's room.

Sandra hadn't expected that.

She stood in her room and called to Honey,

softly and with invitation. Honey sat next to Barbara's bed and stared back at Sandra.

Fine. Honey could sleep in Barbara's room. Sandra would leave the doors open. Honey could come in or not, as she chose, and hopefully Sandra would be able to hear her if she started breathing heavily or had any problems.

Sandra found a knee-length T-shirt in her aunt's closet that would work for a nightgown.

"There you go, Honey. Now I'll even smell like my aunt, right? Not that you are invited on the bed. No, indeed." She kept up a running chatter, hoping that Honey would settle, but she didn't. The dog sat there. Waiting.

Then it hit Sandra. Honey's sleeping pillow was still outside under the oak tree.

"Wait here, Honey."

She put on her shoes, then stood at the kitchen door, allowing her eyes to adjust to the darkness. She turned on the backdoor light, which was helpful, at least as far as being able to pick her way through the excavation. There was no bold moon tonight, but the pole light lit up the open area of the yard, giving it a fishbowl feeling. It also cast long, dark shadows.

She'd left the door open a couple of inches. She didn't want to risk locking herself out, and, being honest, she might want a fast retreat back inside. She told herself there was no reason to feel unnerved out here. The smell of ashes in the fire pit reminded her of the fun the evening before. It was all good, right?

As she touched the dog pillow, she heard a short, sharp bark. She grabbed the pillow and spun around. Honey was several yards away. Staring. Sandra followed her gaze. She was staring at the woods to her right.

Creatures lived in the woods. This could be innocent. A raccoon. A squirrel. Any small critter might be on the move tonight. Honey barked again.

Sandra moved toward the house, clutching the pillow and keeping Honey between herself and the woods—and whatever might be the subject of her attention. She kept moving, mindful of the flashlight man she'd seen a few days ago. A man who hadn't been Colton. As for Trent . . . anything was possible, but it seemed he'd be more likely to drive up to the house than to lurk in the dark woods. Trent hated the outdoors. As she reached the house, she called out, "Come, girl. Come to me, Honey."

The dog gave one last bark and then trotted obediently to the door. Sandra saw a small animal, maybe a raccoon, run out of the woods across the yard.

"Is that who you were barking at?"

Inside, with the door locked, her tension eased. Not a big deal after all. A woodland critter was to blame for the excitement. But she left the outside lights burning.

She knelt and hugged Honey. She expected to find tension, but there was none. She seemed unconcerned. That encouraged Sandra. Nothing to worry about.

Honey watched Sandra put the sleep pillow in her room. The dog walked over and sat next to it for a few minutes, watching Sandra.

"That's where it belongs now, Honey. Go ahead and settle down."

Honey did. But Sandra sat there in bed, upright and wide awake. The adrenaline rush caused by a dog growling into the dark night wasn't diminishing. Honey was sleeping well. Sandra was the one here with a problem.

She eased out of bed and went to the window. Honey continued snoring, sleeping undisturbed.

Sandra lingered at the window overlooking the backyard. Then she stood for a few minutes at Barbara's window overlooking the front. No one seemed to be wandering out there tonight.

She hadn't seen Trent since yesterday. So much had happened. Could it really have been only a day ago? She hoped he'd gone home and back to his job at O'Toole & Sons.

As she turned away, the ambient light in the room hit the bed and the items she'd left scattered there. She folded a pair of jeans and hung a blouse back on a hanger. There was the manila folder. It had come from one of the drawers, but she wasn't sure which.

Choose a likely drawer, she thought, but when she went to put the folder there, she fumbled it in the poor lighting. When the corner of the folder hit the floor, a few papers spilled out.

Not her business, but she needed better light to fit the pages back in properly. She was about to close the blinds when the light from the window touched the headline. It was impossible not to see the tall, bold letters.

Clifford Shoemaker Deceased at 65.

Still in the semidarkness, she sat heavily on the corner of Barbara's bed, her knees suddenly weak. She and Trent had been living in Arizona at the time. Their second marriage had begun with a new job for Trent at an engineering firm that would give him greater opportunity than he'd had before. It was a fresh start for the two of them. Nothing was holding her here in Virginia, including her parents. After expressing their doubts, they stopped voicing them, but Sandra could see and feel them in their eyes. Part of what had drawn her to that second try was the idea of a whole new environment, new friends, new everything. Two years later, they were back in Virginia, this time in Martinsville. The Arizona job hadn't worked out, and Trent was looking for another fresh start, but that was after her uncle had passed.

She'd seen her uncle maybe once since the first wedding. She and Trent had never made the trip out here to the country, and Uncle Cliff didn't like to leave the homeplace. The few family gatherings seemed to happen when she and Trent were elsewhere or otherwise tied up. When her uncle died, her mother called in Arizona, saying, "Uncle Cliff died. They found him this morning."

"I didn't know he was sick," Sandra said, sitting abruptly. "What happened?"

"It was unexpected. They think it was a heart attack."

"When is the service?"

"In a day or so. We don't have that nailed down yet. It will be small and quiet. Family only. You don't need to fly home."

Sandra had been relieved and hurt at the same time. She exchanged good-byes with her mother and then told Trent. He agreed with her mother.

Trent said, "It's a long way, and it's expensive. For what? A short service? Besides, you have that big job interview you're so hot for this morning." He was smiling. He was also speaking in a loud, sarcastic voice. He'd been against her getting a job from the start. "You need to worry about that job, not some funeral for an uncle you rarely saw and hardly knew."

She was already dressed, wearing the outfit she'd bought after their disagreement about the motorcycle. Except for putting on her shoes,

254

she was ready, but it wasn't time to leave yet. She had a couple of minutes to think this through. She'd walked away, wordless, deep in thought and maybe a little in shock, out to the patio. The Arizona sun was kind that early in the morning. The pool was a few feet away. It was a small pool with a little waterfall, and she loved the sound of the water cascading over a rock wall. Usually it calmed her, but today, with Mom telling her not to bother coming east for the funeral, in effect that the family didn't need her, her heart ached. It seemed like the greatest blow of all. True, it would've been nicer for her uncle if she'd visited more while he was alive, and she felt plenty of guilt about that, but it should take a family for a proper, final send-off. A family. But Uncle Cliff had been correct back at the schoolhouse years before when he drew the diagram in the dirt. There was family at the heart of it, and there was family on the fringe. At best, Sandra was fringe.

Trent followed her out to the patio. "Don't sulk. We can't afford the trip even if they wanted you there."

Ignoring him, Sandra ran her fingers around the edge of the phone case. Was she hoping it would ring again? Would her mom call back? Should Sandra call her mom back and tell her . . . what?

Trent, so much taller and with such broad shoulders, picked up Sandra like she weighed nothing. "No sulking, Sandy." He laughed. "Not allowed." He carried her. She didn't object or kick because she was shocked. She was still lost in that world back east, where her mom didn't want her. Yet she was also suspended in Trent's arms as he headed toward the pool.

Finally realizing his intent, she squirmed to get away. "No, Trent. Put me down."

He laughed again. "Yes, ma'am." And he dropped her into the water.

She came up sputtering.

From his vantage point, high and dry beside the pool, he said, "You can't let stuff like that get you down, Sandra, or you'll never succeed. You have to do or not do and then move on. It's all about making choices—choices that lead to success or failure. Make sure you're on the right end of the decision."

"I can't believe you did this." She was drenched. The water was chest high. Her dress. Everything. Sopping wet.

He leaned forward, extending his hand. "Need a helping hand out of there?"

Sandra backed away, clutching her dripping phone. The water streamed from her hair and across her face. The long strands stuck in her lashes, her eyes, her nose, her mouth.

"Suit yourself, then. As I said, it's your choice." He walked away, went into the house, and shut the door.

Her silk blouse was ruined. Her phone . . . did she remember something about dropping it in rice to pull out the moisture? Probably a waste of rice, but she could at least give it a try. It was something to do when she had no idea what could possibly come next.

She waded to the end of the pool and climbed the steps. She hadn't been wearing shoes, so she was grateful for that. Her red skirt might recover with a trip to the cleaners.

Trent, in his "guy" way, had been trying to cheer her up. Totally inappropriately, of course. Sometimes guys went too far. That's what her mom would say.

And yet, this was Trent. With Trent, every action was deliberate. This felt like an escalation. He'd trained her well. What was that term? Stockholm syndrome?

No, she rejected that. She stood taller. She had a right to be listened to, to be respected, and not to be dumped in the pool because he thought she needed to be taught a lesson.

What would she say to him? Deep breath. She pulled on the door handle. The door didn't move.

She tugged again. Nothing.

Her breath caught. Had Trent locked the door?

No. It was either stuck or he'd locked it out of habit. He was very conscientious about keeping the doors locked. He wouldn't allow her to keep a key under a brick or flowerpot. He said it was too cliché, that anywhere they could think to hide something, thieves would know to look. She had to admit the truth of that.

She'd have to knock. Heaven knew she didn't want to, didn't want to see him at all, but he'd hear her knocking, come to the door, and apologize for locking her out. That might open up a conversation about how he should give her emotional space when she was down, that not every action, like a dunk in the pool, was helpful.

She knocked and waited. Then she knocked more loudly. No answer.

The house wasn't that large. He had to have heard her, unless he'd gone upstairs. OK. She'd go around front to the doorbell.

Wet and barefooted, she went through the privacy fence gate and made her way, despite her tender feet, over the gravel path. By the time she reached the front door, the last of her righteous anger had faded, and she just wanted to get in the house and get dry and decent again. She had no hope of salvaging the phone. It was clearly dead.

She pressed the doorbell and listened to the peals reverberate throughout the house before she released it. Again, she waited. When he didn't come to the door, she squeezed her finger against the button and held it there, hoping the peals would drive Trent crazy, hoping she was disturbing him, wanting to get even, at least a little. When he got angry and came storming down, she would make it clear who was at fault here. She hit the doorbell again. She leaned against the door, her face on the metal, gradually realizing that Trent wasn't going to answer the door. He wasn't coming to unlock anything.

The sidewalk wasn't far from the front door. A man, a stranger, walked by, and she felt exposed. She tried to remember what her mother had said—her mother had said a lot of things—that you can pull off pretty much anything if you act like you mean it. Sandra tried to tell herself that no one would give much thought to the ruined blouse and the tangled hair and her red skirt that apparently didn't fare well when mixed with chlorine.

She didn't know any of the neighbors well enough to knock on their doors looking like this. What would it accomplish if she did? None of them had a house key.

She was going to be late, too, for that interview, and she couldn't even call them.

At this hour, the street was empty now that the man had moved on down the road.

Sandra returned via the gravel path to the backyard. She went through the gate and sat at the table. Now what?

She pulled her legs up into the chair and hugged her knees, tugging her wet skirt around them. She hid her face. No friends. No family. No key. She didn't cry. There was no point.

It seemed like she crouched in that chair forever. Finally she decided to bang on the door again. If Trent still wouldn't let her inside, then she'd find a rock or a brick and force her way in. The broken glass would be his fault.

She went to the door, and habit caused her to pull on the handle. The door opened.

How long had it been unlocked?

Sandra slid it open. How easily the door moved. She went inside yelling, "Trent!"

No answer. Both locks on the front door were engaged. She ran upstairs and looked in the two bedrooms. No one. She went back down and looked in the garage. The car was gone.

How long? At what point had he unlocked the sliding door and driven away?

She heard his voice in her head, so calm and cool, saying, "Too bad you were so busy sulking, so busy feeling sorry for yourself, that you didn't notice there was no need for it. That's a failure on your part, Sandy."

My fault. My fault. My fault. Never mind that he'd mocked her for being sad about her uncle, hurt over her mother's attitude, and had dumped her into the pool and locked her out. No blame on him. It was her fault that she'd been miserable and hadn't noticed the door had been unlocked almost immediately. Self-pity, Trent would call it. A point of failure. One of her many failures.

She called to reschedule the interview, and they told her there was no need.

When she'd confronted Trent and blamed him for the ruined clothing and the lost opportunity, he'd laughed.

It was then that she began assembling her stash of money and personal items, because she could see their second hoped-for happily-ever-after was already rewriting itself, and she wasn't going to be on-set for the ending.

Chapter Twelve

The first time Sandra left her marriage, she hadn't prepared ahead. She'd been unbelievably naive and gullible and driven by her emotions. She didn't want that to happen again. In Arizona, when she saw the second end looming, she set about seriously and surreptitiously packing and stashing. She managed to eke a little money out of what Trent gave her for expenses and hid it around the house. He always seemed able to read her so easily. If he found her hidden cash in one place, he wouldn't keep looking. Who would hide it here and there and all around? He'd never think of that. She thought it was a good plan, until the day she saw him pulling into the driveway in a rental truck with a couple of strangers.

"Hey, Sandy," he said. "Guys, start with the sofa and chair, why don't you?"

The men started hauling out the furniture.

"Trent, wait." She moved aside as the two men carried out the leather chair. "What's going on?"

"We're going back to Virginia. I know you've been homesick, so we're moving back. Happy?"

"What? No, I mean yes. I mean . . . we aren't moving because I'm homesick. Tell me what's going on."

Trent stopped and reached down. "Hey, what's

this?" he asked, holding the cash that had fallen from under the sofa cushion. He winked at her and put it in his pocket. "I have a new job opportunity. A much better one. None of the crap I've had to put up with at this firm." He stepped aside to make room for the men to carry out the kitchen table. "Careful with that, guys."

She ignored the wink. It could mean anything or nothing. She raised her hands. "Wait, Trent. Please. I have to pack things up."

"No time to waste, Sandy. Take what's most important and toss it in the back of the truck."

"No. My dishes, my glassware, toiletries and groceries . . . it all has to be boxed."

"Do you have boxes? I sure don't. Figure it out, Sandra, but don't take too long. Don't worry over it. When we pull out of this place, we won't look back."

He meant it. For now she'd gotten as much of the story as he was going to share. Some people worry themselves to distraction. Some people bluster and threaten. Some people do it, whatever it is. Trent was perfectly capable of driving away and leaving everything they owned if it suited him.

He moved toward her and put his hands on her shoulders, then slid them down her arms and around her back, pulling her toward him. He embraced her. She felt him willing her to cease questioning and join in his mania. Sandra relaxed consciously. She had no choice, as she saw it. She'd get more cooperation from him if he thought she was on board.

She tried to smile. "OK, then. We're moving back to Richmond."

"Not Richmond. But Virginia, yes. Martinsville. An engineering firm I've been talking to offered me a great job. They were so impressed they practically begged me to join them."

She didn't bother to ask, if they were so serious about him coming to work for them, why weren't they paying for a proper move? Why the sudden, hasty rush to leave this place? She didn't ask because her time was better spent trying to recover her cash before it was found or lost, and in trying to quickly pack the breakables into whatever containers she could find, but she had to ask, "What about this place? This house?"

"It's a rental. Not our problem."

"And in Martinsville?"

"We'll find a house. A big one. Things are a lot cheaper there. We'll get a mansion."

There was no point in discussing it further. The furniture was disappearing fast, and she was running out of time. She had to get to the items where the cash was hidden. She was going to need it sooner rather than later.

A little cash wasn't enough, but it was better than nothing. The less she had to depend on her parents, the better. And yes, Mom had mentioned the possibility of her and Dad moving to Florida. Sandra hadn't taken it seriously. So, she prepared to leave Trent, including rehearsing a cool speech that she'd give to Trent as she stood on the threshold with the loaded getaway car ready and waiting in the driveway, in case he didn't take the news well. But preparation and actuality were different things. Sneaking off in the dark of night and letting a few handwritten words on a piece of notebook paper speak for her was the actuality.

She fell back onto Barbara's bed, drained. The contents of the folder spilled across the covers. All she could see was Barbara's mural by starlight. By whatever light was making it through the window. The bed bounced, and Honey curled up beside her. Great.

"Honey. I'm not staying. I'm not. I'm getting up in a sec. I'm going to bed and getting some real sleep, so don't get comfortable."

Honey was snoring within moments.

Sandra lay there without the will to move. She shoved the clipping and other papers onto the floor, then rolled over onto her side, a hand on Honey's foreleg, and fell asleep.

She awoke with the sunrise and with a stiff neck, feeling like she'd been breathing in dog hair all night. She brushed at her face. Honey yawned.

Her jaws opened wide, and she stretched out a leg and paw.

Sandra sat up, and as she put her feet to the floor, the clipping caught her attention. She picked it up. Her Uncle Cliff's obit. In the daylight, the small print wasn't a problem.

The obituary was surprisingly simple. It said he passed unexpectedly, and a small, private service was planned. And that was it.

He drank, she remembered that, of course. Mom had said they thought it might be his heart, but that was it. It was odd about the lack of a public service. At least, that was odd for the south, and for someone who must've known a ton of people. He was in his sixties and had lived in the area his whole life.

Honey was already waiting at the top of the stairs. As soon as she saw Sandra walk into the hallway, she made her way down the stairs, gingerly but reasonably well, and went straight to the back door. Made sense. That was where Barbara had let her out to do her business. Sandra fidgeted with the clasp on the end of the leash and, satisfied, opened the door and guided Honey through the construction area toward the oak.

She remembered how Honey had barked the night before, and prickles raced up her spine. Then she remembered the raccoon and relaxed.

Sandra wanted to get on with the garden, and she didn't want worries about Trent to spoil that.

It would be ironic, and yet so typical of her, to spend time worrying over the wrong things and miss the important ones.

Be mindful, she told herself. *Be aware.*

The memories were a surprise. They were coming back stronger and stronger. Who knew she had so many memories from her childhood? And they all seemed eager to be acknowledged.

Was it due to coming back here to where she'd spent so much of her life—her very young life? She, and her mom and dad, at the Shoemaker homeplace. At Cub Creek. It touched something in her—something that wanted to be heard. It seemed to her that things changed abruptly after her grandmother passed. She'd stopped coming here. The connection was lost. And then, more and more, she'd lost other close connections. She'd never had an easy relationship with her mother. The relationship with her father was the last to erode. Maybe fate knew what it was doing when it pulled her back here. But also worrying about Trent? Fate was trespassing too much on what didn't concern it.

Suddenly, she remembered her mother's voice over the telephone that day in Arizona. "Uncle Cliff died. They found him this morning," Mom had said. Sandra had assumed they'd found him in his bed.

Not that it mattered, but she was curious. She might ask her. Surely now, two years later, her mother wouldn't be squeamish about giving the details. Maybe her mother needed to be more open with her, and Sandra needed to be more specific and insistent with her questions, since neither of them seemed to have the talent for gentle persuasion.

When Colton and Aaron arrived, they brought sandpaper for her.

"Why, what a thoughtful gift," she joked.

Colton smiled and pointed to Barbara's table and chairs. "You'll want to sand off the rough areas before repainting those."

"What a great idea." She was thrilled to contribute beyond fetching iced tea and lemonade.

The dogs were nearby enjoying the grass and fresh air. Colton and his helper, Aaron, set the fence stakes. The fenced area wasn't huge, but the grass enclosure alone was more than triple the original area. The bushes still in place around the patio area provided a satisfying definition.

The table and chairs were in pretty good shape. She was done with most of the sanding before midafternoon.

"The stakes are in deep, but not in concrete," Colton said. "We can still move them if we want to make any adjustments before the wire goes up." He pointed at the excavated area. "I'll set the block tomorrow or the next day. I might have to be on the work site tomorrow. All this rain has wrecked our schedule. Work will probably be picking up and might impact our project here."

She liked how he said the word *our*. She confirmed it, saying, "Our project can take all the time we need." It didn't sound quite like what she'd meant to say, but maybe it said enough, because Colton smiled.

Sandra kept Honey quiet the rest of the day. The next morning after breakfast, when they went out for Honey's business, the dog pulled at the leash. Sandra decided that if Honey felt up to it, they'd take a walk. They started down the path. It was wide and clear and made for easy walking. Honey moved slowly but steadily and was panting soon, though it wasn't hot. They stopped, and Sandra sat on a downed tree trunk while Honey rested. In the distance, over the sound of the breeze rustling the leaves far overhead and the occasional squirrel scooting past, she heard the sound of running water.

When she stood, so did Honey, and they continued walking.

Cub Creek ran under the wooden bridge on Shoemaker Road, near the state road. This was the same creek, but now they were upstream. Way upstream. The woods were pretty here, as was the creek. Brown water, but it wasn't thick and heavy-looking as it was down by the bridge, and trees arched over it all. At the bridge, the creek hardly seemed to move because it was so deep. Here, the water streamed over and around rocks, making little waterfalls. It gurgled under the bank, and here and there along the creek, rocks stuck out. Below where Sandra stood, a long rock jutted out into the creek, and in its cleft, ferns grew.

Green, green, green. Everything was so green, a fresh spring green, so that the air itself seemed green.

In a nearby spot, the bank sloped down. Honey was already there, carefully positioned with her nose near the water, lapping at it.

When Honey returned to her, she sat at Sandra's feet surveying the area. They were both relaxed. She hoped they hadn't walked too far. She couldn't possibly carry Honey back. But no, Honey's eyes were alert, and while she panted a lot, she didn't seem to have any trouble breathing, plus she was sitting up and not flat out on the ground in exhaustion.

Sandra scratched Honey's neck. A few more minutes of rest and then they'd head back. The house, the clutter and the dust, needed her attention.

They were hardly back from their walk when a visitor arrived, and Sandra wished they'd stayed longer at the creek.

Margaret Shoemaker Lovett, more commonly known as Meg, stood in the open doorway. She was about two inches shorter than Sandra, but her posture was such that people, including her daughter, thought of Meg as taller than she really was. Sandra looked at her, then beyond her. Her mother was alone and carried a small suitcase.

Honey brushed past Sandra and went to greet the new arrival. She sniffed the woman's pants legs and then stood, waiting to be petted.

"Well, hello there. Honey, right? Barbara told me to say hello to you for her." Mom straightened back up and looked at her daughter. "Nice dog. She seems to have recovered well."

"Yes, she's a good dog." Sandra left the obvious question unspoken. She stepped back and invited her in. She could hardly refuse her own mother entry into her sister's house, but it did recall the memory of her own poor welcome when she'd last arrived home.

Her mother walked past and set her case on the floor by the stairs. Mom saw her looking at the suitcase but didn't refer to it. Instead, she said, "How are you doing, Sandra? You look better than I expected. I'm relieved."

Mom paused, waiting for a response, but Sandra thought it best to keep her reaction to herself.

She shrugged. "OK. Have it your way. I had to return to deal with some last things, some financial and other business we still have to finish up in Richmond, and I wanted to see you, to see how you were doing."

Sandra moved toward the kitchen. "Can I offer you iced tea or lemonade?"

"No, thanks."

She stopped, turned, and crossed her arms. "Are you here because you're worried I'll mess up Barbara's house or lose her dog?"

"Actually, I was about to say it looked better in here than I remembered." She walked past her daughter and into the kitchen. "Your aunt will say she's guarding the family memorabilia, the history. I call it being a pack rat." She waved her hand at the room. "She saves everything. I save almost nothing. There has to be a balance somewhere. Neither of us has been able to find it."

Sandra followed, mystified. Her mother stood at the kitchen door and looked out through the window.

"Go on outside. Take a closer look, if you like."

"No need. I've never been a fan of dirt or insects." She continued staring out the window.

Sandra waited. Her words and feelings were immaterial. As were her efforts. She felt the condemnation growing, the criticism about to be expressed. She tensed and crossed her arms again, ready to receive it.

"Well, that's a mess," Mom said. "Barbara let it go, didn't she? To be fair, this kind of upkeep has simply gotten beyond her." She turned to face Sandra. "She was never an outdoor person. She'd rather be at her easel or in her knitting chair, anywhere doing anything that wasn't actual cleaning or other dirty work." She shrugged. "But that was her choice. And she never complained or asked for help."

"Unlike me."

"You are my daughter. Ask away. But when you ask me or anyone for help, you invite them into your life. Why are you so defensive? Is this about Trent? Still? You're an adult, Sandra, and I'll do you the favor of being honest with you. You wanted us to like your choice of boyfriend, then husband, and we did, for your sake. When you no longer wanted him, we disliked him for your sake, though we didn't understand what was wrong."

"I told you."

"You told us some things, but we didn't understand why those things were a problem. But for you they were, and we wanted you to be happy, so we supported you regardless. When you decided he was worth marrying again . . . But I don't get it. I never have. I know you feel like we've let you down, but you can't expect us to keep changing our feelings on a whim."

"Not a whim."

"Bad choice of words, then, but that's how it felt."

How could words hurt so much? "I tried to share. You didn't want to hear." She sighed. "Mom, how did Cliff die?"

Her mother's face went blank. "What?"

"Uncle Cliff. He died while I was living in Arizona."

"I know, but why are you asking? You haven't asked about him since he passed."

"Being here has brought back memories. I always felt a kinship with him that I never felt with the rest of the family. But, no worries, if you don't want to discuss it. I'll call Aunt Barbara and ask her."

"Please don't discuss Cliff with Barbara. If she wants to talk about him, she will. Otherwise, leave her in peace."

"Uncle Cliff was kind to me."

"What does that mean, Sandra?" She was angry suddenly. "As if we weren't loving parents? As if your father and I somehow . . ." She pressed her fingertips to her forehead. "What does that mean? He was civil? He gave you a candy bar a few times? Save your sentimentality, your . . . your affinity, for those who actually cared for you, fed you, and taught you."

"Uncle Cliff taught me an important lesson about him and me and the rest of the family, and about not fitting in or belonging."

Mom pressed her lips together. She looked down at the floor and saw the suitcase. She pointed at it. "There are some things in there that belong to you. I don't know whether you want them, but I was flying up here anyway, so I figured I'd deliver them in person."

"That's not . . . I thought maybe you were staying over."

She looked at Sandra, her eyes wide with incredulity. "Well, then, I'm sure you're pleased to discover that's not true. As for Uncle Cliff, if you feel he treated you better than we did, keep in mind that my sister and I were busy seeing our mother out of this world, doing what we could to care for her while she was suffering." She waved her hands. "Uncle Cliff was never more than marginally productive or helpful. The least he could do was to spare you a few minutes of chatter while we did the heavy lifting—literally." She paused halfway down the front steps and turned back, her finger pointing. "And if you felt ignored or excluded, then I repeat: I'm sorry. I did my best. Whatever you see as my failures, then learn from them and do better. But don't waste your time holding a grudge against me or anyone else. It's really all on you, Sandra. In the end, that's what you'll have and what you must live with—the results of your own decisions."

Her mother's voice dropped so low it was difficult to hear her. Sandra moved closer despite herself.

"Cliff wanted to farm. It was all he ever wanted to do. He did it as long as he could scrape together the cash or get loans to fund the next season, but people who don't farm don't understand. They don't get the increasing debt, the disaster of one or two bad harvests on a small farm in an already marginal industry. Maybe smarter or luckier operations could make a go of it, but not Cliff." Her dark eyes, the Shoemaker eyes, looked haunted. "When he gave up his dream, he gave up on pretty much everything except his alcohol."

"You did your best to hide his failures from the rest of the world, didn't you?" Sandra smiled unpleasantly. "Didn't want to embarrass the family with a real funeral? Or maybe he wasn't worth the expense of a big send-off? Is that why you didn't want me to come home for it? You and Trent agreed on that, didn't you? I wasn't needed."

"Trust me, I wasn't concerned about the family reputation." She spread her arms wide. "Who was here to be embarrassed anyway?" She looked across the old cornfield. "It was to protect him. To let everyone remember him as he used to be." She looked at her daughter. "If you care so much, then go pay your respects at his grave." She pointed at the fallow field. "He's right over there."

"Is that legal? Cheap, I guess, but legal?"

Her eyes looked like those of a stranger. "Your concern would be more appreciated, genuine, if you weren't trying to use it like a club against me. Yes, it's legal, since it's already in use as a family cemetery." She waved her hand. "Know this. Regardless of his failings, I loved my brother. And I want the best for you. Happiness, or the closest you can get to it. Because whatever hurts the child also hurts the parent. And no one can hurt a parent like his or her child."

Her mother moved to get into the car but stopped and added, "Don't look to others for approval. Finding your worth in the eyes of others is the quickest path to failure, or madness."

Sandra clutched the fence rail. With her parting shot, Mom got into the car. There'd been no hug or kind words exchanged between them. It hadn't been that kind of visit, had it? Though, in her mother's own backhanded way, she'd said she loved her, right? Worthy or not, because they were parent and child.

She was hurt and angry. And cruel, according to her mother. Sandra thought she might be right. She didn't want to be that person. She wanted to be kind. To be able to forgive and forget and turn the other cheek, and all that good stuff. But what had that turn-the-other-cheek approach ever solved? Trent took it as permission to do worse. Her mother was different, in that she seemed to read passivity as approval or agreement—as permission to move on with her life despite her daughter's needs. To leave her behind and go with her husband and sister to Florida as if . . .

She hugged her arms closely around her. Mom and Trent had a lot in common when it came to advice about not seeking approval, or one's worth, from others. A breeze wafted by and touched her hair and her cheek. Sandra pressed her hand to her cheek and saw the fallow field again. Not dead. Fallow. But Uncle Cliff? He rested in the cemetery beyond, past enjoying what he had loved, past altering or adding to his legacy on this earth. She and her mother had differences, in personalities mostly. Her mother wasn't evil. Her intentions were very different from Trent's. Did she, Sandra, have to get mean so quickly? She hadn't done that with Trent despite multiple, significant provocations.

Trent battered her psyche. He was smart enough to refrain from obvious cruelty or outright manipulation when others were around. He avoided being with family and friends, and when they were, he managed his behavior and their interaction with deft orchestration guaranteed to make her the envy of every wife and sweetheart who wanted to be as cherished by their spouse as she appeared to be.

She knew her mother loved her. But was her mother so different from Trent? She knew how to hurt Sandra with words, too.

Even so, the flaw in her thinking was unmistakable. Did Sandra need people to ask if there was a problem before she could speak? Did she need to know others would believe her before she could tell the truth of her life? Did she need their approval to approve of herself?

Wasn't that how she'd been brought up? If her

mother hadn't wanted her to learn that lesson, then she shouldn't have taught it so well.

Dad would've counseled patience. He would've recited Poe.

She spread her hands. They felt empty. Her father's book, their shared bonds, were an important part of her history. He would tell her to be careful of time . . . that time can't be held back. There were no do-overs in life. He would caution her against stubborn pride and anger. He would advise her to look around, listen, and consider whether she was really all that unhappy with being where she was. He would say not to squander the moments.

The breeze stirred again, and Sandra laughed. She could appreciate irony. Despite the hard words she and her mother had thrown at each other, regardless of the emotional words about love and hurt, Mom had left without answering the question about Cliff's death. Sandra realized she still didn't know how her uncle had died.

Sandra sat on the porch with Honey. Colton had left a voice mail. They wouldn't be coming over today. Work-related, he said.

She put her arm around Honey and scratched her neck. "What do you say, Honey? Let's not squander the day. Let's see if we can open up some windows and disturb some more dust?"

Honey whined and put her chin on Sandra's thigh.

"None of that, Honey. We're a team, and Barbara and the house need our help."

She stood. Honey didn't. She wasn't leashed.

Sandra didn't want to leave Honey outside alone, so she added, "Didn't I see a box of treats in the pantry?"

At the word *treat,* Honey rose and went directly to the door. Sandra opened it wide and said, "I guess I'm not above a little manipulation myself."

Honey barked from the kitchen. Sandra laughed and closed the door.

Chapter Thirteen

Colton and Aaron arrived with John. While the men unloaded the stone blocks, Aaron set up his work space in the shade of the oak.

Not knowing how else to be helpful, she offered refreshments. "Can I get anyone something to drink?"

"Thank you, ma'am, but I'll be taking off as soon as we're done unloading."

"John came along to help with the stone, but he can't stay. He has another job this afternoon." Colton set the last stone onto the ground. "We can't thank you enough for your help, John."

John slapped his cap back on his head. "Happy to help. Good luck with your dog, ma'am."

Colton walked with John to his vehicle.

Sandra stood at the stack of stone and tried to lift one. "Heavy."

"Yes, ma'am," Aaron said.

"Well, what about you? Cookies or lemonade? Both were made fresh this morning."

"What kind?" Aaron asked.

"Oatmeal raisin."

He smacked his lips and rubbed his stomach in exaggerated motions. "Perfect."

Soon after, Sandra was in the kitchen getting the cookies and pouring tea and lemonade. The screen door slammed and Aaron was suddenly there, standing at her elbow.

"May I help?" he asked.

Honey barked, and Sandra heard men's voices. "John's back?"

Aaron looked out the back door. "No. There's a man out there talking to Dad."

"Another helper, maybe?" This whole thing was going so well. She could hardly believe her good fortune. "Can you get the door for me?" She held up the tray.

"Yes, ma'am."

Sandra watched her footing as she crossed the construction zone and looked up only when she reached the grass.

"Trent," she whispered, going cold.

When he saw her, he smiled. She kept her eyes straight ahead, not wanting to look at Colton. She didn't want to see the two men together in the same frame.

Trent asked, "Mind if I join you all?"

An abyss opened. Her world cracked wide and ugly. Vaguely, she was aware of Sammy and Honey moving. No one else did.

"You aren't welcome here," she said.

Whose voice was that? A woman's. Hers. Her lips had moved. It was like she was watching herself speak in a much stronger voice than she was capable of. "You aren't welcome here."

"I was telling your friend"—he nodded toward

284

Colton—"that I missed you and wanted to make sure you were safe living alone in the woods." He grinned. "Hey, young man. What's your name?" He held out his hand.

Aaron accepted his hand, and they shook. "Aaron."

Trent nodded. "Pleased to meet you."

"Go into the house, Aaron. Please," she said.

"No need to send him away on my account, Sandy. I want to hear about all this work going on. I have to admit I'm impressed." He smiled, nodding toward Colton. "Of course, you have help. Everyone needs help, and you're lucky. Clearly you found the right person."

Aaron looked from her to Trent, then at Colton, and back to her. She held the tray out to him. "Would you take this inside for me? And call the dogs? Take them inside and give them a treat."

"But—"

"Please." She could count on Aaron's courtesy and cooperation. She looked at Colton and nodded but spared him only a quick glance. She waited to hear the door shut. When she did, she felt freer to deal with Trent, but before she could speak, he did.

"Seems like I've interrupted a party here. Or a break, I guess. I'd love a glass of that iced tea, Sandy." Trent kept grinning.

Colton gave up trying to figure it out. He stood.

"What's this about, Sandra? Should Aaron and I leave?"

"Hey, not on my account," Trent said. "I want to meet Sandra's friends. Get to know them. And I can see you've been real helpful to her. I appreciate that."

"Sandra?" Colton prompted her.

"I know you don't understand, Colton. Frankly, I don't understand what he's doing here, either."

Trent turned away from her and faced Colton. Trent was taller and broader, but Colton's stance looked like he was telegraphing that he could take care of himself regardless. This was wrong. All wrong.

"As I was explaining before Sandra joined us, I'm Trent Hurst."

"Sandra mentioned she'd been married. That would be you?" Colton didn't sound friendly.

She stepped between them. "Leave, Trent. You don't belong here."

He turned toward her. "Maybe you don't want me here, but you're lucky I was, weren't you? What would have happened to you and Honey if I hadn't been there with you?"

Colton frowned. "What's he talking about, Sandra?"

She closed her eyes for a split second and then responded. "It's a long story, Colton. I'll explain it later. For now, Trent, you are trespassing. Leave."

"Not so fast, Sandra." Trent shook his head. "I'm not trying to embarrass you in front of your friend, but I happen to value the truth. Honesty and honest people." He nodded. "I might be a little old-fashioned in that way. But that's how it is. Someone who fails at honesty—"

"She wants you to leave," Colton said.

"Colton, please. Don't engage him. He must simply leave. In fact, you should take Aaron home, and I'll call the police and let them work it out with him."

Trent laughed. "That's not funny, Sandra, but if I don't laugh, I may cry. You're breaking my heart here. What exactly do you think the police will say?"

The authorities always believed Trent. He didn't have a record. He was confident and self-assured. He stayed cool under pressure.

"Don't talk to him, Colton. Get Aaron and go."

"I can't leave you here alone with him."

"Then let's go inside. We'll go in, and Trent can leave as he pleases."

"Whoa. Hold on a minute." Trent waved his hands. "I'm not saying Sandra and I haven't had our troubles, but it takes two, right? Our first marriage ended in divorce, but we both got smarter, didn't we, Sandra? We were both much smarter and wiser when we went into marriage the second time."

Colton spoke calmly. "But that didn't last,

either. So why not do as Sandra asks? Why stay where you aren't wanted?"

"Because you will? You'll stay, won't you? You two must've gotten real close real fast. Maybe you can explain this to me: Since when does being a friend outweigh being a husband?"

"Ex-husband," Colton said.

Trent looked at Sandra and laughed ruefully. "We've been married twice but divorced once. The second marriage is still in force. Or didn't Sandra tell you? Did she tell you she was single? Or did she let you come to that conclusion on your own?"

Colton looked confused. "Sandra?"

It was all too distracting. She felt everything she'd built in the last few days, all that was good, crumbling.

"Technically we're still married. I left him for the second time more than a month ago. We are over, forever."

"But you aren't divorced? Legally separated?" Colton's voice was quiet.

"No." She could barely get out the word.

"Did you know she left in the middle of the night? She gave me a kiss good night before bed." He pointed at Sandra. "I went to bed and got up during the night only to discover she'd run off." He looked down and closed his eyes. "I can't begin to tell you how that made me feel."

If she hadn't known the truth, she might have fallen for it, for his sad tales, all over again, so she could hardly blame Colton for the doubt on his face.

Aaron hadn't stayed in the house. He approached Colton, his small face pale and his limp pronounced. Colton looked down at the boy, then back at Sandra. His expression looked like that of a man caught between bad options, with no good choices at hand.

"Do you want me to stay?" Colton asked.

Yes. The word reverberated in her brain. But Aaron continued to stand there looking shocked, so she said, "No need. Trent is leaving."

Colton looked doubtful.

"I'm fine. Truly." She hesitated, then urged in a stronger voice, "Please go now. Get Aaron out of here."

Colton gave Trent a look that might have given any normal man second thoughts, but his words were meant for Sandra. "I'll call you later," he said.

"Aaron! Sammy!" Colton called out. "Get in the truck."

He nodded to her as he walked past. His eyes were cold. Aaron went to the kitchen door and opened it enough to let Sammy out.

She watched Aaron limp to the truck and Sammy trot alongside him. Aaron looked back as he reached for the door handle. Colton did the same before climbing into the truck and driving away.

Trent was still there. Instead of anger, Sandra felt cold inside, an icy sensation that made her forget about actions and consequences. All she wanted was a world without Trent, and for once she agreed with him, that everything one did should be focused on achieving the objective.

"I presume you accomplished what you wanted," she said.

"You need to get a better grip on the truth, Sandra. Not everyone will put up with your flaws and screwups like I will."

"Leave, and this time, stay away. All I want from you is an address for my lawyer, because the next time we communicate will be over divorce papers."

Trent had an odd expression on his face. One she didn't recognize. He started to walk away. Then he stopped halfway across the yard and looked at her. "Why are you so shocked? You wanted me to leave, so I'm leaving. I'll do anything for you, Sandy. Say the word." He waited. "No? Nothing more to say? Then I'll be on my way." He disappeared around the side of the house.

She looked at the stacked stones for the patio, the roll of fence wire, the black metal table sitting nearby. The icy feeling inside melted instantly as panic rushed in. She ran around the house to see where Trent was. There was nothing she could do if he refused to leave or decided to return. Nothing. She couldn't keep him out of the house, not if he decided he wanted in. Her only option would be to call the authorities and hope they believed her.

The truck engine kicked alive. He drove off down the dirt road.

Sandra went up to the front porch. She fell onto the top step, leaned against the post, and hugged her arms, feeling almost like that child again with her sick grandmother upstairs, the women tiptoeing around and Uncle Cliff due out of the woods any time now holding his bottle wrapped in a twisted brown bag and wearing his shy smile.

Trent. She could no longer avoid thinking about or dealing with him. When she left Martinsville, she'd been concerned about getting away, had discovered her mother's welcome was limited, but it met her needs because her goal was to avoid Trent at all costs. She couldn't deal with Trent alone. Not even to get that divorce. She had no money. She barely had clothing. Hence the constant raiding of Aunt Barbara's drawers and closet.

What a disastrous failure her life was. What could be forgiven in a younger person was unforgiveable in someone her age, someone who should have learned from prior experience.

Some people learned. Some were destined to

repeat the same mistakes over and over again. Unfortunately, it was clear which one she was.

Sandra wanted to hide in the house. She didn't want to run this time. It wouldn't matter if she wanted to run because she had nowhere else to go.

Halfheartedly, she returned to the storage room. She pulled out some items, but the interest wouldn't stir, and finally she sat on the sofa, grabbed a pillow, and curled up around it. Honey lay on the floor alongside her, and they slept.

Sometime later, the phone rang, waking her. She grabbed it without thinking.

Colton said, "Sandra?"

"Yes, I'm here." She sat up, pushing away the pillow.

"You're OK?"

"I am. He left right after you did."

"You mind if I drop over later to talk?"

"I'll be here."

An hour later, Sandra heard Colton's truck. She waited for him to knock, but he didn't. Finally she stepped outside onto the porch. He was sitting there alone.

He was dressed in his usual blue jeans. He wore boots, but not work boots. These looked more like dress boots, but well worn. His shirt was blue and flattered his eyes and hair. She congratulated herself on not bursting into tears.

Or offering self-serving excuses. She just waited.

Colton reached up and scratched his head. His burnished hair was orderly and unruly at the same time. He said he'd lived a wild life for a few years, until Aaron's mother showed up, had her troubles, and left him with her child to raise. Sandra had an idea that Colton had been pretty popular with the women.

He leaned forward and tapped one boot on the wood plank. "Why didn't you tell me about Trent?"

"That I was still legally married?"

He nodded.

She leaned back against the railing rather than join him on the bench. "Because I didn't want to discuss him."

A momentary expression of confusion touched his face. "I get that you might not want to tell me about him. I don't like it, but I can understand. But the story about Honey's rescue . . . it wasn't true. Don't you think the truth matters?"

"It matters, but some things matter more." She held up her hand. "You don't have to question me. I'll tell you anything you want to know. Trent brought himself into the conversation, so I guess it doesn't matter now. If I'd told you he helped rescue Honey, then I would've had to talk about him. If I'd told you I wasn't officially, legally single, then again, I would've had to talk about him. It wasn't that I didn't want to tell you about him. I simply and absolutely didn't want to talk about him, say his name, or think about him in any way. Is that plain enough?"

Colton spread his hands as if to ask another question, but then placed them together and interlocked his fingers. Hooked together, they looked like one huge fist to Sandra. He studied his interwoven hands for a moment, then nodded.

"I can respect that. Not wanting to speak about someone from your past. Wanting to keep him in your past. And maybe it's not my business, but I thought it might be. I thought you might want it to be. Maybe I assumed too much. If I misread the signals, I'm sorry. I'm out of practice, I guess. But I'm a big boy, and I can deal. Aaron's different. He's vulnerable." He stood and brushed his hands together. "Let me know when, if, you decide you want to discuss him and what's going on between you two."

"Nothing is going on between us. Nothing good anyway. I want him to go away."

"You married him twice."

"I'll get the second divorce as soon as I can." The words sounded brave. Braver than she felt. "What did you tell Aaron?"

"That you used to be married to him and still have stuff to work out."

"Had," she insisted. "We're done."

"Did you tell Trent that?"

She stood, feeling stunned. "What do you

mean? I left him twice." It sounded ridiculous and humiliating. "I told him to leave and stay away. You heard me yourself."

"Women can say things like that when they get angry. Men, too. Next thing you know, they're making up. It's not a good place to be when you're caught in the middle. I've been there, and I know."

Fire rose in her. "You have no right to say that to me." She struck the porch rail with her fist. "What is it with people? Why do I have to justify my choices? My actions? No one's blaming Trent, and he wouldn't care if they did. It's always on me. My mistakes. I'm either overreacting or making too much of something, or I'm condemned because I didn't speak of it sooner. People are so—"

"Stop, Sandra." His voice dropped to a lower tone. "Stop before you say what you can't take back." He paused, then added, "If you want me to leave, say so."

She stopped, and her anger evaporated immediately. The fire had been only a flare, protection for her sore spots. She covered her face, sighed heavily, and said, "It's instinct, I guess. Either an instinctive reaction or a conditioned response." She ran her fingers through her hair, remembering. She'd come so far. She didn't have to start throwing bombs as soon as things got tense. The person who deserved that treatment was Trent, and she never fought him outright. Why? Because she was afraid of him. Her family and friends deserved at least as much courtesy out of love as she gave Trent in fear.

"As far as Trent goes, I've told him we're done. I've told him that if he trespasses on this property, I'll call the police. I've been clear, but I can't make him believe it if he refuses."

"Sounds clear to me." He leaned forward. "Don't be so hard on yourself or others, Sandra. Human nature can be messed up. It's not your fault."

She shrugged. True was true, but it was still hard. "Thank you. Trent has a home and a job in Martinsville, so hopefully he's on his way back there. If not, I'll deal with it then."

Colton moved to the stairs. "Give me a call if you want to talk." He paused midstep. "Do you feel safe here?"

"From Trent?" She rested her hands on the railing. "He wants me back. My sanity is at risk more than anything else."

"Have you talked to the sheriff's department?"

Sandra frowned. "And tell them what? That my husband followed me here?"

"He's trespassing, isn't he? You said it yourself."

"He is."

"That's against the law. Also consider an order of protection. The sheriff's office can give you some information about that, too. Look, Aaron's at the house alone, so I've got to get home. If you need a place to stay, let me know." As he reached the truck, he called out, "And keep your phone charged and on your person. In case."

She nodded.

Was he really ready to take in another needy woman? At least this one didn't come with a child. She smiled. Besides, if there was danger, it was to her, and bringing it to Colton's house and to Aaron didn't seem reasonable. But she bit her lip and didn't say the words aloud.

He'd done the gentlemanly thing—he'd offered, had seemed concerned—but in the end, he left. She was still on her own.

Sandra stared down Shoemaker Road as far as she could see. Beyond the bend in the road, anything could be happening, and she couldn't, wouldn't know. For the moment, assuming Colton hadn't run into Trent's truck on his way out, things were quiet for now. She needed a plan.

This was really between Trent and her, and only she could solve it. Bottom line: she'd been clear with Trent, but she couldn't make Trent believe her. It wouldn't matter if he did believe her. Trent did what Trent did, and he'd do it for as long as he wanted to. That was his bottom line.

Mom and Dad had paid for her college until she dropped out to get married, and then they paid for the wedding. Four years later, when she left

Trent, they paid for the attorney for the divorce. The real break between her and her parents came when she told them she and Trent were giving it another try.

Why a second try? She didn't know how to explain it in a way that didn't reflect badly on her. She couldn't find a decent job? She was tired of living on her parents' charity? Trent was so charming and strong, and the laughing personality that had attracted her before was back? She saw what she wanted to see and what he wanted her to see. They promised each other that this time they'd do it right. But they hadn't. It went south quickly. It killed her to admit a second failure for all the world to see, and so she left, running in the dark of night. And she didn't call ahead. Thinking the words was hard enough. Saying them aloud to someone, anyone, was too humiliating and a testament to her lack of courage. Yet another failure.

Somewhere along the way, she'd picked up the habit of living with fear and personal paralysis.

After tossing and turning for hours, and occasionally falling asleep only to wake in fleeing nightmares, she stood at the window and observed the night. The moon highlighted the patio area below. The pallet of block, the bags of sand. The end of the roll of fencing.

There was no movement out there. Not even an

opossum. Behind her, Honey whimpered on her bed pillow. Sandra gave her a quick look.

Dreaming. Maybe she was having nightmares, too.

Alone again? Colton and Aaron had been temporary anyway. Friends. Maybe friends again one day. But Sandra had a job to do. Help was nice, but she also could do it on her own.

The hardest work had been done. The rest, Sandra could manage. She was pretty sure she wouldn't see Colton or Aaron again anytime soon, and if they did show up, hopefully it wouldn't be to retrieve the stone and fence materials, because she needed them.

Sandra started with breakfast. Fueled, she went out to build a patio. Honey wanted to come out, too, so Sandra tied her leash to the stake in the shade. She stood facing the work area and tried to remember what Colton had said about laying the block.

The stone blocks were rough and heavy. Her DIY manicure was doomed.

Sandra laughed, surprising herself.

Her mom had said she was no good alone. Trent said many times that she failed at everything. They'd both been right thus far. Maybe it was Sandra's turn to be right. However that looked. Maybe her "right" wouldn't look like theirs, and that was perfectly fine.

She pulled back the tarp and used the rake to smooth the sand, while envisioning how to place the stone blocks.

Block by block by block—each stone was heavier than the one before, and her back protested. She stood and stretched, then went back to work. Halfway through, Honey barked, and Sandra accepted that as a signal for break time.

She refilled Honey's water dish and brought out food, too. Sandra moved their stuff to the other side of the oak, where the shade was denser. They faced the back woods, and Sandra was content not to be looking at the construction project for a few minutes. She sat in the chair next to Honey. Honey's eyes were bright, and she was moving well. The dog sensed she was being watched and left her food to come nuzzle Sandra's hand. Sandra returned the favor with a scratch around Honey's neck. Her heart moved despite herself.

"You're a good girl, Honey."

A squirrel shook a branch somewhere up above her head.

"So was I, Honey. A good girl. Look where it got me."

In the fringe of the woods, bright specks caught her eyes maybe thirty feet away from where they sat. She thought it must be mica in the soil picking up glints of sun-dappled light. She waited, watching for it to recur, and saw a patch of tan moving among the trees. A deer. A doe, surely. Near her a spotted fawn moved, and then two more. Triplets. Sandra didn't breathe or move. All things considered, this was pretty cool. Slowly, she reached over and placed her hand on the dog's back. "Be still, girl."

They sat until the deer moved on. The last one spotted them, and, after a frozen pause, she took off, suddenly seeing she'd been left behind.

"A good girl, and where did it get me?" she asked aloud. Honey rolled onto her back. "It got me here, Honey," Sandra whispered. "I'm here, and that's good enough."

Chapter Fourteen

After two days of concentrated effort, Sandra assessed her progress.

The patio block was in. She needed to wet it down again to settle it and then add another layer of sand over it, sweeping it into the joints. Her fingernails would grow back, and that was the best thing she could say about those poor broken nubs.

There had been no word from Colton or Aaron, but no sign of Trent, either, so that was a relief. Maybe he really had gone home to Martinsville.

She had almost finished painting the table, and up next would be the fencing. That intimidated her. Maybe she'd trim the bushes first while she considered how best to approach the fencing. She had a vague idea that the fence wire would settle into those upright slots on the fence stakes, and if she steadied the roll against the nearby stakes, it might not fight her too much. Maybe. Fencing didn't seem like a one-person job.

She examined the table and chairs looking for missed spots.

"Your patio is almost ready for you. Not half bad if I say so myself."

Honey woofed in agreement.

"You deserve a w-a-l-k." Not until after supper,

though, so she had to spell it out. A walk down Shoemaker Road was a good way to stretch the muscles and relieve tension before calling it a day. She was so pleased. Colton, assuming they resumed their friendship eventually, would surely be impressed. Barbara would be absolutely thrilled. No question.

After a light supper, she called to Honey. Honey had been recovering for a week and seemed back to normal. Sandra felt pretty confident that Honey would stay with her during the walk, so she took the leash but didn't fasten it to her collar.

They were a short distance down the dirt road when Honey stopped and looked back. Sandra turned. Sammy and Aaron were walking toward them. She stood there, staring, realizing how filthy she was, yet hoping Colton would come into view. He didn't.

"Hi, Aaron."

"Hi, Miss Sandra. Going for a walk?"

"We are. Would you like to join us?"

"Yes, ma'am."

She nodded. His limp was evident. Honey and Sammy walked ahead of them, sometimes stopping to sniff a ditch or investigate a noise in the outermost edges of the fields.

"The patio looks good," Aaron said.

"Thank you." She kept it polite. No questions about Colton. Aaron was a child, after all. "The fence is next, but it's intimidating."

"Dad will take care of it if you wait. He's been working extra-long days lately, making up for the rainy days while he can."

"Is that so?" She said it coolly. "I thought he was angry or annoyed with me."

"You mean about that Trent guy?"

"Yeah. Something like that." Or about honesty, or openness? Really, how on earth would it have sounded to a guy—even a really nice, helpful guy, but one she'd met only days before—that she was technically still married? Kind of presumptuous. She'd been attracted to him, though, and apparently he was to her also. Mother was right. Did Sandra hate being alone so much? Was she so fearful of depending on herself that she would get close to the first male, still a stranger, who came along?

"Well, we'll see about the fence. I might give it a try. It isn't fair to expect your dad to spend so much time helping me. I could never have gotten this far on my own, though. I'm very grateful to both of you."

His cheeks pinked up, and he didn't speak for a few minutes. The old schoolhouse came into view. The dogs ran ahead. It was nice Honey wasn't traumatized. Sandra might've been, but if Honey wasn't, then who was Sandra to whine?

"The hole was under there? You called it a pit?"

She nodded. "It was very dark and scary. I'd say pit sounds right, wouldn't you?"

Aaron nodded. He joined the dogs at the school-house and peered through the open foundation. His limp had vanished again. Eventually, he'd be able to give it up completely. She smiled, feeling that kinship again. Patience, she told herself. Everything worthwhile takes time.

"It's deep," she said. "My aunt said some kids dug it out a long time ago."

"Lucky that guy came along."

His words startled her.

"To help you get out?" he prompted.

Sandra took a breath, then said, "Do you understand why I didn't mention him when I told you about rescuing Honey?"

"Because you didn't want to talk about him, right? He's mean or something?"

"That's right. No excuses, though. I'm an adult. I should've been upfront and honest about him."

"Nah, I understand."

"Do you?"

"Sure. I used to get teased a lot until my dad worked it out for me to study at home while my leg gets better. I'd come home, and he'd ask how my day was, but I didn't like talking about those jerks and what they would say to me, so I wouldn't tell him." He kicked at a rock. "I knew they were bullies, that it meant stuff was wrong with them, not me, and all that stuff grown-ups say, but when they said mean things, it felt true. The way they acted wasn't my fault, but it still felt like my fault. You know what I mean? Like, if there wasn't something wrong with me, then how would they think up that stuff?" He shrugged. "I didn't want to talk about them at all, not to anyone."

She did know. "What did they tease you about?"

He surprised her by laughing. "I'm a nerd. They teased me about that, and so I got all stupid and tried to do tricks on the skateboard, and now I'm a cripple. I'm pretty sure you noticed." He patted his leg. "And then they teased me about that, too."

Inwardly, Sandra cringed. Outwardly, she touched his yellow hair and smiled. "I noticed you are smart and clever and talented."

"Thanks. But it's hard being different. Sometimes I'd rather be big and mean. No one would mess with me then." He shrugged. "It's not so bad if you have someone to be different with. I had a friend, but his family moved away. After that, well, I still didn't fit in with those guys, and then I was alone."

Trent came to mind. "Trust me, Aaron—you don't want to be mean. There's no future in it. Some people are so insecure and so messed up that they try to make others feel more messed up than they are."

"Sure. I know. But knowing doesn't make it feel better."

"I know that, too."

They resumed walking, and the dogs caught up. They stopped near the bridge. Beyond it and that next short stretch of Shoemaker Road, cars and trucks whooshed along the state road. Over the sound of the creek running and with the buffer of the woods between them and the state-owned asphalt, Sandra heard the sound of traffic. Her hand twitched. She considered the leash.

"Let's turn back. I don't want Honey near the main road."

Honey and Sammy ran onto the bridge but not across it. They were more interested in sniffing below where the bridge supports met the weedy grass and mud and rock. Sandra didn't know what they found so intriguing. Compelling smells? Maybe tasty creatures or other potential snacks that might not be good for an old dog's recovery.

"If she falls in, she's on her own," Sandra said. Then she called out, "Honey! Come here. Here, Honey."

Both dogs looked up, and Aaron whistled. Sammy came immediately, and Honey followed close behind. They all turned and headed back.

"I'm glad you came to visit."

"I'm glad, too. I didn't really start out to visit, but Sammy was leading the way, so . . . I guess she missed Honey." He grinned.

She stopped herself from asking more. For instance, was Colton angry? Would he really come back and finish the fence? All were self-serving questions no matter how you looked at it, so she didn't ask.

"What about that Trent guy?"

"What about him?"

"Are you still married to him?"

"Yes, but . . . yes. I'm not going to be married to him much longer, though. I haven't gotten all the official legal stuff done yet."

"But he followed you here?"

"He did. I'm surprised he remembered my Aunt Barbara lived out here." She was assuming he'd lost her trail back at Mom and Dad's house. Maybe he hadn't. Somehow he'd found her here, and that was what mattered.

"What's wrong?" Aaron asked.

How quickly ugly memories had swamped her present. She touched his shoulder.

"I was just thinking. I guess he doesn't want the marriage to be over, but it is. We tried twice. That's enough, I think."

He nodded. During the conversation about teasing, his limp had returned. She wondered if he noticed how it came and went.

"What about you?" she asked. "What do you do for fun? Are there any kids your age around?"

"I know some guys through the home-schooling program, and I have Sammy." He paused. "Besides, Dad goes where the jobs are. When he's finished at the new subdivision, we'll move on to the next jobsite." He showed a little swagger as he added, "We like that I'm free of schedules and stuff so I can go along with him."

She felt a blip of sadness. *Moving on?* Both them, and her, too, when Barbara returned.

"But if you ever want to play a game or anything, let me know. I'm pretty good at chess."

Sandra laughed. "I'll bet you are. I'm not. Maybe you can teach me."

"I was thinking about something." His expression was suddenly serious.

"What's that?"

"I wondered if you might be interested in going somewhere with me. You can drive, and I wouldn't have to bug Dad."

"What is it?"

"Remember that shelter? The one where you got upset?"

She stammered, "Y-yes, I was upset, but—"

"No, I get it. It's hard having them all looking at you. It's like you can feel all their thoughts and wishes hitting you . . . like spitballs or something." He shrugged. "It's hard seeing them, knowing they need a home, but you're helpless to help."

Helpless. She shivered and rubbed her arms. "What did you have in mind?"

"I want to visit them. Talk to them."

"Won't you get their hopes up?"

"I guess, but everyone needs hope, don't they? Dogs, too." He sighed. "I saw something about kids reading to dogs in shelters. The dogs enjoyed it, or it seemed like they did. I thought I might try it."

Could she go back there? With all those dogs and their needy eyes? Yes. She could. "Sure. I'll go along. Maybe we can find some other ways to help out, too."

They stopped in front of the house. Aaron looked subdued again.

"Do you mind if I ask you something else?"

"I don't mind."

"You said that when you were a kid, you got teased about your name."

"Cassandra? Yeah, but like you said, people who are going to tease you will find something, no matter how hard you try to fit in."

"Yeah. So I was wondering . . . you said that teacher suggested Sandra was a better name, and you told people to call you that instead. Are you sorry?"

"I don't understand."

"It's kind of like a nickname but not really."

"I'm the same person, no matter what I'm called."

He shrugged. "I guess that's true. But it would be different, you know, if you'd decided on your own. Did your mom or dad mind? I mean, they were the ones who chose the name Cassandra, right?"

She stopped and tried to recall. "They were surprised, I think. They didn't make a big deal out of it. If they had, if they'd cared a lot, I would've stuck with Cassandra." A bird took flight from a nearby tree, and she watched it soar higher and higher. "It seemed like it didn't matter much to them."

"They were probably trying to be . . . what do they call it? Supportive?"

Sandra looked down at him, his skinny frame, his tousled hair, and said, "Maybe."

"Did you ever regret it? Changing yourself because you thought it might help you fit in?"

Stunned, her careful expression flickered for a heartbeat, and Aaron must've seen it.

He spoke abruptly. "Sorry. That was rude, wasn't it? I'd better get on home." He patted his leg. "Come on, Sammy."

"Aaron," she called out.

"Ma'am?"

"Be smart. Be yourself. Don't change who you are to suit anyone."

Aaron grinned. "Yes, ma'am."

Sandra waved. " 'Bye," she said, still feeling oddly unbalanced.

" 'Bye," he echoed and took off across the yard with Sammy.

Sandra looked up at the sky and laughed. The

joke had been on her. She'd changed her name and still hadn't fit in. How had her parents felt about it? She'd never wondered.

Aaron, heading toward the woods with Sammy close behind him, looked back when she laughed. He raised his hand in another wave, and she returned it. Honey followed the boy and dog at first, but then realized Sandra wasn't keeping up. Honey turned and looked questioningly at Sandra before trotting back to where she stood.

At some basic level, didn't everyone want to fit in? Was it a bad thing? Not necessarily, but it could be. Maybe it depended on the lengths one would go to fit in, blend in, with the rest of one's world. Was Aaron considering trying harder to fit in? She thought that would be a mistake, but she sympathized with the instinct to belong.

Instead of relaxing her, this walk had backfired. It had gone from solitary to having company, to sharing deep, complex, emotional topics. And it had been delightfully satisfying.

Already in the backyard, she walked over to the fencing and wrapped her fingers around the rolled bale. She'd give it a true effort tomorrow. This evening she'd get the feel of it and overcome her anxiety about attempting to erect the fence.

Sandra negotiated the bale over to the first stake, then dropped it on its side and unrolled it until she was past the second stake. Then she stood it on end, leaned it against the second stake.

She could see it was doable but required skill and experience she didn't have. And a second set of hands. Maybe if she'd had the Internet and could've done some online research . . . She could go to the hardware store and ask questions. Yes, that she could do. In fact, she'd do that in the morning before getting dirty in the garden area.

She gave up the trial effort in favor of a soak in the tub. The ache eased out of her shoulders, arms, and back. Even the tension. It wasn't only about the labor she'd done today. She was taking control. Responsibility was a heavy burden, but the lack of control was the true anxiety-maker.

Finally, she climbed carefully from the tub, toweled down, and then enjoyed her aunt's rose-scented powder. She felt pampered and decided she could get used to this. Alone wasn't so bad.

Honey had already tucked herself into bed on her pillow. Sandra did a quick survey of the doors, including flipping on the outside lights and such, took a glass of water up with her, and settled into the bed while her muscles were still relaxed. She suspected she might be sore in the morning.

She awoke in the night. The outside light lit the back window. It glowed in the dark room. She listened and heard nothing, but the room felt a little warm and musty. She wished she'd left that window open. She reached toward the nightstand for her glass of water and saw Honey. She was standing in the doorway, not moving, and appeared to be watching Sandra. When Sandra moved, Honey barked. It was one low bark, not much more than a chuffing sound.

Sandra froze, listening intently. Nothing. She ran her hand up her arm, feeling the goose bumps, and wondered what was going on. Did Honey need to go out?

In the near dark, the dog's eyes were bright and unblinking. Sandra kicked off her sheet and blanket, then set her feet carefully upon the wooden floor and stood. Honey was gone.

Sandra didn't follow her immediately but went to the window and pushed aside the thin curtain.

The exterior light on the pole and by the back door lit the backyard, creating bright circles that overlapped and intersected and shadows that stretched long and dark across them. Sandra saw no movement and nothing that didn't belong.

She went into Barbara's room to look out the front-facing window. Nothing unexpected. Night. Trees. The glimpse of fallow fields across the road.

No visitors. No flashlights.

She would've heard Trent's truck . . . unless he'd left it parked down the road and walked up.

His obsession frustrated her. It would be easy for him to find someone else, maybe someone who would actually appreciate his overwhelming and controlling personality. Maybe in his own crazy way, he loved her, and this was how he showed it. What about his own life? His job?

He wasn't here, and still he interfered with her life.

Honey was waiting by the front door downstairs. Sandra didn't bother with the leash but let her out. She waited on the porch while Honey went down the steps.

She paused by a bush to do her business, but then continued across the grass to where the dirt road began. There, she stopped and faced down the road, standing and staring. Sandra watched her from the porch but saw nothing out of the ordinary. She called to Honey to come back. Honey gave up on whatever had her attention and returned to the porch, trotted up the steps and into the house.

What had that been about? Something was going on, but Sandra couldn't make sense of it.

Sandra felt well rested despite the middle-of-the-night excitement with Honey. She fed Honey and fixed breakfast for herself. She made a list and took a couple of twenties from Barbara's envelope. She was headed to the hardware store for advice and to the grocery store for bread, milk, and eggs. She could live indefinitely on a few staples combined with what her aunt had packed into her pantry, cupboards, and fridge.

She put the car back into drive and moved forward. Her heart felt heavy. Her peace of mind, her growing comfort here at the homeplace, kept being eroded as it was trying to grow. Trent. Her own fears. It all took potshots at her confidence. She had some thinking to do unless she intended to continue as a victim—a willing victim who always seemed to volunteer to be pushed this way and that by others.

After breakfast, she called O'Toole & Sons in Martinsville. It was the last engineering firm that had hired Trent, and it was the job for which they'd made that hasty move from Arizona to Martinsville because it was going to be the opportunity he deserved, that he'd been looking for in each job he'd ever had, and that always failed to materialize. While the phone was ringing, Honey made the "out" noise at the door, and Sandra opened it for her, saying, "Don't go far."

A woman answered the phone. Sandra asked for Trent. The woman said he didn't work there.

"Oh," Sandra said, her heart sinking. "Are you sure he's not there?"

"Definitely."

She played dumb. "Do you know how I can contact him?"

"No, ma'am."

"Perhaps his new employer?"

"No. Sorry. We couldn't share that information

anyway. I have to go now. I have another call coming through."

"I understand, thanks."

They hung up. Honey was back at the door, and Sandra let her inside.

Trent was out of work—whether voluntarily or not didn't matter. Apparently, she was now Trent's job.

After their first divorce, when he was chasing after her again, trying to convince her to come back, he'd said she was his good luck. She was his reason for getting up in the morning and living each day. She'd thought it was romantic hyperbole, but it did make her heart go all warm. He apologized, saying he'd taken things too far and that he would try harder to be a good husband and friend. The friends she still had at that time thought it was sweet. Most said, "Give him another try." But there was one who said, "Your chemistry is bad. You two don't do well together. Good intentions or not, it's bound to go bad." That last voice had been Tammy's. Sandra wished she could call her now, but Tammy had died soon after that, unexpectedly and much too young, when her brakes failed and her car hit a tree.

Seeing and being reminded of how uncontrollable, how unpredictable, life could be had steered her back in Trent's direction.

Sandra was living in her parents' home and

going from temp job to temp job, feeling like a constant disappointment and failure. She thought her dad had had it with her, as he didn't seem to want to hear or understand her worries. But that was before the dementia had progressed to the point that they understood something bad was happening to him. She was seeking constancy and security, even to the point of blinding herself to the truth. And to be wanted—and Trent had wanted her.

It made her sad. Standing here in her aunt's home, surrounded by family stuff if not by family, and with a dog who wasn't hers but who felt like hers, she was nearly overwhelmed by mixed feelings but mostly good feelings. She grieved for the girl who thought she was chasing love and hadn't understood she was settling for far less than she deserved.

Sandra left Honey shut up in the house. Honey looked bemused, as if she knew she should go along, but Sandra scratched her head and said she'd be back soon.

"Watch out for the house, Honey," she said.

"What's wrong?" the clerk asked at the hardware store. He tugged at the front of his work apron and touched his name badge.

She'd seen the price of the rolls of fencing wire in the H-frame and that the rolls of fencing looked an awful lot like what Colton had brought to her house. And the green stakes in the bin next to the H-frame. Not cheap, either. This project was an expensive proposition, more expensive than she could afford even if the materials were leftovers . . . and, except for the stone, the materials Colton had brought to the house didn't seem like cast-offs.

"I was looking at the pricing."

"Yes, ma'am. There are different types of fencing with different prices, but you're saving on labor, right?" He looked doubtful, but that passed quickly. "You said you were looking for information on how to erect fences. Here's the pamphlet I was talking about, and I have another idea. Let me get my pen." He scribbled a web address on the pamphlet. "This is a really great place to check for information. Unchain Your Dog. Yes, ma'am, I was showing this to another customer the other day."

"Unfortunately I don't have a computer or access to the Internet."

He looked at her like she'd grown a few extra ears on her forehead and cheeks.

"No problem. Come with me."

They went back to the customer service desk, and he pulled up the website on their computer. He motioned her closer and turned the computer so she could see.

"This website shows you how to do it," he said. "In fact, they have a PDF. Hang on a minute."

He opened the PDF, hit some keys, then reached below the counter and came up with some papers. He grabbed a stapler and put the finishing touch to it.

"Here you go. This should give you what you need."

It gave her the information she needed, but what she really needed was a fatter wallet. "Thank you so much," she said. "I really appreciate this."

He nodded. "No problem. Glad I could help. Call me if you need anything." He handed her his card.

She left, but all the way home she was thinking about what she should do. There was the right thing to do, the expedient thing to do, and the practical thing to do, and they were whirling in her head all the way through the grocery store, which was a quick stop. She tossed a candy bar into the basket because sometimes chocolate was essential. Then she was back in her car and feeling almost dizzy with the need to make a decision. As she arrived home, she saw a pickup parked in front of the house. A green pickup.

Colton's truck.

Chapter Fifteen

Sandra went directly into the house because she had perishables, pausing long enough to shove one bag in the fridge and deposit the other on the counter, then went straight to the kitchen door. Through the glass, she saw Colton working on the fencing.

She celebrated silently, doing a little happy dance.

When she looked back out, she saw Aaron sitting in the shade concentrating on something on his laptop. He had the look a kid gets when he's struggling with schoolwork.

Colton was wearing jeans and a T-shirt, his usual attire. He looked serious, very serious. And tanned. And fit. Sammy was napping in the shade near Aaron. In the kitchen, Honey was lying up against the door as if by being closer, she might manage to squeeze out under it. She looked up at Sandra with a hopeful expression.

"Just a moment." When Sandra tried to open the door, Honey moved only enough to allow it to open a few inches, and then she scooted out.

Colton looked up when he heard the door. Different emotions played across his face, but nothing Sandra could read for sure. He said, "The patio looks good."

She followed his glance. "Thank you."

Aaron was peeking over the top of his computer, and he looked away real fast. Honey and Sammy were running around the yard and the tree. Sandra thought she would give almost anything not to disturb this scene.

But she didn't have that choice, or at least it wasn't her choice to make. Right was right. Convenience . . . well, sometimes it didn't measure up to right. In the end, you paid for everything one way or the other.

Sandra walked carefully across the stone to the grass where Colton stood. "Don't think I don't appreciate this," she said. "I was at the hardware store, and I saw what this fencing costs, and I saw what the stakes cost, too. Even sand costs money."

Colton held up his hand to signal her to stop. It had taken a lot for her to say what little she had, so she was fine with stopping for the moment.

"Remember I told you I got a good deal on the stuff? A very good deal."

She almost quipped, "What? Did you steal it?" But she sucked those thoughts back in quickly before they were spoken aloud. Some might regard snarkiness as wit, but she didn't think Colton would appreciate it. She didn't believe in a million years that Colton had stolen materials from a jobsite.

"Besides, this has been an excellent project

for Aaron. It's about math skills and project planning. It's also given him something positive to be involved in." He nodded toward Aaron. "I would've paid the full cost of this project for that alone. But the fact is, I did get a good deal. A very good deal, so don't worry about what I've spent. I can manage my own finances."

"How do you feel about the other thing? What we discussed? And seeing I have a temper?" she said.

"You do. You might have been justified, too. Let's forget what was said and move on."

"Pretend it didn't happen?"

"No. We both said things we needed to say. What I mean is, don't harbor it. Let it go and save recriminations for more important stuff."

"I like that approach, but I have to be honest. I did send signals, but I don't have the right to, not yet. I have to deal with Trent first. I have to be free and clear of him before I can consider getting close to someone. For more than friendship, I mean."

"I agree. I have Aaron to consider, so we'll keep it friendly for now. But honestly, when I thought about it later, about Trent and the conversation you and I had, I realized we hardly know each other, at least in terms of calendar days. I couldn't blame you for not telling me everything about your life." He paused, watching her face. "And don't forget the rest of the deal," he added in a somber tone. "You still owe us that meal, and we have high hopes for it."

He smiled, and her heart warmed, almost too much. Her face felt hot, too, and she turned away, seeking a distraction.

She said, "So you really think the patio is OK?"

"It looks great. Seems stable. I'll do some finishing up around the edges, tweak it a bit, and water it down. Another thing. I was thinking we might want to expand this fenced area. It'll be awfully hard to cut the grass otherwise. There's not much room to maneuver a lawn mower this close to the house."

"I guess that depends on how much wire we have." She couldn't help herself. "I thought you might not come back. Or if you did, that . . ."

"I'm here, so that's that."

Was she blushing? She thought so, but she refused to touch her cheeks. It seemed safer to move a few feet away. "I'll go say hello to Aaron."

Colton nodded. "He's writing an essay. He needs to stick with it. We agreed he could do his work here if he didn't look for excuses not to get it done."

"Understood."

While Sandra was saying good morning to Aaron, Honey, who'd settled onto her pillow, lifted her head to look at the woods. It reminded Sandra of last night, but since she didn't want to get into anything that had any possibility of being connected to Trent, she didn't choose to mention it or do more. Maybe after Colton and Aaron left, she'd take a look.

Honey stood and trotted to the edge of the woods. What was it that so fascinated her about that spot? Sammy followed. But after giving it a short stare, she moved on. The two dogs walked along the woods' edge, heading toward the back of the yard.

Sandra held the wire while Colton hooked it on the stakes. He handed her a pair of worn work gloves.

"Put these on and pull the wire and stake toward you while I pull it this way."

She did. The metal bit into her fingers and palms despite the gloves, but it didn't cut the flesh.

"What am I going to do about a gate?"

"No worries." He looked at her. "Hold that tighter." When he was done, he said, "I have one in my truck." He looked up at her again. "Used, of course. Got a great deal."

"Aaron said you build all sorts of things. I'm glad that includes a dog's garden." That sounded better than calling it a dog's toilet. "Barbara owes you a lot of thanks."

"I'm not doing it for Barbara."

He said it with such sincerity, her heart blipped.

"I'm building this for Honey," he said.

"I'm sure Honey appreciates it."

"And you."

She answered with a smile, saying, "I appreciate it, too."

He spoke in a low voice. "That wasn't my meaning."

She tried to appear unmoved, but inside, her heart did some sort of tap dance. She didn't know what to say. They'd already agreed to keep this "friendly," but she didn't want to ignore what he was trying to communicate. She touched his arm. "Thank you." Then she grinned. "Aunt Barbara thanks you, too. Or she will when she sees it."

Sandra waved at the area again. "It was a garden a long time ago, but nothing useful or pretty has grown here in a long time."

Colton disagreed. "Honey has. And she's thriving. She deserves at least as much consideration as a squash plant or a rosebush." After a few moments of silence, he said, "I notice you didn't secure her to the stake today."

"I hope I'm not making a mistake. She's doing well staying in the yard so far, and when I'm not outside, I keep her in the house with me."

"She's a lucky dog."

There it was again—the heart dance and the flushing face. She fought the urge to turn away again. Instead, she said, "If you aren't too picky, I could rustle up a little food."

"That would be great. Maybe that meal you promised?" He laughed. "Seriously, anything is fine and would be much appreciated."

She fixed what she had the makings for. There was plenty for three, and it didn't have to be defrosted. Pancakes.

Sandra woke in the night. Her arm. Someone had touched her arm.

She sat up abruptly, ready to fight and trying to remember where she'd left the knife, and then saw Honey. Sandra touched her arm. It was wet.

Honey was developing a bad habit—late-night trips outside. She'd moved away from the bed and was now standing on her hind legs at the back window. The curtains bunched and draped around her shoulders as she stood there.

Sandra eased out of bed, trying to be quiet. On tiptoe, she crossed to the window. When she moved aside the curtain to look out, Honey dropped to all fours and left. She padded out of the room and left Sandra standing there. From below, she barked. One bark. The "out, please" bark. OK. So that's all it was. Good.

She left the window and made her way in the dark down the hall and then the stairs. All seemed well in the house. Honey was waiting at the back door.

In the dining room, the curtains at the wide patio doors were open. The night looked like a big-screen movie. The pallet was now mostly empty of stone, and the unrolled fencing had an interrupted, abandoned feel. The patio table and chairs made an odd, shadowy configuration half-concealed in the darker area under the oak tree.

Honey barked again. Sandra joined her at the kitchen door. When she opened the door, Honey was out and moving fast. Belatedly, Sandra grabbed the leash. She followed Honey outside but moved more carefully, picking her way through the patio-garden area.

What was Honey focused on? She'd done this at this same location before, standing and staring. Suddenly, Honey trotted forward, toward the woods. She disappeared into the brushy growth along the trees. Sandra was left cursing under her breath and holding the pointless leash.

Sandra stayed in the area lit by the exterior lights. Should she go back into the house or wait here where she felt exposed? She slapped her hand lightly with the leash, uncertain. She was fidgety herself, on edge, and trying to shake the feeling of being watched. It was all too strange. And what about Trent? He'd never been a woodsman. It was hard to visualize him hiding with the squirrels and snakes in the dark, but she couldn't dismiss any possibility.

"Honey," she called out.

As she moved to walk back to the house, Honey came out of the woods. Sandra took the opportunity to leash her while she could, though they were so close to the house. Honey gave one last bark in the direction of the woods and then walked with Sandra back inside.

A nonevent. Nothing had happened, and yet she felt unnerved. It could be nothing . . . or anything. Or . . . It made her angry. Even here, even now, without being present, Trent managed to mess things up for her. But it was her fault for allowing it.

Maybe Colton was right. She should talk to the sheriff's office. She should have done that already and gotten a protection order. Would the authorities be sympathetic? She'd told Trent to leave, and he had. She hadn't seen him for several days. But in her heart, she knew it wasn't over.

There was very little between her and the night. Ordinary household locks in wooden doorframes. Glass. So much easily breakable glass. This house wasn't secure no matter how many latches were locked, no matter what. Not if someone really wanted to get inside.

Locks and closed windows were sufficient if the predators were possums or raccoons. Probably enough against a bear, too. But two-legged predators? Like Trent?

She wasn't armed. The steak knife in the bed-room was mostly for show, so that she didn't feel empty-handed. Tonight, it didn't seem enough.

Likely, her uncle's or grandfather's guns were stored somewhere in this house along with everything else the family had ever owned, but even if she found them, she had no idea how to use them. Could she shoot Trent anyway? For any act short of an outright physical attack?

Vigilance and her phone were her best weapons.

Sandra went upstairs and grabbed one of her mother's blankets, took her pillow and Honey's bed, and carried them back downstairs. She fixed her bed on the sofa and put Honey's nearer the patio window.

She might doze, or she might not, as she kept watch. She would deal with tonight, tonight. Tomorrow, she'd figure out what to do going forward. Honey was already peacefully sleeping. Her back was toward Sandra, but Honey slept on her side, and she could see the easy rise and fall of the dog's chest. Reassured, Sandra rested her head on her pillow and tugged the blanket up around her neck.

The next day was overcast, and the clouds spit rain on and off. In the morning, Colton called to say he was inspecting interior work today at the jobsite and wouldn't be coming by. It reminded her of the interior work she'd planned to do in her aunt's house, which had taken a backseat to the work on Honey's garden.

She stood in front of the refrigerator. While

cleaning, she'd found a listing of emergency numbers for Louisa County and had stuck it under a magnet on the fridge.

Colton had recommended she call the sheriff's office. She liked that idea. She'd called them every day when she'd been searching for Honey, and they'd been patient and helpful. Calling them would help her peace of mind.

A woman answered. Sandra cleared her throat and identified herself.

"I'm Sandra Hurst, out on Shoemaker Road. You might remember me. I was looking for my lost dog, Honey."

"Yes, ma'am. I do remember. I heard you found her. I hope she isn't missing again."

"Oh, no. She's doing fine. I wanted to thank you all for helping me with that."

"Happy to." After a short pause, the woman asked, "Is there another problem?"

"Oh, well, maybe. I'm not sure, but I thought I'd ask. I'm sorry to have bothered you." Sandra couldn't find the words.

"I'm Deputy Wilkins, Ms. Hurst. Please feel free to say whatever you'd like to share. I'm happy to help if I can."

She sighed. "My husband. We're estranged. He followed me here. I told him to leave, and I think he did, but I'm not sure. A friend suggested it might be a good idea to let you know."

"Are you feeling threatened?"

"Not at the moment. Honestly, he's never been violent. I don't want to misrepresent anything."

"Why don't you give me his information? We'll keep an eye out for him. But if anything changes or he returns, and you're concerned, please call us."

She gave Deputy Wilkins Trent's information, and when they disconnected, she congratulated herself on taking a big step forward. Trent, if he found out what she'd done, would be very angry. She pushed away any second thoughts. If Trent didn't like what she'd done, then he should leave her alone.

Making the call had provided an adrenaline boost. There was no way she could spend the day going through more of Barbara's papers or magazines. She had other plans.

Her bedroom needed help. A few creature comforts. A chair and table would be nice. Maybe a dresser. Items that declared she wasn't an overnight guest. Ultimately, her choices would be guided by what she could reach and what she could move.

She opened the doors to the three storage rooms upstairs and tried to guess what was in each one. Was there a theme or a hint of organization? It made sense that the most recent things to be put into storage would be in the former bedroom rather than the gable rooms.

Honey joined her. Other than a few quick

off-leash trips outside, she seemed content to lounge on the smooth, cool wooden floors of the hallway, even rolling over onto her back for a while. She looked like she was airing her belly. Sandra was pretty sure she heard a soft snore or two.

A wooden chair was in the front, and she moved it out of the way. Beyond that was a dresser and an upholstered chair that she wanted. She thought they'd be perfect if she could maneuver them out of the room, but first she had to move smaller items stacked against the legs and sides of the furniture.

A stack of worn, dusty books was in the way. Hardy Boys books with some Nancy Drews mixed in. Sandra set them against the wall in the hallway. Next, she moved the picture frames that were leaning against the side of the chair. These weren't fancy frames. They were old and tarnished. There might be a few faces she'd recognize if she tried hard enough, and she'd take a closer look later. One was different. It was a thick, rough frame, like a homemade shadow box. There they were—the orange monarchs. Someone had pinned several perfect butterflies into the display.

She remembered these from her trip upstairs that day long ago, the day she thought she'd heard her name called from inside the house and had left the porch and her dolls. She'd gone in and followed the voice up the stairs and down the hall, into her grandmother's room. Mrs. Shoemaker. The first Cassandra.

It had been shocking to be in the room. Hot. Dark. The bright spot had been those butterflies.

The air was thick with pain and despair, and with a stink that the open windows couldn't overcome. The sick, elderly woman was lost amid the pile of blankets and pillows, still calling out. Young Cassandra had stood near the bed, disoriented and frightened. She wanted to run. But from among the jumble of blankets, a hand reached toward her, the thin fingers grabbing at the air, as her grandmother spoke garbled words. The only words Cassandra understood were her name and the plea to come closer.

Cassandra wanted to move closer, but her feet were fixed to the floor. She couldn't move. She couldn't help.

That memory had stuck with her like a permanent mark. As an adult, Sandra still felt guilty. Her grandmother had been dying. Seven-year-olds could feel compassion. Shouldn't that have been enough to overcome the fear?

Her mother had found her within moments and had taken her daughter's arm to pull her out of the room, but the old woman's hoarse, mumbling voice continued to call after her. Mom had paused in the doorway. She knelt, asking Cassandra if she wanted to go back to the bedside and speak to her grandmother. She had shaken her head no, but the word had also escaped her lips, loud and panicky. She still remembered the feel of it, the frightened "no," and the old woman going silent. Mrs. Shoemaker hadn't passed that day, but the silence and her own childish refusal had firmly woven itself into her memory and mixed with her memories of the first Cassandra's death.

Mom had ushered Cassandra out of her grandmother's room and down the hall. As they descended the steps, her mother, still clutching her daughter's arm, spoke in harsh, low tones. "Why did you go in there? Why did you leave the porch?"

"Someone called me. I heard my name."

Her mom stopped at the foot of the stairs and looked at her. "Nonsense. Who would call you up there?" She put her hands on her daughter's shoulders. "Please be a good girl and stay on the porch as you're told." Mom opened the screen door and motioned her out.

She remembered hearing her mother call out, almost breathless, as she ran back up the stairs, "I'm coming, Mother. I'll be right there."

Who could blame a child for being afraid? No one, not even her mom. But each time she heard her name, she remembered her grandmother, and she felt the guilt and fear again. In retrospect, she suspected her discomfort with her name,

Cassandra, had contributed to her being teased about it. It had made her a target.

Later, after her grandmother had died, when Mom was going out to the homeplace, she'd ask Sandra if she'd like to go, too. Sandra declined, and Mom hadn't pushed her.

Sometimes it wasn't what you'd done that stuck with you. It was what you hadn't. Mom had said many times you couldn't reap what you hadn't sown, but that wasn't true—you could reap without sowing, but the result was often hollow and unsatisfactory. It was more commonly known as regret.

All these years later, here she was sleeping in this very same room. It looked so different. It felt different. Far different from that memory. But that was life—an uneasy blend of chance and fate. If she'd never heard her name called that day, she would never have come up here on her own, been frightened, and carried the encounter with her into her future.

In fact, holding the frame, she saw the butterflies weren't real.

Someone had painted fake monarchs. They were exquisitely done; the colors and markings looked real. Maybe better than real. The wings were thin, perhaps painted onto parchment or tissue paper, something that could be delicately shaped to mimic the fluttery shape of the insects' wings.

The artist had wanted to capture the beauty of the butterflies, but perhaps not the butterflies themselves, and had mounted them in the frame as if they might fly away at any moment.

Sandra hugged the frame to her. She used her sleeve to wipe the tears from her eyes, then carried the frame to the bedroom. As she set it on the bed, she saw words on the back panel. *To Mama,* it read, and it was signed by Clifford Shoemaker Jr. Not in a childish scrawl, but youthful, like the penmanship of a young adult. Uncle Cliff?

Her mother had another question to answer.

She turned the frame back over again, admiring the butterflies and touching the glass, then laid it on the bedspread and returned to her work.

Next, a stool. It was old but cute. The chair was stuffed and plump and looked comfy. She worked it out of the room, then put a blanket under the claw-and-ball feet to slide it. Hopefully, the cushioning would protect the floors. The wood floors were scratched and stained, but the old scars contributed to the floor's patina. She wanted to avoid new damage.

Honey had moved, and Sandra was pretty sure she'd gone down for a drink and snack. No barks, so she wasn't asking to go out yet.

She pulled the chair carefully down the hallway and through her bedroom door to the fireplace. She pushed it near the window. It would be a wonderful spot for reading or daydreaming, especially in the winter.

Well, but she wouldn't be here come winter. Never mind, this was a cozy spot for summer, too, here next to the window. She put the framed butterflies on the mantel. It was the only spot of color in the room. She'd have to do something about that, too. She had a lot of work to do.

Honey had rejoined her. She'd settled herself half-under the chair and had resumed napping.

Late that afternoon, Sandra kicked the small suitcase sitting next to the stairs in the foyer. The kick was accidental, and her foot was bare, so she jumped around for a few moments holding her toes. Honey was waiting in the kitchen for her supper and appeared unimpressed. What could be more important than supper?

Sandra had forgotten about the suitcase. Her mother had left it when she'd stopped by. They'd argued. She felt badly about the harsh words she and her mom had shared. Probably, she'd been avoiding that memory, and as part of that had stopped seeing the suitcase.

She stared at the case. It was scuffed and looked familiar. Her mom had given it to her when she was a kid. Sandra carried the case over to the sofa and sat down. She flipped open the two locks and lifted the lid.

Her favorite doll, Felicity, was on top. Someone must've stored her in the case with Sandra's other childhood friends. Rather, Cassandra's friends. Her Barbies were layered below Felicity, neatly lined up on top of the assorted clothing.

Sandra's hands stopped. They hovered, her fingers spread, hesitant to touch.

Mom must have packed these away, probably after Sandra left home for college. She'd arranged each doll with care and consideration, and she'd stowed the case safely away. Sandra had never missed them. Hadn't given them a thought in years, except in an occasional memory.

She smoothed the doll's hair and touched the fabric of the dress. Honey had come from the kitchen to sniff the case and its contents. How many memories could Honey smell? Was the air, the scents of the days spent on the Shoemaker porch trapped in here? Along with much of her childhood?

"Careful, Honey. Watch your nose." She closed the lid and snapped the locks. She carried the case upstairs, but Felicity rode in the crook of her arm.

After such a solitary yet pleasant day, Sandra gave no thought to the distress of the night before. She saw last night as an overreaction, a product of too much happening in her life, good and bad. The garden work was moving along, and Colton and Aaron's help with that was invaluable. Their friendship, too. Trent's appearance had added to the emotional mix, except that he didn't fall under the good category.

She bathed to get rid of the dust she'd collected from the storage rooms, pulled on Aunt Barbara's white cotton nightgown, and then did the nightly pre-bedtime tour of the house, of the doors and such. Honey was already asleep on her pillow and didn't join Sandra on the rounds.

When she tucked herself in, she sat up in bed with her history book. She'd left off while reading about Queen Elizabeth and had marked the page with a scrap of paper, but her heavy eyelids told her pretty quickly that she wasn't reading tonight. Still, she sat awhile, propped against the pillows, admiring her effort at decorating.

The upholstered chair, the round table beside it, and a leather footstool with colorful sections, like pie slices, created a pretty grouping in a space that had been too empty. She'd found a colorful fringed scarf in a box and had draped it over the table to pick up the orange of the butterflies and the burgundy and green of the footstool.

This was the first time in her life that she didn't have to follow anyone else's rules. Not her mom's, not her husband's. She could do it her way. By the time she left here, she'd be a stronger person. In fact, she already was.

Her old friend, her doll friend, sat in the chair. Sandra felt a solitary tear in her eye and a warmth in her chest. She pressed her hand over her heart, struck by a sudden vision of the hands, her mother's hands, lovingly packing away the toys of her grown daughter and saving them for her. Returning them to her.

She set aside the book, closed her eyes, and fell gently into sleep.

Sandra slept, and maybe her dreams were especially charming, because when she woke during the night, she simply rolled over and went back to sleep.

There was no middle-of-the-night toilet trip outside with Honey. It was broad daylight when she woke with the feel of eyes on her and warm breath brushing her arm. A cold nose touched her hand. She opened her eyes slowly to see Honey's warm brown eyes staring into hers.

Sandra groaned, too cozy to get up, but Honey's message was clear.

"OK, you win."

Honey yipped and bounced back, moving like a puppy again and wagging her tail. Amazed, Sandra was certain the day-long rest yesterday had done Honey a lot of good.

Her heart ached, in a good way. She could love this. Maybe Aunt Barbara would want to stay in Florida longer than planned? She tossed back the blanket and went to the bathroom. Catching sight of herself in the mirror, she didn't flinch or turn away. Her hair was a smidgen longer, and her face had lost the gaunt, haunted look.

The Shoemaker eyes. She recognized them now. Her eyes—like her mom's and her aunt's— marked them as family.

Honey barked to remind Sandra that she had responsibilities, including a dog waiting at the kitchen door to be let out.

Sandra flipped the locks and let her go. Honey was in a hurry. Was Sammy out there? What was Honey after?

She followed, stepping barefooted out onto the stone. The morning breeze caught her white nightgown and the hem fluttered. She touched the skirt as it billowed, and then she saw him, standing under the oak tree, waiting for her.

Chapter Sixteen

Honey was already there sniffing around his shoes. His hand hovered above her head, fresh from petting her. He wore a familiar grin, the one that heralded a lesson.

The old battle again—it flared inside her. Old habits of default cooperation versus internal rebellion. She wasn't a child now. Not a student. She was an adult, and she could refuse Trent's world.

Not angry or in fear, she squared her shoulders and calmly called her dog. "Honey," she said.

Honey barely glanced at her as Trent knelt and scratched the furry neck. He murmured soft words to Honey and then looked back at his wife, smiling as he offered a treat to the dog and she accepted it from his palm.

"These are her favorites," he said.

"Let her go."

"Let her go?" He moved his hand a few inches from Honey's body. "I'm not restraining her. In fact, we're good friends after all those middle-of-the-night rendezvous." He gave her another scratch. "Isn't that right, girl? She loves her treats, doesn't she?"

In that cool voice, he added, "Dogs are such good judges of character, aren't they? They like to know who's boss. The alpha, you know what I mean? They want to be trained. Dogs are smart. Smarter than most people."

He rose partway. His fingers snagged Honey's collar, and he pulled. She whimpered as he stood, lifting her by the collar until her front paws barely touched the ground. She tried to move away, but Trent tightened his hold.

Sandra stepped forward instinctively, but Trent fixed his eyes on her, this time with cold intent, and she froze. He released Honey's collar and knelt again, hugging her, apologizing. He returned his attention to Sandra.

"See? Dogs are smart, and they have a loving heart. A forgiving heart." He ruffled Honey's fur and then gave her a shove toward Sandra.

The puppylike quality was gone. Her tail drooped. She ran to the kitchen door and pressed her body up close to it. She wanted in. Sandra didn't blame her.

"No more, Trent. We're not doing this again. Shame on me for taking you back, for believing you when you apologized and made promises that things would be different. I wanted to believe you, and I gave you another chance. That won't happen again. I don't want anything that has anything to do with you."

"You ran away in the night."

"If you somehow didn't get the message before, believe me now—we are done. Don't come back here."

"Be careful, Sandra. Watch who you toy with. Don't play with me and don't play with . . . what's his name? Colton? And the kid? Aaron?" He made a breaking motion with his two fists. "The problem with caring about people is that it makes you vulnerable. Even an attachment to a dog is a—"

"A point of failure?" she interrupted. "Really, Trent? Give it a rest. Caring can make you vulnerable, but it also makes you stronger. Or it should." She felt a sinking sensation. She was getting drawn into his head again. She spoke more forcefully. "What about Leo? You love a dog."

"I liked that dog a lot. He was faithful. Obedient."

Liked? Was? Sandra felt ill.

"But when it came to it, I put him down."

Had Trent moved closer? He seemed closer. She felt herself shrink a fraction. "Leo got sick?"

"No, the hard truth is he made poor choices." Trent shook his head and spread his arms as if indicating he had no choice. "After you left, he had to go, too."

She tried to calm herself. She had to think. Trent had mentioned Leo in the truck. What had he said? "Do you mean because he snapped at me?"

"He shouldn't have snapped at you, true. But what got him killed was that he snapped at me. I can put up with a lot, but I have my limitations."

She wanted to clutch her stomach, to force the

bile back to where it belonged. She didn't want to shake. She refused to retreat into silence.

"Leave, Trent. Don't threaten me—not directly or obliquely. I'm going in the house now, and I'm calling the police. It's that simple." She put her hand on the doorknob. The warmth of Honey's body was between her and the door. She pushed open the door. Honey scrambled inside.

"Don't waste your effort," he said. "By the time they arrive, if they bother to come, I'll be gone. They'll see right away that you are foolish and a liar. If I do decide to be here to greet them, then what?" He mimicked, "Your husband, you say? You're not even separated? And he rescued you and your dog from a muddy drowning?" Trent resumed his normal voice. "The vet will vouch for me." He laughed. "Think about it, Sandra. You will expose your own character and competency to questions. I'm leaving now anyway. Oh, and by the way, that treat? No worries. It was fine. Not tampered with or anything. But you might want to keep a closer watch on that old dog. Because next time . . . Well, let's agree there's always danger waiting for the unwary. Being unwary and assuming you know the rules of the game—that's definitely a point of failure, wouldn't you say, Sandra?"

He left. Finally. She was nearly destroyed in his wake. She was so angry and frustrated she couldn't breathe, and her knees gave way. She caught herself by clinging to the doorknob. She fought the weakness and pushed back up. The sobs began in her diaphragm and ripped their way up through her lungs and throat, jagged and immense. She choked and coughed, nearly drowning in the tears that erupted.

Blindly, she stumbled inside, slammed the door, and fell back against it. She huddled on the floor, and Honey licked the salty tears from her face, and then sat on her. As if she were a lapdog. As if doggy weight and furry warmth were some sort of cure for self-pity and misery.

Not self-pity, but frustration. The inability to make stuff happen the way she wanted it to, the inability to make Trent get out of her life, was too much to accept.

Sandra wrapped an arm around Honey. Her fur tickled Sandra's face. She'd stopped crying, mostly, but the storm had left an ache in her chest that she didn't think would pass soon.

What would she say to Colton? Colton wouldn't care about Trent's threats, not for himself, but what about Aaron?

Could she insist Colton and Aaron stay away? No, she rejected the idea of it.

Was it her selfishness or cowardice that made her willing to put them at risk?

And Honey. Clearly, the dog had no defense against Trent. Maybe she'd remembered him from the rescue? Or from the vet's office. Trent had gained her confidence, but dogs often served unworthy masters. Even children adored bad parents. And what about spouses who stayed long after they should've moved on?

Would he really poison Honey? He was capable of almost anything, and there was something new about his manner. He'd moved from smiling manipulation to overt threats. She'd have to keep Honey inside. And when outside, make sure she was on the leash and not allowed to pick up anything outside, not to sniff or nibble.

That was no way to live. But she had to protect Honey.

If she left . . . if she ran away again, Trent would follow her. He'd forget about her friends here. He'd forget Honey. They'd be safe.

No. She wouldn't run again.

Trent had gained Sandra's confidence at least twice, well enough for her to marry him. He could be charming, and he looked so honest and intelligent and down-to-earth.

There was no risk she'd be fooled by him again. There'd be no third try. But Colton had the right to know Trent was fixing his attention on him and his son as being part of the problem. As part of what might be keeping her from going back to him.

She moved Honey gently off her lap. She got onto her hands and knees and pulled herself upright.

The nightgown. It was ruined, covered in tears and dog hair and dirt. She stood over the kitchen sink and ran the water, wetting and rewetting a towel and holding it to her face over and over. She breathed in the moisture. It soothed her windpipe; it cooled her hot, wet eyes. When she took it away, the window before her showed the backyard, framing the view, green and grassy in the morning sun. The oak offered its welcome shade. The table and chairs below the spread of the branches would return to the garden—its former spot, which was so very different now—later today. Sandra wasn't expecting Colton and Aaron until afternoon, so she had time to think.

Not this time, Trent, she thought. *Not again. This time you don't get to win.*

Sandra stripped off the gown and dumped it in the washing machine, and then went upstairs to get ready for the rest of the day.

It was early yet. Who knew what else he might have planned or what he might do?

Sandra showered quickly, not lingering because how could she know Trent was truly gone or wouldn't come back? Something had to be done. Should she call the county police again? Deputy Wilkins? That was the best choice. But what would happen? Could she actually accuse him? Of what? There were strict laws about domestic violence, but there hadn't been any actual violence, except for Trent scaring Honey. Scaring her, too. But that wouldn't translate well in the telling. If nuance were enough, her parents would've understood. Trespassing, though. Trent was guilty of making threats and of trespassing. That should be enough.

She'd seen a TV show where someone was arrested because the spouse said they'd been attacked. The woman was the one accused and the one arrested. Sandra wouldn't lie about Trent, but Trent was capable of saying whatever would accomplish his purpose. She couldn't imagine being handcuffed and taken to jail. She couldn't risk it. Who would rescue her? Her parents?

Speaking of her parents—it would be humiliating, but she could beg her mother for money and make the divorce happen. Despite their differences, Mom would help. An official divorce filing would make her position stronger if Trent continued to stalk her.

Stalk. Yes, that summed it up. He was a stalker. She'd call the county offices and ask how to proceed. With a protective order, any subsequent complaint she made would be less of a he-said-she-said situation.

Trent would be angry.

Trent's feelings weren't her problem. Correction. He wouldn't be her problem. She was erasing him from her life. He might not believe she could fight him, but lack of imagination and underestimating her—those were his personal points of failure.

By noon, Sandra had called the county and had gotten the info she needed. Protective orders were issued at the state level, and the easiest way was to fill out the forms online.

The Internet. The world turned on it. She'd use a computer at the library, as soon as she located the library. She couldn't wait to have her life back and the means to get a smartphone, computer, and Internet access. Nature was nice, but it was hard to do what she needed to without the connectivity. For now she'd find the library or whatever would work because she refused to be sidetracked by obstacles or derailed by self-doubt.

How would she explain this to Colton? His first concern would be Aaron, as it should be. Trent had relied a great deal on charm to cover his failures and selfish motives. If charm was failing him now, then who knew what he might do?

Colton and Aaron wouldn't arrive until afternoon. Increasingly, she was on edge. It was the waiting. Waiting for Colton because she needed to tell him, to warn him. And waiting to see if Trent would return.

As the early afternoon passed, she went out to the patio table and sat in the shade of the oak. Honey was nearby. She'd been uneasy at first and spent some time with her nose to the ground, going round and round until she was satisfied, and then she relaxed. She'd become Sandra's barometer. If Trent were nearby, Honey would surely react, whether in fear or welcome, and Sandra would know. She reattached the leash to Honey's collar, uneasy that Trent might try to lure her away and into trouble. At the moment, the dog, her aunt's dog, napped peacefully in the sun, clearly not worried about anything. She'd left that to Sandra.

Idle hands. Waiting. She hated it. As soon as she'd spoken to Colton.

Making decisions. Living with the choices, the outcomes. It frightened her. And waiting made it worse.

Sandra walked along the edge of the woods, trying to see into them, past the brush and foliage. This was the section Honey had repeatedly displayed interest in. Due to Trent? There was a hint of a path inside. She walked back in the other direction, past the side of the house and her car, and down a bit farther.

There it was. The beginning of the path.

A few steps in, the foliage surrounded her. Glimpses of the house were visible between the leaves and branches. They'd had so much rain that everything and anything green and growing had overtaken the season. Spring was rushing into summer, at least in terms of lushness.

She picked her way forward, watching her step

and carefully moving branches aside, until she was near the area Honey had repeatedly shown interest in.

Her phone rang.

Sandra stopped and pulled it from her pocket. Colton's number.

"Hello?"

"Are you OK, Sandra?"

Odd greeting. "Yes, I'm fine. What about you and Aaron?"

"I found my tires slashed this morning. The deputies left a few minutes ago."

"Trent."

He gave a long sigh. "That was my first thought. But in fairness, in construction you run into a lot of odd characters, some with real issues, and sometimes you piss people off. They tend to react in a physical way. A punch in the face can get them arrested. Sometimes sneakier methods of getting even, like slashing tires or keying a vehicle, are methods of choice."

"Did you mention Trent to the police?" She tried to sort out her thoughts.

"I didn't. I wanted to talk to you first." He spoke to someone nearby. "Hey, I've got to go. Aaron is all worked up."

"Of course. He must be scared."

"Scared? No, but he wants to catch whomever did it. He's decided he's an expert in forensics. I'll call you later?"

The call disconnected.

She hadn't had the chance to tell him about her own visit from Trent that morning. But he had more immediate concerns. She could tell him when he called back.

A leafy branch brushed her face and tried to entangle itself in her hair and ear. She dropped her phone into her pocket. She moved a few feet forward, thinking again she should leave.

Slashed tires? Of course it was Trent.

She wasn't doing anyone any favors by standing up to him.

Her knees went weak. She didn't fall, but she knelt and pressed her hands to her face. Breathe. Breathe. It struck her that it had been a while since that awful constriction had tightened her chest. It wanted to start up again, and she felt it gripping and pinching her lungs, wanting to spread across her chest. She pushed back up to her feet and screamed, *"No!"*

Honey bounded up onto all fours and barked and barked at the woods where Sandra was.

She called out to reassure her. "I'm fine. Hush, Honey. I'll be right there."

But it wasn't OK with Honey. She continued barking.

"Calm down, girl. I'm coming."

Sandra looked around where she stood, seeking the fastest way out. That was when she noticed the scuffed leaves. Barely noticeable, but nothing that nature would've caused, and she hadn't stepped in that area yet.

Trent had stood here spying on them. He'd probably parked down the road, maybe by the school, and walked up to the house. He would've seen the narrow path from that angle. Day and night? Why not? It was another point of failure for Trent, because compulsion of any kind led to bad judgment and mistakes.

Out of nowhere, she saw the plastic bags in his truck bed again. The ones she'd shoved aside to make room for herself and Honey before Trent pulled her away.

You made bad choices here, Trent. You should've moved on—gone back to Martinsville, or even back to Arizona, while you could, before you took this too far.

Did he disable Colton's vehicle as a warning? As revenge? Or because he had more immediate plans for Sandra that he didn't want Colton interfering with?

Nearby, a twig snapped. She spun around. Nothing but trees. Most likely a squirrel. Nothing more. Nothing except the sound of a motor from the direction of the dirt road and the front of the house.

Blood roared in her ears. Her breathing quickened, but none of the air-stealing tightening returned. Her hands turned into fists, and her nails bit into her palms.

Fight or flight? It was her choice.

Honey barked.

Sandra forced her way through the branches, scratching her arms and legs, taking the most direct path where there was no path, to reach Honey. Honey was fine. Her leash was still secured to the table leg, at least for the moment. But Trent was right. Caring about people, even dogs, made one vulnerable. She would take Honey into the house.

"Hold still, girl." Sandra worked quickly to free the leash. Blood was dripping down her arms from the scratches. Honey was agitated, no doubt smelling the blood and sensing Sandra's urgency. Did she also sense Trent? Sandra cast a quick look around.

Enough, she told herself. One bad choice, repeated, shouldn't condemn her for the rest of her life. He had no right to deprive her of any chance of ever finding happiness. She didn't just want to find happiness, she wanted to *live* happiness.

Inside, finally, with the kitchen door closed and locked, Honey looked bewildered. She stood in front of the closed kitchen door while Sandra went to the sink and grabbed a paper towel. She wet it and held it to her arm. The bleeding was minimal, but the briar scratches stung like crazy.

"We're good, Honey. We're safe." She said the words to reassure herself as much as Honey.

The front door latch clicked. It stole Sandra's breath, but she had the presence of mind to reach into the knife drawer and pull out a long, shiny blade. She turned as Honey trotted through the living room to the front door.

"Sandra?"

She closed her eyes. Mother.

Mom came directly to her. "I knocked, but there was no answer. I used my key." She stared at Sandra. "You're hurt."

Sandra was acutely conscious of the knife she was holding. "I'm . . ."

Her mother took the used paper towel from Sandra, got a fresh one, and wet it. She held Sandra's arm while she dabbed at the scratches, asking, her voice harsh with disbelief, "What have you been doing? Have you lost your mind?"

Sandra put the knife on the counter. "Yes, I believe I have."

Her mother frowned. "What does that mean? What's going on?"

Sandra's lip quivered. She caught it between her teeth to hold it still, but of course, she couldn't talk that way, so she didn't say anything.

"You'd better sit down. You're awfully pale."

Sandra allowed her mother to guide her to the sofa, and she sat, but she was thinking again. Rational, clear thoughts. Lovely words. "I'm fine, Mom. Really. But I need a favor." She had to ask. This was the moment. "It's Trent. I know you don't approve or understand, but he's been stalking me. I'm getting a protective order against him."

"He's here? In Louisa?"

She nodded. "He won't leave me alone. He refuses to accept that I won't come back to him. He even threatened Honey. I don't need money for the protective order but I do for the divorce."

Her mother was staring at her.

"Remember my things that were stolen from the car?"

She nodded.

"Most of it was clothing, but some of those things were precious to me. I put them in plastic bags. I saw those bags in Trent's truck bed. I saw them, Mom."

Her mother's frown deepened.

"I'm serious, Mom."

"I know. I should've told you. One reason I came here today, in person, was to do exactly that, but I didn't want to worry you without reason."

"What else is wrong?"

"Nothing . . . Well, clearly that's not true. Right after Barbara got to Florida, she answered my phone. I was with your dad, so she grabbed it. She didn't see a name on the caller ID, only digits, and answered, 'Barbara speaking.' It was Trent. He must have called from a different phone, because otherwise the caller ID would've identified him. He asked for you, and Barbara told him you weren't in Florida. He told her who he was and asked where he could reach you. She was shaken and wouldn't tell him. He hung up. He must've put two and two together. Her being in Florida and you nowhere to be found."

"Why didn't you warn me?"

"She didn't tell me. Not until we were talking about how you were doing." Mom shook her head. "I decided to come here and see for myself, to talk to you face-to-face. You mentioned getting a protective order. Do you think that will keep him away?"

"It might deter him. It might hammer some sense into him. Or at least he'll see that jail is a real possibility and would be a major inconvenience."

"Morris Ward handled the divorce last time. I'll have him call you, and I'll help with those expenses."

Sandra closed her eyes and held her free hand over them for a moment. They stung like the bleeding scratches on her arms.

"I didn't realize. But, Sandra, if there's any chance you might go back to him again . . ."

"I deserve that. I do, but no. I feel like I'm thinking for myself for the first time in years. I've tried to handle this on my own. I know you didn't want to be involved again."

"No. That's not it. You blamed us for teaching

you to be 'nice' but not how to survive the real world, remember? For the record, I disagree. I think you simply were . . . are nice—a nice person who doesn't like to deal with unpleasantness. But you can't spend your life running away or hiding from trouble. I wanted you to see you could manage on your own." She put her hand to her heart. "Your dad and I won't always be here to take care of you, but we will always love you."

"You see me as a failure."

"Not as a failure. But you haven't found your potential, either."

"My potential?"

"Your happiness. Everyone has something that feeds them, gives them emotional happiness. You've never had that. I thought you'd find it given time and maturity." She pressed her hand on the damp towel again while holding her daughter's arm. "What makes you happy, Sandra?"

"I was happy this morning." She looked across the room. "The sun was slanting into the room through the window, and Honey was waking me with her wet nose. I'm sorry I didn't find a successful profession . . . any profession. I'm sorry I dropped out of college. It didn't fit. But if I'd tried harder, maybe . . . And I couldn't make a successful marriage. I wanted to be happy with my husband. I tried." Sandra put her hand on her mother's. "Don't say it. I know we can't rely on others for our happiness. Is it so terrible that I'm a thirty-year-old woman with no ambition? No ideas, no work, no hobbies. How can that be?" She sighed. "I do know that I wanted a marriage that was forever. I wanted a happily-ever-after. I'm certain Trent did, too. But our visions of what that meant didn't mesh. Now I understand they never could."

"So what now?"

"A protective order."

"Of course, but I mean about you being out here. It's isolated."

"You think I should leave?"

She looked away and then back at Sandra. "You could come to Florida."

Sandra opened her mouth to speak, closed it, then opened it again. Finally, she shook her head.

"I thought you were afraid?" Mom said.

"I am afraid, but it doesn't matter. Trent can't win this time. He gets into my head. That's where the fear is, and I start doubting myself. I have to stand up to him. He's a bully, that's all."

"I don't like any of this, but I'll be honest, Sandra." She sighed. "I don't want you to join us in Florida. You don't belong there."

It hurt, it truly did. Sandra's eyes burned. She kept her hands away and wouldn't rub them or cover her face. Instead, she looked down at the floor. "I know that. You didn't exactly hide it before."

She felt her mother's hand on her shoulder.

"No, Sandra, listen to me. You misunderstand. You've wasted a decade of your life with Trent. I watched my sister and brother waste their best years. Cliff stayed because he wanted what he couldn't have. Barbara stayed to care for our parents. By the time our mother died, Barbara didn't think she could do anything else with her life, that it was too late for her. I don't want that to be you. I don't want you to go from Trent to Florida, where you'll spend the next couple of decades taking care of your dad and me. I want you to find your own happiness.

"Your father . . . I've been gone a lot in a short time. Barbara's good with him, thank goodness, but this is hard on him. Everything is, including the move, but he would want me to put you first."

Sandra patted her mother's hand. "I'll be fine. I don't have it all worked out, but now that I can move forward with the divorce, I can make it work. I can withstand him. And, Mom, one day, I promise, I'm going to make you and Dad proud."

"We were always proud, but we also want you to be happy as the person you are, not trying to fit who you think you should be or who people want you to be."

"Uncle Cliff said he and I didn't fit in."

"Uncle Cliff didn't want to fit in. All he wanted to do was farm, and when that no longer worked, he was a man without a dream. He died of exposure, Sandra. Drunken. Facedown in the dirt. They found him a day later." She paused. "I hate to say this, but Barbara found him at the schoolhouse. It wasn't pretty, and she doesn't sleep well. She has nightmares. I don't care what your dream is—or I do, but what I truly care about is that you have a dream to guide you, to aspire to. Without that, people are . . . lost. No one can give it to you. Find it, Sandra. Not in someone else, but in yourself."

"Mom," she said. "I found the butterfly picture. The orange monarchs in the shadow frame."

Her mother nodded. "Yes."

"Cliff's name is on the back. Who painted those?"

Mom looked at the floor, at Honey, and around the room. Finally, her gaze came to rest on Sandra's face. Her mother's eyes were so sad, Sandra almost stopped her from speaking.

"Cliff," Mom began, but then paused. "Barbara was always the artist. People praised her. As long as it didn't interfere with her household duties, our parents encouraged her to pursue it. Cliff was two years younger. He drew a little, but no one paid much attention because even as a child he helped our father with the farm. That was Cliff's job. And farming is all-consuming. Do you understand that?"

Sandra nodded.

"He got sick when he was fifteen, something

with his lungs, and was confined to bed for a few weeks. No one knew he was painting the butterflies until they were done." Mom paused again and sighed. "When he gave them to our mother, instead of praise, our father made it clear that Cliff's job was the farm. It was one thing for Barbara to dabble, but Cliff needed to keep his attention where it belonged." Her voice dropped almost to a whisper. "I remember how he walked away. He never mentioned it again. I wish . . ."

"What do you wish?"

"I wish we'd spoken up for him. I wish he'd had the chance to pursue art if that's what he wanted. But we didn't. When the farm started failing, I tried to interest him in painting again, but he wouldn't hear of it. And you saw what became of him." She squeezed Sandra's hand. "If we had done more back then, he might still have had something to care about, to engage him in life later."

Her mother breathed in slowly, then sighed again. It was the longest sigh Sandra had ever heard. But Mom wasn't done yet.

"Sandra, something for you to think about while you're going through all this. This was your grandparents' property and your grandfather's parents' before them. Your father and I bought out Barbara and Cliff when Mother died, though they continued to live here. If Barbara decides to stay in Florida, then I'm ready to deed it to you, if you want it. But not while you're married to Trent. Not until after the divorce is final."

"What about Aunt Barbara?"

"I think she'll be relieved to live with me permanently." She took Sandra's hand. "All that said, if you don't want the burden of it, say so. No hurt feelings here. I know it's an old house, and we haven't kept it up the way we should. I'd rather it stayed in the family, and I'd prefer you didn't sell the timber or subdivide it, but I won't tie you up in legalese over that. I've got some ideas for funding that we can discuss later, but it will be your choice, and I won't second-guess you. I've learned some difficult lessons myself about not holding on to the past. No wonder you have that same problem yourself. Think about what you might want to do when the divorce is final. Think about whether you might find your dream here at Cub Creek, and at the Shoemaker homeplace."

So many emotions, recognized and not, slammed into her. Sandra struggled to find the right words. "I feel like I've been waiting all my life for my life to begin." She squeezed her mother's hand. "Don't I deserve a second chance? Another chance at happiness?"

"You do, and you don't need to wait. Get your legal affairs in order and make your plans so when the time is right, you are ready to move forward." She patted her daughter's arm. "But remember, Sandra, life includes everything that comes between what you know and what you don't, and what you think you want and what you get. Make the most of it. Nothing waits. Not dreams, not happiness, not life."

Mom added, " 'Life is but a dream within a dream,' remember? You, your father, and Poe— it seemed like you three had your own little club back when you were growing up." She said with a smile, "Yet if hope has flown away, in a night, or in a day, in a vision, or in none, is it therefore the less gone?"

She continued. "Those are Poe's words. These are mine: Time, life, hope, happiness—they won't wait. Don't be left out or left behind, Sandra. Find your life in each moment."

They walked out of the house together, Honey beside them.

Her mother gave Honey a pat on the head. "I don't care much for dogs, but this one . . . she is sweet, isn't she?"

"She is." Sandra leaned forward and put her arms around her mother and kissed her cheek. "I love you, Mom."

Her mother hugged her back. "I have always loved you, my daughter. I always will."

Mom paused before climbing into the car and looking at the sky. "Look at those clouds rolling in. Nothing but rain, rain, rain lately up here in Virginia. Someone said it had to do with El Niño."

368

She looked back at her daughter. "Be careful, Sandra. I don't know when I'll be back here. When the attorney calls, be frank about what Trent is up to. Spell it out to him, be specific, and don't hint around, trying to be polite. And remember, you can always call me if you need me."

Chapter Seventeen

Sandra said good-bye. She told her mom to give her love to Aunt Barbara, asked her to give Dad a kiss and hug from her, and wished her a safe trip back to Florida. The usual phrases, the courtesy words, all sincerely meant.

Meanwhile, her heart raced. She was frightened.

No, not frightened. At least, she wasn't in fear of Trent, or anxious about disappointing her mother, or daunted by the prospect of owning this house and land.

It was something different, something she was unaccustomed to feeling and had trouble recognizing, and it shook her.

Her mother drove away, and Sandra stood on the porch. She looked around with new eyes.

That ivy climbing up the house. The rutted, weedy road. The incursions of the creek. The bridge. And that was the outside. She couldn't begin to count the work needed inside.

She wasn't afraid of work. The thought of the potential expenses did give her pause.

It was like standing on a threshold. She could see the goal on the far side, glowing so blindingly bright that she couldn't quite figure out what it was, but knowing that to reach for it, to grasp it, would require . . . something . . . perhaps extraordinary . . . on her part.

Was it commitment? Courage that she could face up to possible failure?

No, she didn't think that was it.

Maybe it was facing the truth about herself. Being willing to stand alone and hold it together, alone.

She thought she'd already done that. Apparently not.

Was it about being willing to screw up without seeing it as some sort of judgment against herself? Or that her life wasn't really about her? But maybe about something less easily defined?

Honey sat at her feet, looking up expectantly.

They walked inside together. The view into the living room and down the hallway to the kitchen was filled with the piles and stacks of Aunt Barbara's junk. Overwhelming. Some instinct told her that Barbara wouldn't want any of it. It would be Sandra's burden to sort through and deal with. If she moved it all out, would the house fall down?

Of course not.

This could be mine. Not my aunt's junk, but the walls, the floors, the ceilings.

That sounded stupid. She didn't know how to express it.

Mine. With no strings attached.

Except taxes and such. Mom would help her

with that. She knew it. Her mother wouldn't give her this and then saddle her with expenses she couldn't possibly meet.

Uncle Cliff didn't die of drink and exposure. He'd died because he lost his dream and couldn't, or wouldn't, accept another.

That wasn't her. Had she never had a dream? Or had they been too small?

As she stood there thinking, it hit her that she'd never had a dream that was all her own, a dream that was independent of being a daughter or wife.

A shiver raced along the length of her body.

She felt weightless. Her worries about Trent, her desperation and frustration, seemed to have evaporated. She could handle Trent. It might be unpleasant, might be a little dangerous, but she could do this.

Sandra walked out the back door to the garden—now both a patio and a dog run and still being renovated. The large, open backyard surrounded by acres of woodland and running creeks was an invitation, but as she looked, she saw the eyes that haunted her memory—the abandoned, the unwanted, the damaged—and felt momentary terror.

Whose eyes? Her eyes as captured in the park restroom mirror, the eyes in the kennels behind fence and wire—all spoke of so much loss and fear.

She fled back to the house, away from those

eyes, and found herself on the front porch, huddled on the top step with Honey beside her.

One of Trent's points of failure concerned survivors and victims. In his view, victims settled for supporting the dreams of others. Like parasites, they attached themselves to the dreams of the strong, the survivors, because they couldn't come up with their own. They lived vicariously. In Trent's world, survivors were concerned only with themselves and their goals. The day he'd said that, she'd answered, "You're talking about leaders and followers. What's wrong with that? If everyone was a leader and no one wanted to follow, where would we be? Without the volunteers and worker bees, we'd be in a mess."

"Not bad, Sandy. You're close, but no prize this time." He'd laughed. "Those people are a means to an end—the leader's end. When they no longer serve the end, then they have to go."

"But loyalty and devotion, those are qualities everyone should have."

"Let me clue you in, Sandy. Loyalty and devotion? They aren't qualities of any kind; they are tools. If you use them right, you can have your way and make others happy to help you get what you want."

How strange to stand here now on her aunt's porch—*her* porch, or soon to be—and hear Trent's voice ringing in her ears from a

374

conversation from many years ago. That conversation hadn't caused her any concern back then. In fact, it had been back in the early days when she'd admired his strength and belief in himself. She'd been certain that, if she was patient, one day he'd see he was wrong about certain things. Several years had elapsed between that chat and the event that drove her to finally leave. Leo had snapped at her, and she'd decided to push the issue with Trent.

"Your dog snapped at me, Trent." Leo had always looked mean. She was more than afraid of that dog. She hated him. It was safer to blame, and despise, the dog than the man.

"He didn't bite you."

Trent had been only mildly curious, and she'd lost her temper. The snap was a nothing issue, she knew that, especially when so much else was so badly wrong, but she couldn't help herself.

"That's right. But I never know when he's going to be aggressive." She struck out with her words. "It's me or the dog, Trent."

Trent had smiled and placed his hands on her shoulders. "I'm so sorry, Sandra. I didn't realize how uncomfortable Leo was making you. We can't have that, can we?"

He took his hands off her, and she realized she'd been holding her breath. Her chest ached, and she wanted to gasp but controlled it lest Trent see she was in pain. He didn't like it when she showed she was ill or hurting. He'd walked across the room in thought.

"Training. He needs training." He stopped near Leo.

Leo was sitting upright watching his hero and master with ever-adoring eyes. He leaned a little to the left, and Sandra knew it was due to arthritis in his right hip. He was no longer the young, energetic dog he'd been when they were married the first time. The arthritis made him cranky sometimes and had probably contributed to him snapping.

Already regretting taking such an extreme stand, she said, "But he's older now. I don't know if he can be trained—"

She'd been about to say more but never remembered what. Trent took his booted foot and slammed it into Leo's side. Leo went airborne and then rolled a few feet, hitting the wall.

Sandra felt it herself, the kick, the shock, the spinning. Leo's bewildered, pained expression was her own. The sharp agony in his side echoed in hers. She bent over, grabbed her ribs, and cried out.

Trent turned back to her. "I think he's learned a lesson now. Satisfied?" He left the room.

She would've gone to Leo and offered comfort despite the risk of his teeth, but he struggled to his feet, unsteady and dazed, and limped out of the room, following Trent.

She dropped to her knees, still holding her ribs. Leo. Was she so different? Was that her fate, too? Spending her days, her years, with such a man? Whose failure, whose fault, was that?

That night, Sandra decided she'd stashed sufficient cash and clothing. The cash wasn't much, but she had enough for a tank or two of gas and, beyond that, her mom and dad would be disappointed in her, but they would help her. In retrospect, she was embarrassed she hadn't thought to call the local authorities. It was illegal to abuse pets, right? But Leo wouldn't tell, and she wasn't going to be there to testify. No one would've believed her anyway. Not against Trent.

And where was she now?

The wood planks of the porch at Cub Creek were back under her fingers, and her side ached again in sympathy and remembrance. Several years had spanned the distance between that conversation with Trent about survivors and victims and leaders and followers, as well as the horrible scene with Trent and Leo in their living room in Martinsville, but it was all present with her that day on the porch, and it came to her that there was a flaw in Trent's thinking, besides the obvious, of course.

Per his points of failure, when the follower-victim ceased to be with the program, he or she was no longer useful and must go. Clearly, she was no longer a supporter and of no use, and yet he was here, almost like a follower himself, needing to force her back into the subordinate position so that he could be the leader again.

It was *his* point of failure. She wasn't Leo. She wouldn't be kicked with impunity or disposed of or discarded at his will or whim. Or driven away. Instead, she was moving forward to her own goal. She didn't need someone else's dream to inspire her. She'd have her own, and she'd do it with or without help. Help was a tool, not necessarily a weakness, and only one of many resources.

The clouds had gone from thick and white to dark and dramatic. A freshening breeze rolled across the treetops and then bent the weeds in the fallow field. It stirred Aunt Barbara's wind chimes and set them singing. When the wind reached her, it blew the last of the ugly memories clear, and she stood and held out her arms to receive the new.

Honey was there beside her. Her face was tipped upward, into that breeze, and her eyes were mostly closed. Her fur rippled in the wind. She sensed the change, too, and they both welcomed it. Even the prospect of more rain seemed to be a promise of growth.

"Honey," she said, "we have work to do."

She went back into the house and called Colton. She had to leave a message. "I need to talk to you. It's about Trent. Watch out for him. He's still around and looking for trouble." Sandra placed a second call, this one to the Louisa County Sheriff's Department. Deputy Wilkins wasn't on duty so she told the deputy who answered, "My estranged husband is in the area. I can't be sure, but I believe he slashed the tires of a friend of mine this morning, Colton Bennett. He was also here at my house this morning and directly threatened me, my dog, and my friends."

The dispatcher recorded the information and asked if there was a current threat. Sandra said there was no way to know for sure, but at that precise moment, the answer was no. The dispatcher said a deputy would drop by to talk to her, but if the threat status changed at any time, she should call 9-1-1 immediately.

The call, though short, had been exhausting. It was a huge step forward for her, and suddenly she was waiting again, and not wanting to wait.

She felt like she'd moved on from what had been but was now caught between what was and what would be. Thunder rumbled in the distance. She went out to the porch and greeted the coming storm.

The skies opened, and rain poured forth. If she'd thought they'd had a lot of rain and mud before, she realized now they'd barely made their acquaintance.

Drops hit the roof like hail, melted and merged into a liquid sheet, and poured over the gutters like a wall of water. Sandra stood on the porch, getting wet from the splashing as the water hit the edge of the porch, the rails, and the steps, and couldn't see beyond the solid curtain of water that pounded from roof to dirt.

Honey whined from the doorway. Sandra had left the front door wide open, allowing in that supremely fresh air that accompanied the downpour. Electrical energy charged the air, embedding a sharpness in the scent of the rain. The thunder stayed distant, and this downpour was a gully washer and also a head-clearer. It was basic and elemental.

She thought of the creek and that miniature, charming waterfall she and Honey had visited in the woods. The waterfall was probably more churning than charming right now. And that pit beneath the schoolhouse where Honey had nearly been lost was likely awash with swirling creek water by now. Uncle Cliff had died in that schoolhouse clearing. The soil had been washed clean long ago, and she hoped he'd found peace.

Sandra wanted peace, too, and happiness, not as a gift but as a reality. She sensed that it had always been waiting for her, waiting until she was ready to receive it.

Her house? Her property? Her Cub Creek.

She'd need to have the creek dredged through the schoolhouse area so it wouldn't so easily overflow its banks. Same with the road. It needed grading and restoring.

How would she ever afford that? The rain didn't care, and she didn't, either. She had goals—tough but achievable goals—and she fastened on them, seeing the creek in her mind. The creek widened and deepened as it passed the schoolhouse, and by the time it neared the front of the property, it ran dark and deep. With this much rain upstream, there could be a problem. She should call Colton again and tell him to avoid the bridge today. She didn't trust that bridge on a good day, and the new pounding by the water flowing downstream might be a problem. So next on the list was to get someone with an understanding of structural stuff to take a look at the bridge. She wouldn't mind it being built a little wider, longer, and broader. Talk about expense. But one step at a time.

She realized she was smiling and her pulse was racing but steady.

It all looked different to her now. Knowledge. Potential. She would work out an actual plan—like a business plan. She could do that. For now, she would brainstorm. When Trent was no longer a factor, it would be the time to make it all official.

She was grateful to her mother for having bought her siblings' interest in the property all those years ago. She'd never dreamed of this while playing on the porch. She might have taken more walks in the woods if she'd known she would own them one day.

She was very glad her mother hadn't deeded her the property while Trent would also have a claim on it. Trent. She shivered in reflex and rubbed her arms, then stopped. Fear of Trent was an old habit—a habit she was trashing.

The rain eased, and Honey joined her on the porch. Everything seemed so fresh. It made her heart hurt and soar at the same time. She stumbled backward and sat on the blue bench. The water that now wet her cheeks hadn't come from the rainstorm.

"Do you mind if I stay, Honey? Will you accept me in place of Barbara?"

Honey rested her muzzle on Sandra's thigh.

The last, fat raindrops hit the ivy clinging to the porch and the house. The leaves danced and jerked as the storm subsided.

Time was running down, too, and seemed to be rushing headlong into inevitability.

What would she do when Trent came back?

Her cell phone rang. Colton's number. "Hello?"

"You OK?"

"I am."

"I have new tires. Luckily, I know a guy with a tow truck. The flatbed kind. He took us into town. We're on our way back now. Any sign of Trent?"

"Not today, but I have some news to share, and to warn you to be careful of Trent. The tire slashing sounds like his style. But I'm sensing a change in him. I don't know what he might do. I found out he doesn't work where he used to. I suspect he's unemployed right now."

"That explains why he has the time to hang around harassing you. He's a bully, Sandra. I've known guys like that, and mostly they back down when confronted, but you can't count on that. You can never tell what will flip a guy from unhappy to desperate. Everybody has a different trigger. If you see him, lock yourself in the house and call the police. Don't confront him."

"I understand what you're saying. I don't know what I'll do. How can I? Because I don't know what he'll do. But I'll be careful. I did call the police and told them what was going on. They're going to send someone over to talk to me."

"Hang on a moment."

She waited.

"Well, we're sitting here at your bridge now. I don't like the looks of that water. The creek's high and rising. Not worth the risk to cross the bridge. We're going to drive home and walk over by way of the path."

"Please be safe. Maybe the high water will discourage Trent, too, and keep him away today. That truck of his is massive."

"Remember what I said. You can't predict what people like Trent will do. Any sign of anything, call the police and then call me."

"I know. I understand. I have other news, too. I can hardly wait to tell you."

"Aaron and I will be over as soon as we can."

They disconnected. She hugged the phone to her chest, thinking the high water and the low bridge might be a blessing. Trent wouldn't want to risk his truck. Whatever else he was, he wasn't an idiot.

Unless . . .

She stared at the dirt road.

Unless he was already on this side of the creek.

If he was, then he was stuck on this side. He and his truck.

Trapped animals could be all the more dangerous. Trent might not know he was trapped. Aside from the middle of the dirt road, the only option for parking was in the schoolhouse lot, and that was probably flooding.

She tried to visualize it. If—a big if—he was on this side of the creek, then the rising water in the school yard would force him to leave, and he'd be sitting in his truck down at the bridge thinking, as Colton had, about whether driving across the wooden structure was worth the risk.

If he decided it wasn't worth the risk, then the obvious choice would be to drive back here, to the house and to her.

She needed to know. If she went around the curve and a short distance farther, she'd be able to spot his truck if it was down by the bridge. If not, she'd come back to the house, feeling a lot easier in her mind, to wait for Colton and Aaron.

There was no point in driving. With so much rain and mud, her old car might get stuck. Besides, if Trent was out there, he'd hear her car motor.

She kicked off her sandals and tossed them in the house. No sense in losing them in the mud. Mud wouldn't hurt her bare feet, and she was familiar now with the territory and hazards. She patted her pocket to ensure she had her phone.

Honey whined. She wanted to come. Sandra paused. Suppose Trent was in the woods nearby, watching them at this very moment?

"Come in, girl." Sandra brought Honey inside and locked the front door. She knelt and scratched the dog's ears. "I'll be back."

Honey looked confused as she watched Sandra leave via the back door, yet wasn't allowed to go, too. Sandra locked the back door and pushed the house key deep into her other pocket.

She walked out to the oak and fidgeted with the chairs, trying to act natural. She didn't sense anyone around. Really, the rain had been so heavy, it was unlikely he was lurking in the woods. Honey barked from inside the house. She'd settle down once Sandra was out of sight.

Sandra wouldn't put Honey at risk. Better that Honey should be unhappy but safe. She didn't need the mess, either, that would surely result if Honey went for a walk in the mud. She went around to the front and started slogging down the road.

That blue dirt was like a fine clay, the sort of material that was slick when wet, like the mess she was walking on.

Most of the land in this region seemed to be red clay or a darker loam flecked with mica and minerals she didn't recognize. Lots of minerals. The nearest town was named Mineral for a reason. But the dirt on Shoemaker Road was this bluish gray clay, and where the mud was deepest, it sucked at her feet. Her sandals would've been goners for sure.

In the near future, she hoped to see some grading and filling and a good thick layer of gravel overall. Definitely on the to-do list.

No sign of danger. No sign of Trent. The schoolhouse sat lonely in its wide clearing. The trees bunched thickly in spots near it, and the brush grew in thickly, adding to the screening. The creek had clearly overflowed its banks. Water lay like a clear slick over the bare earth. Its edges crept beyond the foundation of the building.

It had been a long, slow trudge. She'd come this far with no sign of Trent, so she continued on to the bridge. She'd been hearing the roar of the creek since before the schoolhouse. She stood on the bank but didn't try to descend the short slope to the bridge because the footing was too risky, more like a mudslide.

The water licked at the planks. The bridge itself didn't look any different, but the water must surely be undercutting it. She was glad Colton had been cautious. It would take a huge emergency to convince her to drive over it today. She turned to walk back.

She hadn't gone far when she felt a faint pain in her back, right between her shoulder blades and along her spine. She stretched her neck and rolled her shoulders, hoping to work out the pinch before it tightened and worsened. She remembered what she'd been taught in high school about the brain stem. She kept a keener watch on both sides of the road as she picked her way along. In fact, this rain could flush all sorts of things out of the woods, not only unwanted spouses.

But as she walked, that old enemy, the tightening in her chest, returned, and it tried to squeeze her lungs. It wasn't painful. It was more like a ghost of a memory. A warning. She stopped and breathed deeply, holding her breath and easing it out. The freshness in the post-rain air filled her lungs, her senses, and she began to move again, looking forward to Colton and Aaron arriving. Perhaps they were already there. She could share her news. She wanted to discuss the possibilities with friends and allies.

Her quickened pace was ill-advised. She slipped, waving her arms, and regained her balance. As she congratulated herself, she noticed something shiny off to the left. Small glimpses of something black and shiny peeked from among the branches and leaves, and as she looked, it came together into one image. Despite the camouflage, it was obvious. The side of a large vehicle. Trent's truck.

The schoolhouse was a short distance ahead. The angle would put the truck there, but she hadn't seen it before because the trees and bushes shielded it. He must be parked partly behind the building, next to the creek. He might have been there for days, for all she knew.

Was he in the truck now? She started forward abruptly. The mud made a smacking sound as she pulled her foot free.

Why would he hang out in the truck? Now that the rain had passed, it was more likely that Trent was at the house, where Honey was locked in, and also where Colton and Aaron were headed.

She pulled the phone from her pocket to call the police. She'd also let them know to be careful of the bridge. She dialed the phone, but when she put it to her ear, she heard a series of quick beeps, then nothing. She looked at the screen as the battery died and the screen went black.

Sandra closed her eyes. She'd screwed up again.

No. That wasn't it at all. She opened her eyes. She hadn't screwed up. This wasn't an indictment on her or her abilities. She just needed to choose another option.

The useless phone went back into her pocket. She would focus on getting home. Her charger was at the house, and Colton and Aaron might be, too.

She whispered, "Please don't let Trent be there."

The mud was like a slick, gluey paste, and Sandra slipped again, again catching herself. Her legs and arms were muddy, and her clothing was liberally speckled.

The house would be visible when she rounded the bend ahead. It seemed so far away. She was anxious to close the distance. Then she heard the sound of an engine. She stopped. The noise was coming from behind her, from the schoolhouse.

She turned slowly and walked back toward the school, but then stopped short of the clearing.

The truck's engine was being gunned or revved. It was an intermittent sound, indicating the truck was stuck in the mud. Suddenly the noise changed as the truck powered forward, appearing with force from behind the building and the trees. The truck kept moving, yet it also appeared to be swerving and fighting for traction at the same time, as it barreled forward toward Sandra.

Had he seen her? Not at first, certainly. It was fate that pointed his truck in her direction.

She scrambled away, avoiding the drainage ditch beside the road. As his truck exited the clearing, the rear end spun out, and, once again, the truck was pointed in her direction. This time, she knew without a doubt that Trent saw her. The truck jumped forward. She ran. Unfortunately, she was headed toward the bridge, not the house.

There was nowhere else to go. There was nothing between the truck and the end of the road except her. Drainage ditches lined both sides of the road. In the ditches and beyond them was shrubby, scrubby growth; sticker bushes; and snakes. If she could beat Trent to the end of the road to the creek, she could get onto the creek bank, and his truck couldn't follow her there or he'd end up in the water.

The engine noise dropped to an idle. She looked back. The driver's door opened and swung wide. Trent stepped out. He was drenched, so he hadn't been in his truck during the storm.

"Hey, Sandy, wait up." He spread his arms wide and opened his hands, palms up. He called out to her over the low hum of the running truck, "I wanted to give you a little scare, that's all. The mud was slicker than I thought. I took it too far. I forgot you don't have much of a sense of humor for jokes like that, and I can't blame you. I wouldn't really have hit you. You know that, right? No matter what our differences, I could never hurt you."

As he stepped toward her, she backed up. He stopped. She did, too. She was pretty sure she could run faster than he could because she was barefoot, and he was bigger and awkward in those boots. If he moved to get back into the truck, she'd take off again and be all the better for having the breather and thinking time.

"I'm sorry. I mean that. I love you, Sandra. I always have. All this stuff we've been through recently hasn't changed that." He waited, then resumed. "I didn't see you at first. By the time I did, I thought you'd earned a little scare, but that's all it was. You've really tested me, but I shouldn't have given in to it."

His pants leg was torn. The khakis were light beige, and a darker area had spread below the tear. Blood.

"What happened to your leg?" she yelled.

He pulled at the fabric. "This? Yeah, it hurts. She got me, all right. That dog of yours. Sort of ironic, right?"

"She's in the house."

"I wanted to check on you after that storm. That was some crazy rain, wasn't it?"

"The house was locked."

"Was it? Didn't seem to be. Door opened pretty easily. But you and me, we must've just missed each other."

Sandra tried to beat back the anger. It was difficult to think. Forget running to the creek. She needed to get back to the house and to Honey. The truck took up most of the road, but there was a narrow space on either side.

She ran.

Trent rushed to intercept her, expecting her to emerge at the other end, beyond the truck. She didn't. She threw open the passenger door, dived across the seat, grabbed the driver's side door, and slammed it closed. She locked it and then flung herself back to the passenger side. As he reached for that door, she yanked it closed and locked it.

His fingers left muddy tracks on the glass as he missed his grip.

She had to move fast before he could grab onto the side of the vehicle or jump in the truck bed. Despite the mud, she reversed full force, and within several slithery seconds was back in her front yard, slamming on the brake and skidding to a halt. Behind her, Trent was running, his boots pounding around the curve, and he fell. Good. It bought her a few more seconds of time.

She fell out of the truck, controlling her descent by hanging onto the handle, and raced toward the house. The steps slowed her down. She grabbed the doorknob. Yes, it was unlocked. She hadn't left it that way.

Trent's breathing was loud and heavy as he ran across the yard. She threw open the door and tried to get inside, wanting to find Honey, when she was slammed aside. Trent grabbed the neck of her shirt. He pulled her backward, and they grappled. The edge of the porch threw them off-balance and also kept him from securing his grip. They fell together, half flying and thumping down the wooden steps, propelled by black-and-white fury and a howling snarl. Somehow Sandra rolled free.

Honey was protecting her. Trent was kicking, and all Sandra could think of was that Honey was old and had recently been sick. Honey had sunk her teeth into his other, previously unbitten leg. Trent kicked at Honey's head with his big boots. Sandra threw herself on top of him, taking the blow herself, before he could land another on Honey.

His fist grabbed for her hair, but her hair was still short, and his hands were big and muddy. He lost his grip and instead went for her neck. Again the mud prevented a good grip, and Sandra twisted away. Suddenly, Colton was there. He knelt calmly but forcefully, with one knee landing on Trent's throat.

It stopped.

"Settle down or I'll crush your windpipe."

They were a jumble of fur, mud, flesh, and blood. But it had stopped. Trent believed Colton. He raised his hands, as if in surrender.

"I called 'em, Dad. 9-1-1 is on the phone. The police will be here soon."

Breathless, but in a good way, and flushed with triumph and relief, Sandra crawled aside. Honey still had her teeth sunk into Trent's leg.

"Honey," she said. "Stop. Let go." She tried again. "Come, Honey. Come here."

The dog released the flesh and fabric and stepped back with one bark. Job done, the snarling, teeth-filled face was suddenly panting and sweet again. Honey walked around Trent to reach Sandra and began licking her hand.

"Good girl, Honey," she said.

She was hugging Honey when Trent's legs moved, and Aaron shouted. Sandra turned, ready to fight again, but saw that Trent was on his feet and running. How had that happened? Colton appeared unhurt. He'd moved away and was motioning to Sandra to stay back. Honey's muscles bunched, and Sandra tightened her hug and tried, despite her distress, to make soothing noises.

"Stay on the porch," Colton called out to Aaron.

The truck came alive. Trent backed and reversed direction. The tires squealed despite the mud, and the truck roared forward, away from them.

Enough, Sandra told herself. Her heart thumped and raced. Part of her was ready to resume the fight, but instead she closed her eyes and tried to reset her emotions. She pressed her face into Honey's fur and held her breath.

Trent was running away, and if he beat the

arrival of the cops, Sandra thought this defeat would be enough to keep him moving. She'd get that protective order and start legal actions for the divorce. Those thoughts happened in mere moments, and she looked up at Colton. He was already staring down the dirt road as if he could see around the curve.

"The bridge," she said.

The two of them took off down the road. Sandra felt like she'd found her "mud" legs. She aimed for the weed clumps as she ran along because they were less slippery.

The rains from upstream, from the mountains, from the lakes, were still making their way into and down Cub Creek, and its banks continued to disappear as the water spread and deepened.

"Slow down, Sandra. You'll get there soon enough. He'll either be gone or he'll be caught. Either way . . ."

It was true. She knew he was right, but she kicked up her heels anyway. Not a single slip this time. It was as if her feet had grown wings.

Lights were flashing red and blue on the state-road side of the bridge. Trent's truck was about as long as the creek was wide, and it was canted at a strange angle, wedged between the banks of Cub Creek. The water continued to flow, and it was building up against the side of the truck and putting pressure on the soil that currently held the truck in place.

"Wait!" Colton called out after her.

Through the back window, she could see Trent in the cab of the truck, moving. A deputy stood on the far side. He looked interested but content to wait for Trent to emerge from the vehicle on his own. Where else would Trent go, after all? More emergency vehicles arrived with their lights flashing, but they were on the far side. The deputy began to angle downstream, moving closer to the creek. She could've told him not to worry about Trent making a swim for it. Trent couldn't swim. Another failure on his part.

Sandra eased down the short slope, careful where she placed her feet.

"What are you doing?" Colton asked.

The front end of the truck was lower than the truck bed. The top was almost level with the ground. The truck shifted a fraction, but Sandra didn't weigh much, and if she moved quickly, she could get it done.

The officer called out to her, and so did Colton, but she didn't have time to talk. She unhooked the bed cover and pushed it out of the way as she moved onboard. Trent paused halfway out of the front cab and looked back at her. The truck jolted abruptly in favor of the downstream side. Sliding, she grabbed the first plastic bag and tried to toss it back to the creek bank. The angle was awkward. Colton came closer.

"Forget it, Sandra."

"Cassandra. Call me Cassandra," she said. "Here, catch this."

He grabbed the first bag, and she went for the second one. The truck moved again, but she was done and returning to firmer ground.

Trent was finally emerging from the cab. Honey had arrived on the bank, along with Sammy.

Sandra dragged the second bag along with her as the officer on the far side kept his eyes on Trent. Trent was hanging onto the door handle and the top rim of the door. The water wasn't swift because so much of it was being dammed on the upstream side. At some point, something was going to give, but she was on relatively firm, if muddy, ground, and she grabbed Honey's collar. They were muddy, but they weren't going swimming today in Cub Creek.

"Hey, Trent!" He turned her way, and she lifted the bag, holding it up like a trophy. "I win."

He grimaced as he lost his footing. Now his only hold was the door handle, and his booted feet were underwater.

"Everyone stay back," the deputy yelled. Another deputy joined him, and they sorted out a rope. Colton put his hand on her arm.

"Don't distract them. Let them get the job done. I'm pretty sure he got your message." He eased the bag from her hand. "What is this stuff, anyway?"

She laughed at Colton's question as she pressed her hands against the bulk of the bag. Finally, she felt the harder form, the edge and surface of the Poe anthology in its waterproof wrappings.

"My stuff. Just my stuff, Colton. I've got it back now." Then, she turned her attention to the spectacle of the deputies fishing Trent Hurst from the creek, and she smiled in satisfaction.

They walked back to the house to await questioning. Each had a plastic bag slung over a shoulder.

"I'm glad he didn't drown," she said. "I don't want that as a permanent memory on this property."

She paused to look at the schoolhouse. Had the roof sagged more? She thought so. And the water was pooling. The ground was no doubt saturated.

"What a mess," Colton said.

"This is where he was parked. Back behind the trees." She didn't mention this was also where her uncle had died.

"I'm thinking a small lake would be nice. With a bench. And maybe a small garden." She added, "With butterfly-friendly bushes." She thought Uncle Cliff might like that. She waved her arm at the area. "Instead of dredging the creek to keep it confined, I'll dig out the dirt, use it to grade the road, then let the creek fill it in as a small lake." She nodded, then hefted the bag back onto her shoulder, and they resumed walking. "Maybe some ducks will move in."

"Ducks? You've lost me now." He scratched his head. "Seems like a strange time to think about altering geography."

"I'm making a list." After a pause, she asked, "How long do you think we'll have to wait?"

"For the deputy? A little while. They'll have to drive around and take the path, I believe. Might be state police instead of local, or maybe both."

Aaron was standing on the porch waving as they reached the house. Judging by the fresh mud on his shoes and the tracks on the steps, he hadn't stayed there the whole time. They dropped the bags near the steps.

"I hope you weren't worried," Sandra said.

Aaron's eyes were bright with excitement. "The 9-1-1 lady told me what was going on. Man, they're gonna need a big tow truck. Can I go down and see?"

"No," Colton said.

They sat on the porch at the top of the steps. The mud was churned in the yard, a reminder of the struggle. "I thought Trent had forced open the front door. I know I locked it."

"Oh. A little bad news. He forced the back door. Looks like he kicked it in. The doorframe is splintered. Probably unlocked the front door to get out. Looks like Honey gave him some encouragement." He laughed.

"Of course. Count on Trent. Will it shut?"

"No worries. I know a guy. I'll give him a call." Colton grinned. "Don't worry, he owes me a favor."

"Does he build bridges, too?" There was grit in her mouth. "Aaron, will you mind fetching me a glass of tea?"

"Me, too?" Colton added.

"Happy to." The screen door slammed behind him.

She looked at Colton. "I'm stuck here, aren't I? Until the bridge is fixed, that is."

He nodded. "Your car is. You can always take the path over to visit Aaron and me."

"I might do that. But tell me this—why'd you let Trent go?"

"I weighed the problem versus the possible outcomes. Seemed to solve the issue either way. I didn't have to maim him or risk crushing his windpipe and killing him."

She waited.

"Let the cops deal with Trent. The investigators and prosecutors can take care of him."

Sandra smiled. "Thanks for neutralizing him. Maybe now he'll leave me in peace." She asked as nonchalantly as she could, "Aaron mentioned you two move around, following the jobs. Any plans to move on anytime soon?"

"No." He frowned. "I don't plan to move at all. I move to other jobs, I guess, but I'm born and raised here in Louisa County." He gave her a look. "How do you think I know everyone around here? Fencing, tow trucks, deputies . . . I either know them or I'm related to them. In fact, this may surprise you, but the Shoemakers and Bennetts have shared property lines for about a hundred and fifty years."

She smiled, then tilted her head. "I guess I made some assumptions."

"You wouldn't be the first person to do that."

"I might need your help."

"You can safely assume I'm happy to help."

Aaron returned with their tea. Before she could say more, the deputy arrived.

"Mrs. Hurst?" He was young but professional looking. The walk through the woods hadn't done him any harm. He smiled.

"I know," she said. "I'm a sight. Looks like I've been mud wrestling." She looked down. "I guess I have."

"Are you injured, ma'am?"

"I think I'm fine. I'll know for sure later." She was covered in gray mud. It was drying and was cracking at her elbows and finger joints.

"The gentleman in the creek . . . Is that your husband, Trent Hurst?"

"We are estranged."

"But still married?"

"The divorce is in process."

"Is this the same man you called about earlier?"

She nodded. "I told him to stay away, and he threatened me. Today he saw me walking down there." She pointed at the dirt road. "He tried to run me down with his truck."

"You live here with him?"

"No!" she shouted. "Sorry. The idea of him living here is so . . ." She shivered. "This is my aunt's house. I'm house-sitting and dog-sitting. He followed me here." Her voice rose again. "He also threatened my dog and my neighbor and his son. He would do anything to get his way. Anything."

Colton spoke up. "Someone slashed my tires. I found them like that this morning and called it in to the sheriff's office. While I was getting them fixed, he must've come back over here."

"Are you two in a relationship? Perhaps that contributed?"

Sandra crossed her arms and spoke distinctly, laying it out as clearly and specifically as she could. "As you noted, I'm still technically married. Colton and his son are my friends and neighbors. Longtime friends with my aunt. If not for Colton and Honey, I don't believe we'd be talking here now."

They were out by the garden, and Sandra was using the hose to wash the worst of the mud from Honey and herself. Honey was surprisingly patient and accepted the cold water better than

Sandra did. Colton kept a hand on the dog, speaking in a soothing voice, but as soon as Sandra switched off the faucet, Honey began shaking her body and water flew everywhere. Aaron came out holding a towel and went to work rubbing her down.

Colton put his hand on Sandra's arm. "Want to talk?"

It was a request more than a question, but it was kindly asked. She followed him over to the chair and tables, still under the oak, but now she and Colton were far enough from Aaron not to be easily overheard.

"What about Trent?" he asked.

"What about him?"

"You don't have the protective order yet, and when you do get it, you're still isolated out here. They'll probably lock him up for assaulting you—for battery, too—but it will be temporary. For now we're good. They'll give us a head's up if it looks like he'll be released for whatever reason. What will you do if he comes back here?"

Sandra ran her finger around the edge of the table, feeling the bump of the pattern. She nodded. "Sometimes things don't work out right the first time. I used to be terrified of him, of confronting him. I know he might be dangerous, but I can stand up for myself now."

"True, but . . ."

"Trent will figure it out. He's not stupid. He

won't like the attention of the authorities, and he'll understand I'm not his wife, and I'm not his victim anymore. Trent wants someone to support his ego and his insecurity. That's not me. Once he believes that, he'll move on."

They gathered around the fire pit—Sandra-Cassandra with Colton, Aaron, Honey, and Sammy. They didn't have the makings for s'mores, but they had everything else they needed.

"I hope hot dogs will do." She offered the plate of buns and hot dogs. They passed it around.

Aaron said, "Hot dogs are great. Do you have chili?"

"Right here." She handed him the bowl.

"Hot dogs are fine. It wasn't your responsibility to feed us this evening anyway, though we appreciate it, and comfort food is welcome considering the day we've had, but so we're clear, I'm still expecting the meal you promised us in the not-too-distant future. I hope you understand that."

"We'll save a fancy meal at the table for later. Right now I prefer this." She balanced her plate on her knees and reached for the mustard.

The flames danced in the fire pit as the logs popped.

Colton nodded. "Suits me."

It suited Honey and Sammy, too, and they snuggled up close, their eyes begging.

Aaron asked, "May I?"

"Table food?" Colton asked.

"A small bite."

Aaron took a nonanswer as assent and shared a little of his food with the dogs.

Sandra and Colton shared a smile. It warmed her more than the food or the fire.

"Aaron, I have a question for you," she said.

"Yes, ma'am?"

"Remember what you were saying about the animal shelters and volunteering?"

He leaned forward excitedly. "Yes, Miss San . . ." He stopped. "What should I call you?"

"Whatever you like."

"Miss Cassandra, then, if you don't mind. I like it because it's a little different. I think Dad's right. It's OK to be different. To be yourself."

"I agree, Aaron. The trick is to know who you are, so you can be you."

"It can be hard," Colton said. "Choices, decisions, trying and hoping you're doing the right thing. I've made enough mistakes to know, but sometimes"—he smiled at Aaron—"sometimes you get lucky."

Sandra said, "You have to take it on faith and move forward."

"And trust yourself?" Aaron asked.

"As well as others. I've also learned that if you don't know who you are and don't have 'you' inside your head, someone else might try to own that space." The night was silent except for a chorus of insects, invisible but very vocal. "Thank you both for your help with Honey, the garden, and with Trent."

"You're welcome," Colton and Aaron said in unison.

Hearing her name, Honey moved closer. Sandra ran her hand along Honey's back, enjoying the silky feel of her fur.

Aaron nodded. "Are you thinking about volunteering at the shelters?"

"That, but more. Remember how that shelter was so full? The woman said the animals kept coming, and she mentioned fostering."

He leaned forward, excited. "Are you going to foster dogs?"

"That's what I'm thinking."

Colton interrupted. "That's a pretty big commitment."

"It's not like adopting. I don't dare adopt. I wouldn't know where to stop. But fostering? I can do that." How far had she come in such a short time? She couldn't even take care of herself before, and now she was certain, absolutely sure, she could take care of others in need.

"What about the expense? What about Barbara?" Colton paused, his expression changed from curious to speculating. "Are you planning to stay longer after all?"

"Maybe. I think so. It's not for sure yet." She

smiled, enjoying the list of dreams, the hopes, growing inside her head. "There's a good chance Aunt Barbara might decide to stay down in Florida."

Suddenly Sandra knew she didn't want to talk about owning the Shoemaker homeplace here at Cub Creek, not yet. It would be a while before that actually happened, and things could change. Plus, she didn't want to close off any options or chart a specific course. She wanted to enjoy the possibilities and imagine how they might complement her life—her real life—the life she'd been avoiding for almost three decades. She wanted to build it well and enjoy doing it.

"I won't be rushing off anytime soon, and I don't think my aunt will mind at all. I have to work out the expenses part, but I'm tired of waiting, and I want to begin preparing. However, there's one problem."

Four pairs of eyes focused on Sandra.

"I've already got a pretty substantial to-do list in mind, and, Aaron, I need your help."

"Yes, ma'am?"

"Can you bring your garden layouts back over? And your tape measure?"

"Sure," he said, nodding.

"Could you design a layout that's flexible? One that can be expanded as needed?"

"You mean like with the fencing and adding some kennels and stuff? I have some great ideas."

"Excellent, because regardless of the other projects on the list, one thing I know for certain—Honey and I are going to need a much bigger garden."

She looked down at Honey, touched her silky ears, and scratched her neck. Barbara might miss her Honey if she stayed in Florida, but as her aunt had said, the trip would be too stressful for an older dog who'd lived a hard life, and she'd be guaranteed a good home with Sandra. Besides, Sandra reminded herself, Mom didn't like dogs and would never allow pets in the house. She laughed.

"What's funny?" Aaron asked.

"Nothing. Everything." She smiled and hugged Honey. "I'm just happy."

A Dream Within a Dream
By Edgar Allan Poe

Take this kiss upon the brow!
And, in parting from you now,
Thus much let me avow—
You are not wrong, who deem
That my days have been a dream;
Yet if hope has flown away
In a night, or in a day,
In a vision, or in none,
Is it therefore the less *gone*?
All that we see or seem
Is but a dream within a dream.

I stand amid the roar
Of a surf-tormented shore,
And I hold within my hand
Grains of the golden sand—
How few! yet how they creep
Through my fingers to the deep,
While I weep—while I weep!
O God! Can I not grasp
Them with a tighter clasp?
O God! can I not save
One from the pitiless wave?
Is *all* that we see or seem
But a dream within a dream?

Acknowledgments

Heartfelt thanks to my first readers, Jill, Amy, and Amy, who each bring their special skills, talents, and perspectives to my books and graciously struggle with me through the early drafts to help craft the characters and the story. Special thanks to Lake Union Publishing and my editor, Kelli Martin, for this opportunity and for making the publication of this book possible, and to Lindsay Guzzardo, my developmental editor, for asking all the right questions and her inspired suggestions. You all helped make this a better story, and, together, we have crafted a book worth reading. I hope you, dear reader, will agree.

An important and special acknowledgment is due to Edgar Allan Poe and his poem "Dream Within a Dream." The poem's themes are represented in this book. Time doesn't wait. Life, happiness, and love—it all passes swiftly. We cannot hold it here. We must find our hope and our happiness daily, in between what we think we want or need and what we actually get. A truth we've all heard: life, happiness, and love aren't waiting at some elusive destination but are with us on each step of the journey, if we will open our eyes and see them.

Thank you to my mom and so many others who suffer from Alzheimer's and other forms of dementia. I represent you here with great love, straight from my heart.

Thank you to my husband, who keeps me writing even when life does its best to interfere and interrupt.

An important acknowledgment must be given to the inspiration for this story. She was a friend and coworker who had divorced her abusive husband, and though she tried to make it on her own, it was difficult. He returned, charming and persistent, and she remarried him despite the warnings of friends. I lost touch with her many years ago and don't know if her happily-ever-after worked out. I hope that it did. This book is for her.

Author's Note

No one, no living creature, should be mistreated. Animals don't have much choice, but people do, and no one should ever settle for anything short of what feeds their happiness, because happy people tend to share happiness. Be the person who shares goodwill and also the person who receives it and passes it on.

If you are interested in helping animals, please contact the shelters in your area and find out what they need and what you can do to help.

You can make a difference in a life.

Reading Group Guide

1. Why do you think Sandra tried so hard to make her marriage work? Did she believe it would work if she tried hard enough? Or was it because she was afraid of failure or of being on her own?

2. When does thoughtless and overbearing behavior become abusive? Is it possible that sometimes the personality or chemistry between the people involved can contribute to the negative behaviors?

3. Along that same line of thought, Trent's points of failure aren't very different from the advice Sandra's mother gives her, yet each point can be viewed either as negative or positive. Why?

4. Have you ever wanted to change something about yourself so that you will fit in better with others? Is there a difference between compromising to make relationships work or compromising yourself to fit into work or social circles?

5. What prompted the change in Sandra's outlook on life? Did something change in her that made the change possible? Do you think external events might have prompted her change, or did they encourage or support the ability to change?

About the Author

Grace Greene is an award-winning and *USA Today* bestselling author of women's fiction and contemporary romance set in the rolling hills and forests of her native Virginia (*Kincaid's Hope, Cub Creek, Leaving Cub Creek*) and the breezy beaches of Emerald Isle, North Carolina (*Beach Rental, Beach Winds*). Her debut novel, *Beach Rental*, and the sequel, *Beach Winds*, were both Top Picks by *RT Book Reviews* magazine. For more about the author and her books, visit www.gracegreene.com or connect with her on Twitter at @Grace_Greene and on Facebook at www.facebook.com/GraceGreeneBooks.

Books are produced in the United States using U.S.-based materials

Books are printed using a revolutionary new process called THINKtech™ that lowers energy usage by 70% and increases overall quality

Books are durable and flexible because of Smyth-sewing

Paper is sourced using environmentally responsible foresting methods and the paper is acid-free

Center Point Large Print
600 Brooks Road / PO Box 1
Thorndike, ME 04986-0001 USA

(207) 568-3717

US & Canada:
1 800 929-9108
www.centerpointlargeprint.com